As You Wish

Jennifer Malin

JOVE BOOKS, NEW YORK

TIME PASSAGES is a registered trademark of
Berkley Publishing Corporation.

AS YOU WISH

A Jove Book / published by arrangement with
the author

PRINTING HISTORY
Jove edition / January 1999

The Penguin Putnam Inc. World Wide Web site address is
http://www.penguinputnam.com

ISBN: 0-515-12433-8

A JOVE BOOK®
Jove Books are published by The Berkley Publishing Group,
a member of Penguin Putnam Inc.,
375 Hudson Street, New York, New York 10014.
JOVE and the "J" design are trademarks
belonging to Jove Publications, Inc.

PRINTED IN THE UNITED STATES OF AMERICA

10 9 8 7 6 5 4 3 2 1

Chapter 1

"BEAUTIFUL," LEAH CANTRELL murmured, slowing to admire the canopy of leaves arching over the path. She had enjoyed her tour of Solebury House, but the splendor of the grounds left her spellbound. Maybe ancestors of hers had roamed these very woods. Maybe she felt nothing more than perfect May weather stirring her senses. In any case, every detail of the overgrown park, from the crumbling statues to the scent of sprouting greenery, charmed her.

She heard footsteps crunching in the gravel behind her and turned to see her friend Jeanine approaching.

The tall blonde glanced at her watch and let out a sigh. "Still half an hour until the bus leaves. It's been such a long day that I'm ready to go now. What do you say? Maybe the rest of the group will have the same idea, and we'll be able to start back for London early."

"But this garden is so gorgeous." After four days on vacation, Leah had begun to wish she had a more enthusiastic companion. *Not Kevin,* she told herself when a pair of soft brown eyes sparked in her mind. She dismissed the thought. "I'd still like to find that spring the guide mentioned."

"What spring?" Jeanine squinted back in the direction they'd come from, apparently trying to see the bus in the far-off parking lot.

"The one where the Druids worshiped." She smiled, picturing the mysterious ancient people, cloaked in long robes, walking on the same ground where she stood all these centuries later. "The guide said that our custom of throwing coins into fountains comes from primitive sacrifices to water deities. Isn't that interesting?"

Her friend kicked a large pebble off the center of the trail. "I guess, but why do we have to look for the spring? Do you plan on wishing that Kevin calls the hotel tonight, begging you to catch the next flight home to Philly?"

"Of course not!" Her smile faded, and she stared off into a grove of oak trees. "I just found the story about the Solebury Spring intriguing. The spring was dry for almost two centuries. Then after the heavy rains England had last month, the water suddenly started gushing again."

Jeanine stopped next to her, watching her until Leah met her gaze. "Don't think I haven't noticed that you started wearing that cheap ring of his again."

Leah glanced down at her left hand, adorned with a tiny diamond chip set in fourteen-karat gold. She couldn't argue with her friend's charge of cheapness, but Kevin had never called his gift anything but a friendship ring. Of course, the trinket had always meant more to her.

"After three years of wearing a ring, my finger just didn't feel right without one. I kept thinking I'd lost something."

"Believe me, you haven't." Jeanine crossed her arms over her chest. "I'd hoped this trip would help you forget that moron. Can't you at least open yourself up to the possibility of finding someone *worthy* of you?"

She didn't answer. They'd had this conversation before and she saw no use in repeating her views. Her friend just didn't understand the importance of a first love. She'd never dated anyone long enough to grow really attached.

Jeanine tilted her head to one side, softening her tone. "I'm sorry, Leah, but you have too much going for you to settle for second best. With that cinnamon-colored hair and big green eyes, you can have your pick of men. Why not take full advantage of our vacation and find yourself a nice English 'bloke'?"

She shrugged. "Despite what you think, I *am* open to meeting someone new. I just doubt that much is going to happen on a fourteen-day tour."

"Taking off that ring might help." Jeanine's lifted eyebrows challenged Leah to contradict her. "If you want to wear a ring, buy yourself another one, the kind you deserve. Throw that piece of junk in your wishing well—or spring. Whatever. Personally, I'm too tired to walk any more. I'll be waiting back at the bus." She flickered a final half-smile and trampled up the path.

Leah let out a sigh and leaned back on a stretch of wooden fence. Now that her friend had gone, she had to admit Jeanine had a point. Unfortunately, Kevin had been a part of her life for so long that she couldn't imagine being without him. He may have broken up with her two weeks ago, but he'd done so before and always ended up coming back.

And always left again, too, she could almost hear Jeanine

object. Shoulders heavy, she slumped against a fence post and gazed off into the trees.

A sunlit patch of stone and mortar, almost completely camouflaged by leaves, caught her attention. Curious, she stood on tiptoe, then squatted down, distinguishing the corner of a small structure of some sort. Careful not to tear the cream-colored rayon sundress she'd bought for her trip, she ducked between the fence rails and wove her way through clusters of brambles toward a leaf-shrouded clearing.

Her excitement grew as she made out a decaying outbuilding, the foundation of which had partly sunken into the ground. She'd never seen a springhouse, but she imagined one might look like this. When she peered around the corner, a pool of crystal-clear water confirmed her guess. She'd found Solebury Spring.

Setting down her purse, she stooped beside the pool and swished her fingers through the cold water. She was tempted to take a sip but reminded herself it might not be safe to drink. She thought of splashing her face but decided the water was too icy. Her fingers had already begun to turn red.

She rose and walked around the edge of the pool, amazed that so much water could come from a spring that had been dry for so long. When she reached the side opposite the springhouse, she faced a huge oak. Water surged among the thick roots with surprising intensity. She grabbed the trunk, leaning forward to take a closer look.

A dark, round form in the perimeter of the pool drew her gaze. Fascinated, she reached in and plucked out a mud-covered coin.

"Someone's wish," she whispered. From the look of the coin, the wish had been made a long time ago—definitely not in the mere month or so since the spring had bubbled back to life. So the wish must have taken place some two hundred years ago. Could she actually have found a coin that old?

She rubbed the piece in water, and a metallic shine slowly developed—a golden shine. With a little more cleansing, she could see the relief of a man's bust embossed in the precious metal. Inscribed below, she read the words GEORGIVS III. *King George the Third.*

"Wow." To come across such a find during a half-day tour of an estate! The coin had to be worth quite a bit, but the value of the discovery didn't impress her nearly as much as her luck. The piece must have been buried deep in the earth until the resurging water uncovered it.

She wouldn't let herself think what an astounding souvenir the prize would make. The only real choice she had was to turn the treasure in to the estate staff.

Or she could throw the coin back, hoping the original owner had received his or her wish all those years ago.

She looked down at the water, and the sentimental urge overwhelmed her. Someone, long ago, had made a sacrifice to ancient deities here, and, superstitious or not, she didn't want to foil their chances of a return.

Before she could change her mind, she balanced the coin on the side of her index finger and flicked her thumb. The glittering antique flipped head-over-tail in the air until gravity captured the gold and pulled it down to plunk in the water. The coin sank into the deepest recesses, disappearing in the roots of the big oak tree.

"There you go," she said. "I hope your wish came true, whoever you are."

She rubbed her damp hands together, avoiding wiping them on the pale fabric of her dress. The thought occurred to her that if *she* had a wish, she didn't even know what she would want. Not Kevin, she told herself.

"I only wish," she said, looking at the water, "that I knew who that coin belonged to and whether they ever got what they wanted."

With a sigh she stood and turned away. Engrossed in her thoughts, she forgot to watch her step and slipped on a moss-covered rock. She teetered backward, grasping for the trunk of the big oak, but her hand scraped down the bark. Treetops pinwheeled around her, and she glimpsed blue patches of sky. Then she splashed into the pool, backside first, the icy spring water a shock to her body.

Instead of sinking into the muddy bottom, she submerged completely, as though the Loch Ness engulfed her rather than a little pool. Eyes squeezed shut, she struggled to regain balance, but her feet couldn't find the ground, and the cold sent panic slicing through her. The pool couldn't be more than a few feet deep. Why couldn't she simply stand?

Flailing, she fought to hold her breath. The muffled bubbling of her struggles mocked her, and she thought her lungs would burst any minute—or force her to breathe in a flood of water. Adrenaline pumped through her, but none of her efforts brought her to the surface.

Would she die in this shallow spring, thousands of miles away from her family? Her parents' faces flashed before her, spearing her with regret. In another second dizziness muddled her mind until only one thought became clear.

Yes, this was how she would die.

The next thing Leah knew, a pair of strong hands caught her under the arms and dragged her from the water, releasing her onto the grass on her stomach. Someone pressed hard against her back, and she coughed up water, sputtering and wiping her mouth, more humiliated than injured. How stupid to be rescued from a few feet of water!

Anxious to regain composure, she planted her palms against the ground and pushed herself up to sit, legs stretched out. Her head felt light, convincing her not to try standing yet. She swiped soaking hair out of her eyes and got her first peek at her lifeline—a tall, well-built man with a shock of black hair. His inky brows arched devilishly over eyes the color of coal, and his jawline and cheekbones could have been chiseled by a sculptor. He must have worked as part of the tour, because he wore an old-fashioned costume, complete with form-fitting tan breeches and gleaming black boots.

Naturally, the best-looking man in Europe would be the one to witness her making a total fool of herself. She gave him a weak smile. "Thank you for pulling me out."

"I trust you will recover now?" he asked, coolly raising one of his perfect brows.

Despite her unnerved state, she laughed at this prime example of British detachment. "Physically, yes, but maybe not from my embarrassment." She gathered her long, straight hair into a rope-like wad and squeezed out a stream of water.

"If you truly feel any shame, madam, you disguise your sensibilities well. Most women would show a good deal more mortification upon being discovered in naught but a shift." He pulled off his jacket, the thin white shirt beneath revealing contours that rivaled Michelangelo's *David*. "Here, cover yourself with this."

She caught the ornate garment in midair and dangled it away from her wet body. "Oh, thanks, but I wouldn't want to get your costume wet, no matter how cold that spring-water made me." Teeth chattering, she looked down at her sundress and plucked at the nearly transparent rayon—a worthless attempt to keep it from adhering to her breasts. "This was supposed to be dry-clean only. So much for that."

Her rescuer's distinctive brows drew together. "Did you strike your head when you fell into the pool?"

"No, nothing like that. I'll be fine if I can just sit for a minute." The oak bark had scraped her hand, though not badly, and her arm ached, but only from the strain of holding his jacket above the ground. She gave it a little shake. "Here, take this back. I have a sweater on the bus that'll do until I dry out. God, I dread having to face the group like this."

He made no move for the jacket, and his frown sharpened into a scowl. "For God's sake, madam, stop speaking nonsense and put on the coat! I am scarcely in the habit of rescuing damsels in distress, let alone suited to stand here like a monk while a beautiful woman flaunts herself before me in a clinging shift!"

A new wave of humiliation washed through her, but she fought off her self-consciousness. Focusing on the inspiring fact that he'd called her beautiful, she lifted her chin. "Well, you Englishmen really are stuffy, aren't you? If that's the way you feel, then fine. I *will* wear your jacket."

She jammed her damp arms into the satin-lined sleeves, warm from the heat of his body. "I still say that a few minutes of comfort aren't worth ruining your costume. Once I get back to the bus, I'm giving this right back to you."

"What is this 'bus' you keep mentioning?" He kept his dark gaze locked tightly on her eyes.

"The tour bus—oh, that's right. You English call it a coach, I think."

"I can hardly allow you to board a coach dressed in a dripping shift. Where is the remainder of your clothing?" He glanced around the pool, then back at her face.

She had no idea what he meant by "the remainder" of her clothes, but his first statement irked her too much to care. When she'd escaped the suffocation of her father's house two years ago, she'd vowed never to let anyone else tell her what she could or couldn't do. She put her hands on her wet hips. "You're in no position to allow or disallow my doing anything."

He lifted his brows again, then smirked down at her. "I should say you are the one in a rather unenviable position at the moment, madam. Who are you, anyway? You have commented several times on my being English. Where are you from?"

"My name's Leah Cantrell, and I'm an American." She suppressed the memories about her father and fought to restrain her anger. Deciding there was no use debating a stranger's chauvinism, she held out her hand. "I didn't realize I'd perfected my enunciation enough to disguise my Philadelphia accent. I guess a bachelor's degree in language and lit is good for something after all."

He stared at her hand before finally taking her fingers and bowing over them with ridiculous formality. "David Traymore at your service, Miss Cantrell, though I will warn you I am rarely at anyone's service. Unfortunately, I cannot leave you to your own devices. Despite what you claim, I fear you did strike your head."

Had she detected an ever-so-slight catch in his voice? She thought she had and excused his condescension as a macho cover for real concern. Waving off his worries, she absorbed his name and couldn't help mentally comparing him again to Michelangelo's masterpiece. "David, huh? Figures. But wait, you said David *Traymore.* Oh, I get it. That's the *role* you play."

She knew from her tour that Solebury belonged to the

Traymores. Now that she thought of it, this actor bore a strong resemblance to one of the family members whose portrait she'd seen—the late son of the current marquess. Yes, his name had been David, Viscount Traymore. This impersonator had sootier hair and more intense eyes than the real viscount, who had been lost at sea when his father's yacht capsized in the Mediterranean. "You do look a lot like him. But the old-fashioned get-up doesn't make sense to me."

"I fear your words make little sense, either, Miss Cantrell. I assure you I'm not playacting."

Strange that he stuck with his character in this situation. And he took the role so seriously, not like the sing-songing actors at Renaissance fairs and staged medieval banquets. She grinned. "Sorry to disappoint you, but I paid attention during the tour. I know about his yachting accident."

He stared blankly, as though she'd made up the tale.

All at once, she realized the guide might have done just that. She shook her head. "Wait a second. *Are* you actually the viscount? Is that yacht story just a fabrication for tourists? Please don't tell me the one about the spring is made up, too."

Still, he looked at her as if she spoke Greek. "Miss Cantrell, I am, quite frankly, having difficulty deciphering your jabbering. I am indeed David Traymore, but, until now, no one other than myself has ever dreamed of my gaining the title 'viscount.' My father, in fact, has only lately approved my mother's decision to bestow his surname upon me."

She frowned. "Maybe I'm confused about the title. But you are heir to the Marquess of Solebury?"

He laughed, if such a bitter snort could be called a laugh. "You are delightfully misinformed, Miss Cantrell. That honor belongs to my half-brother. Lord William is the marquess's *legitimate* son, you see."

She studied his striking features, currently twisted into a grimace. So he'd been born illegitimately and clearly resented the fact. But why had the tour guide called him "the lost heir" and distinctly told them the marquess had no other offspring? Well, she didn't have the time to get to the bottom of the story. If she didn't hurry back to the bus, she'd hold up the whole group, and an angry Jeanine would not be a pleasant roommate.

"You're right about one thing," she said, carefully hoisting herself to her feet. "I'm definitely misinformed."

He stepped forward to grab her elbow, a good thing, since another wave of dizziness hit her. Still off-balance, she threw a resentful look at the mere puddle that somehow had almost swallowed her. But a glimpse of the springhouse made her gasp. In place of the cracked mortar and crumbling stones she'd seen just a few minutes before, four unbroken walls stood strong and level. She whipped her focus around toward the big oak—only the big oak had disappeared, a fragile sapling sprouting in its place. Her dizziness intensified, and she staggered backward away from the pool, thinking, for the first time in her life, she might faint.

David Traymore grabbed her around the shoulders, his strong arm the only thing keeping her from stumbling to the ground. She grasped on to his waist, terrified that he might vanish the way the tree had. But no amount of anxiety could refute the solid muscles of his abdomen, hot with the energy of life even through the linen of his shirt. Relieved, she let her shoulder fall against his chest.

"Now you see that you did indeed strike your head." He bent and scooped her up like a child, carrying her back toward the path. "I will take you to the manor house. My father's wife will care for you until your injuries mend."

She felt as confused as a child, too, and feared she might start crying like one. Willing herself not to give in to hysterics, she set her free hand against the cool skin of her face. "I just want to get back to the bus."

"We shall send a footman out to your people and tell them to bring the coach around to the stables. Don't concern yourself about their being well received. You will find the marchioness a very kind hostess. How she ever fell into my father's clutches I cannot say."

"I don't understand this," she managed to say. "The guide told us there was no marchioness. I must be hallucinating. Yes, that's it. I didn't get enough oxygen while underwater, and my brain still hasn't recovered."

"Well, your brain will recover nicely under Phoebe's care." He set her on her feet and loosened his grasp, not letting go completely until he saw she could balance herself. "Can you stand on your own for a moment while I untie Reveler? If I mount him first, he should allow me to pull you up without much protest."

Distracted by her reeling thoughts, she hadn't even noticed the enormous black stallion snorting and shuffling on the other side of the path. Never having stood so near a horse, she watched in awe as David Traymore untied the reins and stepped into one stirrup, swinging his other long leg over the saddle. When he motioned for her to come closer, she hesitated. She had never realized a horse could be so large.

"You are frightened of horses?" he asked, eyes narrowing slightly. "I shan't ask why, since your answer would likely make as little sense as everything else you have said. I assure you Reveler will do you no harm. He may have the bearing of a demon, but he is as gentle as a lamb."

He looked down at the animal, scratching him softly behind the ears and getting nuzzled in return. "Of course, he does all he can to mask his softer side."

Witnessing the exchange, Leah judged the horse and master well matched, not only in appearance but personality. Convinced of her rescuer's "softer side," she went forward and lifted her arms. He pulled her up with no trouble, placing her sideways in the saddle in front of him. She leaned into his chest, soothed by the warmth of his body and the faint woodsy scent of his cologne—a brand she didn't recognize.

He put one arm around her midsection and held her tightly as the horse trotted up the path toward the house. She closed her eyes and held onto his hips, a little embarrassed by the intimate position. Luckily, she had plenty of worries to distract her—the prospect of Jeanine's anger, as well as the alarming hallucinations she'd had at the spring.

"Here we are," David said after only a few minutes. "Hold on to the saddle, and I will assist you down after I dismount."

She opened her eyes and grabbed the horn of the saddle as he slid off behind her. He turned and lifted her from under her arms, setting her gingerly on the dirt. Another employee dressed in an old-fashioned costume took charge of the horse, eyeing her soggy form briefly before bowing and walking away.

David took her elbow and steered her across the dusty drive toward the manor. When she recognized the door as the main entrance, she gulped down another rush of misgivings. "I could have sworn this driveway was paved." She tried to shake off the eerie feeling, telling herself she must have been mistaken.

He ignored her comment and led her up three polished marble steps, which Leah knew had been cracked and stained earlier. Another costumed man opened the double doors for them, and they stepped inside the house . . . only the shabby interior she'd seen an hour or so ago had somehow transformed into a beautifully maintained decor.

She slapped her hands over her eyes, then uncovered them again, but the dreamlike grandeur remained. Instead of the faded wallpaper she'd viewed before, intricately carved panels lined the hall. While the walls had been practically bare earlier, they now displayed a stunning selection of paintings. And the ragged, garish red rug she remembered had been replaced by an elaborate paisley carpet in rich, dark tones.

"Oh, my God." She closed her eyes again. "What is wrong with me?"

A feminine voice broke into her thoughts. "What has happened, David? Who is this young lady?"

"You will hardly credit the story when I tell you, Phoebe. It seems I have rescued a helpless maiden from drowning."

"David, this is clearly no time for your nonsense." Warm, slim hands took Leah's own and rubbed them vigorously. "Oh, you poor thing, your fingers are like ice!"

A meeker, girlish voice said, "Beggin' your pardon, ma'am, but I just stoked up the fire in your sitting room."

"Perfect, Molly." The more mature woman took on a tone of urgency. "Let us move her in there."

Leah had no choice but to open her eyes in order to be led through the house. David held her at one arm; at the other, a mahogany-haired beauty, noticeably pregnant and dressed, like everyone else, in costume. The costumes bothered Leah. The employees she'd seen earlier had been wearing normal clothing. And how could she explain the changed appearances of the manor and the springhouse? Could she trust her perceptions at all?

She began to tremble, making out only bits of the others' conversation as they talked above her head: "nearly drowned" . . . "her shift only" . . . "an American" . . . "coach waiting" . . . "brain entirely addled" . . .

They directed her toward a blazing fire, and the heat comforted her a little, but she felt a pang of uneasiness when David left the room. A girl in an old-fashioned maid's cap helped her undress and slip into a flannel robe, then the hostess had her stretch out on a backless sofa, wrapping her in a thick down comforter. She propped two big feather pillows behind Leah and handed her a steaming cup that smelled like some sort of herbal tea.

Leah sipped the somewhat bitter drink, hovering over the cup while the two women fussed with the pillows and comforter. The tea soothed her remarkably—more than she imagined possible under the circumstances.

Her body began to thaw, and the frightening images in her "addled brain" grew murky. A strange contentment settled upon her, and she sank back deeper into the pillows. Gradually she realized her fear had melted right along with the chill she'd felt. Now she felt warm, relaxed, almost blissful.

"The tea," she murmured, gazing into the empty cup. "What was in the tea?"

"Her ladyship put in a black drop, I reckon, miss." The maid took the cup from Leah's yielding fingers.

"A black drop? . . . Sounds exotic." Smiling faintly, she let her head fall back into billowing down. *Wonderful, warm, secure.* She felt as though she'd been cold all her life and now, for the first time, had a toasty blanket to warm her. Her strange experiences took on the hues of a fantastic adventure. She felt as though she'd never known what it meant to be alive, and now she stood at the brink of ultimate knowledge.

David Traymore—where had he gone? She had to thank him . . . for saving her life.

Chapter 2

DAVID TRAYMORE RODE up to his father's residence for the second consecutive morning, setting a personal record in the frequency of his visits. During his childhood, his mother had brought him to Solebury House quarterly, dropping him off at the back door, where she collected him again several days later. As he grew, his service-door entry gained significance, and when he got old enough to understand his position in the family, he stopped coming altogether. He had believed nothing would ever coax him back, especially after his mother, the only person much concerned in the matter, died.

He slowed his horse at the front entrance, mulling over the event that had changed his mind. Phoebe, the only daughter of his late army mentor, Colonel Albert Sheffield, had married the Marquess of Solebury. She had played big sister to David since his father purchased him a commission in the cavalry for his sixteenth birthday. When Colonel Sheffield lay on his deathbed, David promised him to look after her. If he had known the girl would end up marrying his own father, he might have hesitated. But these days, the need to ensure the marquess treated her decently outweighed his own wish to avoid the man. Hence, once again, he found himself visiting Solebury House.

Swinging down from the saddle, he tossed Reveler's reins to a waiting footman, then took the marble steps two at a time. He nodded to the butler and brushed past him into the hall just as the marchioness emerged from her sitting room. Leaving the door ajar behind her, she held a finger up to her lips.

He glanced through the crack, attempting a peek at the beautiful American he had rescued the day before, but a large cabinet clock blocked his view. Phoebe tapped him on the shoulder, and he heeded her motions for him to follow her across the hall.

"Miss Cantrell has just fallen asleep," she whispered, leading him into the library. She collapsed on a settee near the fireplace, leaning back and draping an arm over the back of the seat. "She had a most fitful night, alternately tossing in her sleep and waking in a cold sweat. I fear I gave her too much laudanum. I should have taken into account how petite she is."

"And you should take your own condition into account as well." David pulled up a chair and sat facing her. "Nursing an invalid through the night is hardly a task you should undertake at this time. Now, more than ever, you need your rest."

She smiled and placed a hand on her rounded belly. "You are kind to worry about me, David, but I assure you I have been coddling myself. Molly is the one who sat with Miss Cantrell all night. I relieved her only an hour ago."

"Good." He looked down at his hand, examining his nails for nothing in particular. "Are you certain the laudanum is what disturbed your patient? I judged her state of mind rather fragile even before you gave her the tea."

"I fancy that a brush with drowning would have a similar effect on most of us mortals."

He looked up into her large brown eyes. "But she should have been able to wade out of that pool with no difficulty. Even at the deepest point, I doubt the water rises higher than her waist. Has she said anything more about how she came to fall into the spring?"

Phoebe shook her head. "No. From what you told me yesterday, she spoke more to you than she did the whole time Molly and I sat with her."

"Yet nearly everything she said to me made no sense whatsoever." He stood and walked to the fireplace, staring into the flames with one hand braced on the mantel. "The footman I sent to question your neighbors reports that no one saw the coach she claimed waited for her."

Phoebe's brow furrowed. "Did you have time to inquire in the village?"

"I did, but I had no better luck there. No one knew of a young American of her description, and I should think her unusual hair color would be remembered if seen. Furthermore, none of the innkeepers had served travelers at luncheon or tea. Your foreign houseguest is attaining quite an air of mystery."

"Yes. I only pray that when, or if, she gives us an explanation, the tale is not so horrid as I fear."

Before David could ask her meaning, solid footsteps sounded in the hall, and they both looked to the door. The marquess entered the room, combing his fingers through his thick, salt-and-pepper hair. On spotting David, he hesitated in the doorway, the jamb providing a frame for a more substantial, yet not stocky, version of his son's lean body.

Straightening in reflex to his father's entrance, David considered the irony of their marked family resemblance. His half brother, William, had all the legal claim to being the man's son, while he, David, possessed all the physical evidence. Indeed, the likeness between him and the marquess went so far that they might have passed for brothers, rather than simply father and son. Solebury had sired him as a mere stripling.

His lordship regained his bearing and gave David a stiff nod. He went to Phoebe and kissed her cheek, then walked to a large cherrywood desk, where he picked up a decanter. Without meeting his son's eyes, he said, "Good to see you again so soon, David. Will you join me in a brandy?"

"I believe I will." His father's excellent brandy offered some aid, however inadequate, in tolerating the man's presence. He stood back and watched until Solebury had filled two large snifters, then came forward to claim the one holding slightly more.

After both men had gulped down mouthfuls of the fiery liquid, the elder spoke, his voice slightly unsteady. "Have you learned anything more about the young lady?"

David shook his head and said nothing, stepping back to the hearth to reclaim his post before the flames.

Phoebe looked at him with pursed lips, then turned to her husband. "No one in the neighborhood or village knows anything about her. The whole business is most unfortunate. Whoever her family is, they must be frightened out of their wits wondering what has become of her."

"If so, then why are they nowhere to be found?" Lord

Solebury rubbed his chin in thought. "Perhaps we should call in a constable. With no one nearby claiming a relationship to her, she may well be a runaway."

"No, Harold, please." The marchioness stood and went to her husband, taking up his hand in hers. "If she is a runaway, she may have had good reason to leave home."

"My dear, she is far more likely to have no good reason. I daresay most young girls who bolt from their parents do so because their spoiled nature has not been indulged quite so well as they have learned to expect. We have no cause, nor indeed any right, to keep her from her family."

"But, Harold, have you given much thought to the way David found her? Drowning in a pool only a few feet deep? I loathe to voice such a thought, but do you think she may have . . . may have been attempting something desperate?"

David's focus shot from the fire to Phoebe, and gooseflesh rose on his arms. He had known moments in his youth when Death had called to him with the seductive lure of peace. Schoolboys' taunts had sometimes mounted to a crippling crescendo. And his mother's passing had left a looming void within him. But he had never reached the point of capitulation. Had that beautiful young woman sunken more deeply into despair than he ever had? Unhappily, the appalling suggestion fit the puzzle too well.

The marquess stared at his wife, at last taking another swig of brandy. "You think she may have intended suicide?"

"I don't know, Harold. Indeed, I don't even want to consider the possibility unless she gives us more cause for concern when she speaks to us. But, at all costs, I should like to avoid sending her back to an abusive situation. Let us at least wait until she recovers and see what she has to say."

David watched with balled fists while his father eyed the ceiling in thought. Finally the marquess looked back to his wife. "Very well, love. We shall wait until we know her story. Meanwhile, if her people should turn up, I shall make inquiries before placing her in their charge again. Thus, we can ensure no villainy awaits her at home. Have I satisfied you?"

"As ever." She stretched up to kiss him, but something made her start and shoot a look toward the door to the hall. She held up a hand to silence the others, and the sound of a quiet moan drifted in from the sitting room.

"Miss Cantrell is having another nightmare." Wasting no time, she picked up her skirts and hurried out of the room.

David wanted to run after her but quickly repressed the urge. What good could he possibly do? He exchanged a glance with his father, downed the rest of his brandy, and set the snifter on the mantel. "I suppose I may as well be on my way."

"Stay a minute, David. Please." Lord Solebury held his gaze, his upper lip twitching ever so slightly. "I have been meaning to have a talk with you."

David raised his brows in surprise. As much as he would have liked to escape, the novelty of his father's request intrigued him. He propped himself against the mantel again. "Very well. What did you wish to discuss, my lord?"

The marquess sighed and shook his head. "So much that I scarcely know where to begin." He reached for the decanter and lifted the stopper. "Would you like another drink?"

"I think I will pass this time."

While Solebury poured himself a second brandy, David's mind wandered to the scene taking place across the hall. What sort of nightmares plagued Miss Cantrell's sleep?

"To cut to the core of the matter," his father interrupted his thoughts, "I should like you to take up residence in the gatehouse. The Sargents moved out last month, and the place is left without a tenant. As a bachelor, you will find the dwelling quite commodious, and you can have use of—"

"Wait." Scarcely trusting his own hearing, David held up both hands, palms facing out. "First, tell me one thing: Why on earth would I want to move onto this estate—or anywhere even remotely in the vicinity?"

"Well, I know you like to look after Phoebe, though I assure you that you have no need to do so." Solebury leaned back against the heavy desk. "I also hope, perhaps in vain, that your presence here might garner your brother's notice, possibly even prompt him to come home."

"My brother?" David laughed. "I shouldn't think the prospect of seeing me would provide much attraction for William when he has gaming and women to keep him in London."

"Yes, rather too much of gaming and women. Obviously, you have heard the tales." The marquess swirled his brandy and took a sip, then looked his son in the eye. "I thought setting up a bit of rivalry between you two might do the boy some good."

"Indeed?" David turned back to look into the fire, a burning sensation lashing his guts like the orange flames licked the flue of the fireplace. "So this is all about bringing your heir to heel?"

"Not entirely. Your living here would also give me the chance to come to know you."

Spinning back around, David stared at him. "So you have suddenly decided you want to know me, have you?"

"I have always wanted to know you."

"But not enough to marry my mother." Too furious to say more, he walked to the window and looked out at the meticulously tended park. At the end of the drive the gatehouse stood, a handsome stone building surrounded by a blossoming garden. He curled his lip at the pastoral scene.

"I was young," his father said from behind him. "Tractable. I did what my family demanded, conceding to their ideas of a suitable marriage. Of course, William's mother turned out to be . . . well, let us simply say that I came to regret my compliance. And now that I have made a love match, I fully realize how much I lost when I gave up your mother. Of course, my regret signifies nothing to you. But I should like to make amends."

David continued watching out the window. "I fear you are some thirty years too late."

The marquess paused. "Certainly too late to marry your mother—though, indeed, if we had not lost her so young, I would have offered for her after my first wife died. In any case, I hope I am not too late to do something for you. Phoebe has told me you have taken up importing, but you clearly had better prospects with the army. Would a more valuable commission entice you to return? Lieutenant, perhaps. Colonel Sheffield always spoke highly of your composure during battle. By his account, you would make a fine officer, and I do have some influence in that quarter."

David turned around, teeth clenched. "I am not interested in your influence, my lord. Whatever I cannot earn with my own abilities and hard work means little to me."

"But some goals cannot be reached with only ability and work. As unfair as the truth may seem, certain positions can be achieved only through good connections."

David snorted. "So I have heard. What better place to learn that lesson than in his majesty's cavalry?"

"Is that why you sold your commission?"

When he failed to answer, the marquess returned to his seat, taking a long draught of brandy. "At least consider my proposal about the gatehouse. I truly would like to know my son."

David felt a muscle in his cheek quiver. He could not recall ever before having heard Solebury call him "son." But that fact only illustrated how little the man had ever offered him. He swallowed. "I thank you, my lord, but I daresay we know each other as well as we ever will. Good day to you."

He stalked from the room, nearly colliding with Phoebe in the hall as she left the sitting room.

"I was just coming for you, David," she said. "Miss Cantrell has been calling for you."

"She what?" he snapped, still infuriated by the interview with his father. "I find that hard to credit."

Phoebe cast her gaze downward. "Well, perhaps she has not exactly 'called' for you. But she has murmured the name 'David' several times."

He laughed. "Dear Phoebe, she clearly refers to another David. After all, your patient and I are hardly on first-name terms. We have, in fact, barely met. She likely has a brother named David . . . or a lover." He glanced through the doorway toward the recamier where the young woman lay.

"Or she may be calling you."

He looked back at the marchioness, whose large brown eyes implored him to indulge her.

"What harm can come to you in sitting with her for a few minutes?" she asked.

He stood undecided a moment longer, then lifted his gaze heavenward. "None, I suppose. But I tell you I shan't easily grow accustomed to this angel-of-mercy role."

She rewarded him with a warm smile.

They entered the room, David going to the recamier, while Phoebe hung back near the door. He seated himself in a chair that had been pulled up close to the patient's side, and she stirred at the sound of his movements.

Remembering Phoebe's speculations, he shuddered. Could Miss Cantrell truly want to snuff out the precious, precarious life that caused her chest to rise and fall so softly under the counterpane? He wanted to shake her and tell her never to think of such an abomination again, tell her to grab on to life with both hands and climb on for the ride. Instead, he watched her breathe, silently willing her to continue.

She shifted slightly in her sleep, facing away from him with her hair spilled across the pillow. He had never seen such gorgeous hair, almost unnaturally beautiful in both color and sheen. Though deeper in hue, the lustrous red made him think of candy cane stripes—shiny, cool, the portion one imagined tasted sweeter than the rest of the sweet.

He reached out to touch the spun sugar, but her eyelids fluttered open, and he let his arm fall again.

Rubbing her eyes, she fixed her gaze on him. The corners of her mouth curved upward. "David."

Surprised, he glanced back at Phoebe, who shrugged before he turned away again.

"David with the devilish eyes," Miss Cantrell murmured. "They don't disguise your goodness from me."

He heard Phoebe giggle behind him. "Well, she has your measure, does she not?"

"I should hope my character is more complex than one dazed statement would indicate," he shot back over his shoulder. Feeling a gentle touch on his knee, he swung back around to find Miss Cantrell weakly reaching out to him—a gesture so intimate he longed to crawl under the counterpane with her. Instead, he turned to Phoebe for her reaction.

His young stepmother walked forward a few steps and

nodded. "Go on and hold her hand, David. She needs comforting, and she certainly responds to you."

He looked back to Miss Cantrell, who now stretched both arms toward him. Instead of climbing onto the recamier with her as he wanted, he followed Phoebe's suggestion. Miss Cantrell's fingers felt warm, slender and soft, attesting that she had never needed to labor for her living. But he had already appraised her as gently born. Her speech had distinctly educated tones, though obscured by that strange American accent.

She sighed and closed her eyes, apparently content with holding his hand. He felt absurdly disappointed, as though she might have urged him to snuggle up beside her and sleep. He watched her porcelain face for several minutes more until the even rise and fall of her blanket-covered breasts indicated she had drifted off again.

Clearing his throat, he said to Phoebe, "You did give her too much laudanum, though I believe the effect is beginning to fade."

The marchioness drew closer. "You don't think the drug will harm her, do you?"

He shook his head, eyes still focused on the patient. "No, I have seen soldiers sleep off far worse laudanum stupors than this. I believe she will recover by evening, though she'll likely have a beastly headache for a day or two, especially since she hit her head yesterday. I trust you tended her injury?"

"I would have, had I discovered one, but from what I can tell, she escaped her ordeal unharmed. I believe she received a good scare but nothing more."

"You found no blood, no lump on her head?" He set down Miss Cantrell's hand and moved to examine her scalp, but the thought of taking such a liberty discomfited him and he recoiled. "I suppose she might simply have been in shock. She undoubtedly appeared so, or . . ." He trailed off, unwilling to propose she might be mentally unsound.

"We won't know the whole story until she is well enough to tell us herself." Phoebe smiled gently. "Your presence has calmed her greatly. Perhaps you could speed her recovery if you stayed with us for a few days."

He threw a startled look at her, but her face revealed no signs of cunning. Slowly he shook his head. "No, Phoebe, you cannot pull the wool over my eyes quite so easily. I see through your well-intentioned but misguided motives. You will not convince me to stay in my father's house."

"I had thought about the gatehouse, actually."

"Nor on his property." He stood and turned away from her.

"David, I am not asking this simply for Harold's sake. I truly need you to help with Miss Cantrell. You know I am tired these days, hardly up to nursing her as I ought. She responds to you, trusts you. She is obviously quite frightened of something, and for some reason your presence comforts her."

He sighed and closed his eyes. "I know there is more to this than you contend."

"But you will stay and help me? I need you."

He glanced down at Miss Cantrell's peaceful face, then at Phoebe's childlike eyes. How could he refuse Phoebe, the one person he considered family? If his motives ran any deeper than that, he had no inclination to explore them. "Very well. Tell Solebury I will be staying at the gatehouse for a few days—against my better judgment."

"And we can expect you to dine with us here at the manor house tonight? I hope Miss Cantrell will be on her feet by then and can be persuaded to join us."

He shrugged, his own acquiescence surprising him. "I suppose I may as well come to dinner. Better to suffer his lordship's company for an hour or so than try to find decent fare in the village."

She clasped her hands together in front of her chest. "Excellent. I will inform Cook, as well as ensure the gatehouse is made ready for you. And, by the way, I am expecting a call from your old army comrade, Captain Harlowe, so you may as well come to tea also." She walked from the room, a sly smile playing at her lips.

"Minx," he muttered when she left earshot. He looked back at Miss Cantrell, who stirred slightly in her sleep. "But perhaps the more bewitching sprite lies here."

Unable to resist touching her hair any longer, he took up a thick lock in his hand. For all of the exquisite texture, he might have held a bolt of silk.

Twirling the tresses around his fingers, he could not deny being drawn to the lovely stranger, though mystery women normally held no allure for him. His own dubious position in society provided enough uncertainty in his life. He liked to know precisely where the women he knew stood—usually somewhere in the demimonde.

He studied Miss Cantrell's classically formed profile, attempting to make out her character. Her easy, artless manner demonstrated none of the coyness of a debutante, and he had already ruled her out of the working class. She lacked the boisterous ways of the actresses and opera singers he knew, as well as the guile of a courtesan. Into what notch did she fit?

And why should I trouble myself to wonder? he asked himself, frowning. Wherever she stood in the world, her position would surely prove more sound than his. He might even point that out to her if she showed any further inclination to harm herself.

He let her glossy hair slide from his fingers and took a step back from the recamier, gazing on her one last time. Damn the little hoyden for flaunting her wet, lithe body before him in such an ingenuous way that she *must* have suffered from a head injury, despite having no lump. Damn her for sleepily beckoning him into her arms today. Damn the chit, in short, for making him want her so badly . . . in a way he could never have her.

Chapter 3

LEAH WOKE FROM her nightmares with a start, springing up into a sitting position. Disoriented, she scanned the formal decor of the room. Detailed wallpaper, probably hand-decorated, covered the walls with Oriental scenes. The furniture looked antique—though in perfect condition—including the hard, backless sofa where she lay under a heavy comforter. In a nearby fireplace a blaze flickered and crackled, heating the room surprisingly well. A coat of arms hung over the mantel, the name "Traymore" scrawled beneath the crest.

Oh, yes, the sitting room at Solebury House—the setting for the one nightmare she hadn't been able to shake. Apparently, she hadn't dreamed up her accident at the spring.

She wiped perspiration from her forehead and traces of tears from her cheeks. Her head throbbed, but her mind had begun to clear from the upsetting images that had haunted her all night. *And morning,* she thought, noting the brilliant sunlight that speared through the windows.

Swinging her legs over the side of the couch, she set her bare feet on a thick Persian rug. As she stood, a pain pierced her skull, but her legs held out to support her. She made her way past the fireplace and stopped in front of a window, looking out at the grounds.

A horse-drawn carriage pulled away from the house. Though she guessed the vehicle must be part of a historical enactment, something about the sight made her nervous. As she watched the wheels churn up puffs of dust, she realized what: the dirt driveway again, when she remembered it being paved. Evidently, her night of fitful sleep had failed to put an end to her hallucinations.

Had her brush with death done permanent damage to her brain? Her mind *seemed* to be working normally. She could focus on a single subject without losing concentration. Her thoughts seemed to flow logically. The dreamlike stupor she'd been in all night had definitely lifted.

A costumed gardener passed the window, dragging a wooden cart full of seedlings, and she marveled at the detail of the portrayal. Every aspect of the scene reflected a past age, giving her an eerie sense that instead of watching a depiction—or hallucinating, for that matter—she really had gone back in time.

She forced out a laugh at herself. Her nightmares must have affected her more than she realized. One or two had revolved around the theme of time travel.

"Miss Cantrell, I am so glad to see you up and about," a feminine voice said from behind her.

Leah turned to see the pregnant woman who had helped her the day before. Today she wore a different dress, though one very much like yesterday's costume. The flowerspecked white skirt section started just below her breasts, curving over her protruding abdomen and falling straight down to the floor. A sheer vestlike overdress covered the whole outfit for an effect of casual elegance.

"I am Lady Solebury," she said, dropping a little curtsy. "I daresay you may not recall our meeting yesterday."

"I . . . I remember a little." Gathering that she faced the marchioness David Traymore had mentioned, Leah found herself offering an awkward imitation of her hostess's gesture. "I'm sorry if I'm not greeting you correctly. I'm an American and not used to addressing nobility."

Lady Solebury smiled. "And I am not entirely accustomed to being addressed as such, having married Solebury less than a year ago. Before that, I was plain Miss Sheffield. But you did very well, especially considering the ordeal you have been through. I hope you feel somewhat more yourself today?"

"Yes, somewhat, thank you. I . . . I'm very sorry to be such an inconvenience to you. I can't believe I fell asleep on your couch—and for the whole night, too."

The marchioness looked down to her feet, which peeked out under her gown in shoes resembling ballet slippers. "I fear I had something to do with your fatigue. I put a little laudanum in your tea to calm you, but I must have given you too much. I do apologize and truly hope you can pardon me."

"Oh . . . sure," Leah said, stunned to hear the drug had been laudanum. Wasn't that some sort of old-fashioned opiate no longer in use? She guessed that in England they might still have drugs outmoded in the U.S.—but opiates? Maybe they used the name *laudanum* for some modern alternative. In any case, whatever she'd been given had knocked her for a loop.

"I have had a chamber made up for you," her hostess said with a shy smile. "I would have moved you into a proper bedroom earlier, but I loathed to disturb your sleep. I hope you are not in such a hurry to leave that you won't allow me to show you a bit of hospitality. My maid has laid out some clothing for you to borrow, and I thought you might like a bath drawn and something to eat."

Surprised by the woman's extraordinary kindness, she took a moment to think about whether she should accept or try to get back to London immediately. Jeanine would be worried, but she could call her and explain about the problem at the spring. Considering the tricks her mind had been playing on her, staying put for a while seemed the sensible thing to do.

Before she could answer, the weight of a lingering gaze drew her attention toward the door to the hall. Her devilish-looking rescuer, David Traymore, stood in the doorway, appraising her with fathomless black eyes. The intensity of his stare made her breath come quicker.

Following the path of her gaze, Lady Solebury spotted him, too. "David, I am glad you looked in on us. As you can see, Miss Cantrell is feeling better."

He bowed stiffly, his expression masklike. "I am pleased to hear it."

Oh, he's a cold one, Leah thought, though he had saved her from drowning and brought her up to the manor house to recover. Then she thought of the tender interplay between him and his horse, and her opinion softened. Not cold, she amended, but very guarded.

"Miss Cantrell, do you remember my stepson?" Lady Solebury asked. "Mr. Traymore."

"Yes, of course." She recalled her new English manners

and dipped an amateur curtsy. "Thank you again for rescuing me."

He nodded but let out a snort of scornful laughter. "Pleased to be of service. The role of hero is such a novelty."

"Indeed?" Lady Solebury shot back at him, putting her hands on her hips. "How prematurely you have forgotten the time you spent at war."

He gave her a rueful smile but let her comment pass.

The marchioness looked to Leah and said, "I fear my stepson is a bit wild in his ways, but I assure you he has a heart of gold. Oh, and speaking of gold, I have something of yours." She went to a jar on the mantel and dug inside, offering the contents to Leah. "Molly found this in the pocket of your shift."

Leah held out her hand, and her ladyship placed a coin in her palm. The golden face, scratch-free and sparkling, read GEORGIVS III. How had the coin she'd thrown into the spring ended up back in her pocket?

But, on second thought, this couldn't be the same coin. Not even a nick marred King George's portrait, and the gold gleamed beyond what polishing could have achieved.

Yet she had a strong sense it *was* the same coin, transformed—just like the driveway had changed from pavement to dirt . . . and, now that she recalled, the house interior from shabbiness to splendor.

At the thought of those hallucinations, her hand began to tremble. The coin slipped through her fingers and landed on the carpet with a dull plunk.

"What is it, Miss Cantrell?" David Traymore stepped forward and stooped to pick up the coin, examining the face with a frown. "A King George guinea? Strange. I . . . but never mind. It doesn't signify."

A rush of terrifying images assaulted her, some from her

nightmares, some from the waking horrors she'd experienced. She saw the changes in the springhouse, the disappearance of the big oak tree, and the horse-drawn carriage pulling up the drive. Vague visions from her dreams took shape: the spring surrounded in fog and a spirit forming in the mist to tell her that her wish would be granted. Her *wish*?

Her gaze fell on the coin David held, converted from a battered antique into gold that could have been minted yesterday instead of . . .

Suddenly she remembered speaking aloud at the spring: *"I only wish that I knew who that coin belonged to and whether they ever got what they wanted."* Was this the wish she would be granted? No, she'd only dreamed up that water sprite—but her accident at the spring had been real.

She stared at David and Lady Solebury, who both waited for her to respond. "What is . . . what is the date?"

Her ladyship smiled. "The fifteenth of May, dear. In case you are wondering, you slept through only one night."

Leah swallowed. "And the year?"

The others exchanged glances, then Lady Solebury answered, "Why, 1815, of course."

"Eighteen-fifteen?" Her knees buckled. She would have fallen if David hadn't jumped forward to catch her under the elbows. "Did . . . did I hear you correctly?"

"Yes, 1815." Frowning, the marchioness came forward and pressed her fingers to Leah's forehead. "You don't seem to be suffering a fever, dear, but that laudanum has quite undone you. Come, let us show you to your chamber, where you will be more comfortable."

Leah heard only half of what she said but offered no resistance as Lady Solebury and David led her into the hall. Her thoughts raced back to the moment normality had ceased for her: the moment David had pulled her out of the spring.

The spring had taken her back in time, so she could learn whether the original wish was granted. Of course, the whole idea seemed crazy, but, deep inside, she knew she'd hit on the truth.

"Goodness, you are shaking," the marchioness said as she and her stepson directed Leah up a wide, curving staircase. "We are right here with you, love, and we won't allow any harm to come to you. I promise."

Leah fixed her gaze on the woman's eyes, struggling to regain some semblance of composure. "I . . . I'm sorry."

"Nonsense." Her ladyship steered her into a brightly sun-lit bedroom and sat down with her on a large canopied bed. "Don't even think about whatever is troubling you, Miss Cantrell. You are under my protection now—as well as the marquess's and Mr. Traymore's."

Leah glanced at her rescuer, who stood watching her closely.

"Laudanum distorts reality sometimes, Miss Cantrell," he said, though he didn't sound very confident. "Much of your anxiety may be attributed to the drug."

"How much?" His suggestion didn't convince her, either, but she tried desperately to keep an open mind. "Could I, for example, be dreaming right now?"

He glanced at the marchioness, then back at Leah, his dark eyebrows crunched together. "I fear not, but I, too, would like to assure you of your safety."

Determined to consider her dream theory anyway, she looked around the room. Brilliant sunlight fell on the pastel yellow wallpaper, illuminating the tiny buds that speckled it. Beneath her hands, a matching damask bedspread felt cool and finely textured. Both her senses and her thoughts seemed clear—but dreams could be realistic.

They could also be tested.

A book lying on the nightstand caught her attention. She knew she had never been able to read in a dream; by the time she reached the end of a sentence, the words at the beginning always changed. Snatching up the volume, a leatherbound copy of Jane Austen's *Mansfield Park,* she opened to a page in the middle and skimmed the first few sentences.

She could not respect her parents, as she had hoped. On her father, her confidence had not been sanguine, but he was more negligent of his family, his habits were worse, and his manners coarser, than she had been prepared for.

Her throat constricted. Not only could she understand the words, but the passage made her think about her own parents. Her relationship with them lacked respect, too—on both sides, unfortunately. But underneath all their differences, she knew they loved her. She loved them, too, and now she might never see them again!

She swallowed the lump in her throat and snapped the book shut. Obviously she could read. She wasn't dreaming. Given that, she couldn't bear to think about her parents.

"Do you like to read, Miss Cantrell?" her hostess asked. "My sister left that novel behind last time she visited. She said she greatly enjoyed the story."

Leah looked stupidly at the book in her hand. She had to pull herself together and try to act normal. Lady Solebury and David had been very kind to her, but if she didn't calm down, they would start to doubt her sanity. Who knew what that might mean in the year 1815? Commitment to Bedlam? Being locked in a cell or chained to a wall?

She took a deep breath. "Yes. I've read it."

"Indeed? I had no idea Miss Austen had been published in the States." She paused and looked to David. "Mr. Traymore, I think you can leave us now. Would you tell Molly to have Miss Cantrell's bath brought up? I daresay she will feel better after a good soak. I always do."

"Do you have to leave?" Leah heard the words come out of her mouth before thinking about whether she should say them. As cynical as David seemed, he *had* rescued her, and his presence somehow felt reassuring. But she couldn't cling to him. She had to find her own strength. "I'm sorry. How silly I am. I'll be fine soon. My head is clearing already."

"*Did* you strike your head, Miss Cantrell?" he asked, his eyes intent. "Yesterday you told me you had not."

"Oh. You know, maybe I did." Leah put one hand up to the back of her skull and feigned a wince. "I *am* a little tender. I'm afraid I don't remember everything about my accident. Yes, I guess I must have hit my head."

Lady Solebury laid a hand on her shoulder. "Well, I personally will oversee your recovery, Miss Cantrell. Meanwhile, Mr. Traymore needs to go and dress for dinner, and that will give you a chance to do the same. No doubt you will feel much better by the time you meet him at the table."

"Oh, yes. Yes, of course." Leah gave a nervous laugh and nodded to David. "Thank you again."

"Your servant," he murmured. Turning to the marchioness, he said, "I will send Molly to you directly."

She thanked him, and Leah watched him leave the room, attributing the strong attachment she felt for him to the fact that he'd saved her life. She thought back on the conversation they'd had at the spring and realized how strange some of her talk must have seemed. As for the discrepancies between what he'd told her and the tour guide's stories, now she knew the guide had been describing a different era. The David Traymore in the photograph she'd seen during the tour must have been a twentieth-century family descendant of this one. And the roots of David's bitter nature were clearer now, too. Illegitimate birth would be a bigger problem in this century.

"Miss Cantrell, dear," Lady Solebury said, "I will only trouble you a moment longer before Molly comes with your bath. I don't mean to pry, but I must ask if you have family or friends whom I should contact. I imagine they are quite concerned about you by now."

She looked away, forced to think of her parents again. Were they worried? Grieved over her disappearance? Technically, they hadn't even been born yet, so their grief wouldn't come for almost two centuries. Maybe she could somehow return before they had time to miss her.

Could she get back home the way she'd come here? She glanced out the window toward the wooded area surrounding the spring. Terror at the thought of nearly drowning made her wonder if she should even try. Why had she been whisked into the past anyway? Only because she'd spoken a thoughtless whim out loud as she threw an old coin into a spring? Or did she have some other purpose in this century, something more important?

"Miss Cantrell?" The marchioness leaned closer to her, looking into her eyes. "If you don't want me to contact them, I shan't. If you are in some sort of predicament, I promise to do all I can to help."

"No, it's nothing like that. In fact, I wish we *could* reach my family." She pushed a long strand of hair out of her face. What could she tell this sweet woman? Certainly not the truth, though she didn't like to lie. "They're . . . in the States. For now, I'm on my own."

Her ladyship frowned. "But you cannot be alone. Surely someone accompanied you to England? You mentioned something to my stepson about a coach. Perhaps your traveling companions might be seeking you?"

She shook her head. "I had a friend with me, but she won't be looking for me here. I'm sorry. I really don't mean to sound mysterious. I still can't seem to think straight. Maybe I *am* in a predicament. I appreciate your help, but I think I need some time to sort myself out."

Her hostess watched her with narrowing eyes, but just when Leah expected an interrogation, Lady Solebury got up and went to the door. "Certainly, dear. You take all the time you require to determine what course is best for you. For now, all you need do is relax in your bath until dinnertime. You are joining us for dinner, I hope?"

Leah didn't have much choice if she wanted to avoid starving. She only wondered what she would do once she'd worn out her welcome at Solebury House. "Yes, thank you, if it's not too much trouble."

"No trouble at all, dear. You must stay with us as long as you like. I shall enjoy the company. I often find myself lonely out here in the country. But I shall be quite content for the time being with both you and David visiting." She grinned suddenly. "Your *angel of mercy*."

"Yes." Leah did think of him that way, though it was funny that his stepmother would refer to him so quixotically. "I probably would have drowned if he hadn't rescued me."

"Well, I am very glad he did, but you mustn't bother to feel overly indebted to him. You see, I may very well enlist you to do the same for him."

She had no chance to ask about this cryptic statement, because at that moment her bath arrived. The marchioness stepped out of the way, while a maid and four male servants came in, carrying a tub and pails of water.

"We will speak more on the subject later," Lady Solebury said through rising wisps of steam. She left, and the servants set up the bath before the fireplace. They looked to Leah for more instructions, and she excused them, feeling awkward in the role of mistress.

After they left, she locked the door, stripped off her borrowed nightgown, and stepped into the tub. She eased her body into the soothing hot water, concentrating on breathing slowly and steadily. She couldn't let herself think about magic fountains, ancient Druids, or Einstein's Theory of Relativity. If she did, she really would wind up in Bedlam.

For now, she would do her best to take the Scarlett O'Hara approach and "think about it tomorrow." She would focus on her survival, both physical and mental. Only when she had regained some emotional footing would she worry about getting home again—if she could.

Chapter 4

DAVID EMERGED FROM the back of the gatehouse, pausing to admire the pinks and purples of the setting sun. He took in a long breath of the dew-fresh air and closed the door behind him. As he stepped onto the flagstone walk, a footman appeared at the other end, coming off the main drive.

"Good evening, Mr. Traymore." The young man swept him a low bow, typical of the marked deference David received at Solebury House and nowhere else. "My lady, the marchioness, wishes to inform you dinner will be served in half an hour."

"Well, tell Lady Solebury she needn't worry about my tardiness . . . or absence, if that is what she fears." Never a believer in subservience, he tended to respond to toadies with scorn. Of course, the young footman had been hired to toady and could do little else. He cleared his throat and added with more grace, "I will join her ladyship presently. First, I should like a moment to admire the garden."

"Of course, sir," the youth said, his face solemn. "I hope you find all in order. Lady Solebury also sends word that the gatehouse kitchen has been stocked for your convenience. May I ask if all preparations to the cottage have been made to your liking?"

"Very much so." Though David would scarcely admit the truth, he privately savored this chance to stay in the little cottage. Through most of his boyhood, a childless couple who let the house had indulged him with the run of the place. Their home had become his favorite retreat during visits to his father's estate. "You may tell the marchioness I am quite happy with her arrangements. I need nothing further."

The footman bowed and ran off, leaving him to turn and look back at the house. As he eyed the stone facade, dozens of forgotten memories resurfaced: playing with toy soldiers in the garden, eating biscuits by the kitchen hearth, and enjoying hours of free rein in every room. He realized with surprise that he must know every nook and cranny of the place—right down to a secret passageway he had discovered in the cozy room that served as a study.

A wry smile pulled at his lips as he recalled imagining himself the only living soul who knew about the tunnel. Even all these years later, he clung to a boyish hope that no one else of his generation had stumbled onto the hinged wall panel that concealed the entrance. He would not mind an old retainer knowing—or perhaps even the marquess—but he would rather his half brother William remained ignorant. The tunnel, if no other part of the estate, belonged to *him*.

"Foolishness," he muttered, quitting the cottage garden, along with his memories.

Acknowledgment of his folly, however, did not prevent

his enjoying the dusky landscape. Birds chirped as they took to their nests for the evening. The low sun painted the trees and grass with an otherworldly glow. As he progressed through the park, David himself felt an all too rare glow. When had he last taken the time to appreciate a sunset?

He turned up the drive and walked toward a huge full moon, balanced on an orange and lavender horizon. The brilliant spectacle absorbed him . . . until a crackling of twigs off to one side broke the tranquility. The noise seemed to have come from the path that led to the spring.

Amid the darkened woods, something pale floated, obscure and ghostlike, then gone. Perhaps he had simply glimpsed a dove, but, in light of Miss Cantrell's mishap, he felt a swell of misgiving. Surely, he had no reason to suspect a reprise of her "accident," but his apprehension still stuck with him.

He stole down the path to investigate, praying he would be proved wrong. The stone wall of the springhouse felt cold and damp on his back as he inched toward the end near the pool. He heard no sounds of movement from the other side and began to wonder if his eyes had deceived him. But when he peered around the corner, his stomach clenched. Miss Cantrell, oddly still, stood at the edge of the water.

For the first time in their acquaintance, she wore conventional attire, a maize colored silk gown and overdress that cascaded down her gently curved body. Her rich auburn hair had been subdued into a loose knot atop her head, but small twisting curls escaped, playing on her cheekbones.

"I wish," she said softly to the empty air before her, "that I could go back to the time where I belong."

He contemplated her strange words. There must have been a time when she felt she "belonged" more than she did now—though to what or whom remained a mystery.

With her almost preternatural beauty, she might well have been a Celtic priestess, hovering before the spring to invoke the powers needed for a Druid rite. But he knew her for mere flesh and blood, and his heart sank to realize she must be summoning courage for something far more dreadful.

Reluctant to accept the evident, he resolved to allow her another moment, hoping he had misinterpreted her motives. He waited and watched as she lifted her hand and peered into her palm, then clasped her fist together. Whatever she held had a weighty significance for her. She looked back at the water and took a deep breath. Closing her eyes, she stepped forward, teetering on the brink of the pool. He could no longer doubt she meant to plunge into the water.

"Damn you," he hissed, leaping out from his hiding place.

Still oblivious to his presence, she swayed precariously forward.

He vaulted forth and snatched her around the waist. One yank set her feather-light form aloft, alighting again a yard away with his arms to keep her from tumbling.

"Damn you to hell, woman!" He trapped her against his chest, though she made no effort to escape. "Is that really what you want?"

"Oh, my God," she gasped, her eyes rounded like two green moonstones. She clutched him as tightly as he held her and dragged him yet further from the spring, apparently seized—rather belatedly—by terror.

He could feel her body trembling, and his initial anger melted into compassion. What on earth had she suffered that left her so determined to end her life?

The faint scent of rosewater drifted up from her hair, and he placed his hand on the side of her head, cradling her against his body.

"David," she whispered.

Though she had called him by his given name before, the second time startled him as much as the first. He ought to have found the stolen liberty presumptuous, even rude, but her artless manner drew quite the opposite response. She used the familiar address so naturally that he felt almost as though they *belonged* on intimate terms. He even had a compelling urge to address her the same way.

"Leah?" The word fairly caressed his tongue.

She looked up at him, her eyes still wide and lips slightly parted, as though inviting a kiss. Indeed, everything about their circumstances cried out for kissing, from their intimate embrace to their use of given names. Even the vulnerability he read in her uptilted eyebrows implied a willingness to bend to his will. She moistened her lips, heightening the tension to an unbearable intensity.

But for all the magic of her spell, he could not quite forget himself, his station in life . . . the coil of scandal that originated in the very moment of his birth. The times when he most longed to ignore his unhappy parentage only served to make him feel his disgrace more sharply.

He stared into her eyes, and she returned him a steady emerald gaze. In this overwrought state she might well submit to his advances, but when she recollected herself she would realize how low she had stooped and come to rue her indiscretion. He had no doubt of her proper breeding. She could make a good marriage and live happily—so long as a nobleman's bastard with no prospects did not compromise her first.

"I won't." He let her go and turned his back to her, shamed by his thoughts. At such a moment he ought to be lecturing this young woman on the value of life, not calculating his chances of seducing her. He ought to be delivering a sermon to her that would rival Hamlet's soliloquy.

Hamlet? What an unhappy reference, with Leah now having twice chosen "not to be" over "to be." Had Fate made an equally poor choice in placing *him* in the position of helping this young woman? He hoped not, for her sake.

"You won't what?" she asked from behind him.

He spun around and faced her. She no longer bore herself like a Celtic priestess. Her lithe body had wilted, making her look small and childlike. She waited for him to speak, and he realized, however badly suited, he must.

"I won't simply shrug off these ill-judged attempts of yours." He forced himself to step closer to her. "Whatever your difficulties may be, whatever miseries you may want to escape, I beg of you to confide in me rather than resort to an act of desperation. I may not have the position and wealth that grant worldly influence, but I have connections who do. There must be a way we can help you. There are always alternatives to this."

She watched the motion he made toward the pool, then lifted her gaze back to his eyes. "What do you mean?"

The blank expression on her face bore every mark of confusion, but he had witnessed that form of equivocation before. He threw his hands up in exasperation. "Drowning yourself. There is always another way—and I don't speak as a stranger to desperation."

Her eyes widened. "Did you think I meant to kill myself?"

"Are you claiming you did not?" he snapped, annoyed that she chose evasion over trusting in him. "How else do you explain nearly drowning in water too shallow to engulf an infant?"

For a long moment she only stared, each passing second further depleting his hopes for her candor. Before she answered, she broke away from his gaze.

"I didn't want to kill myself. All I can say is that I slipped and fell into the water, and then . . . well, I can't really explain what happened next. I *did* try to stand and get out of the pool, but I just couldn't manage."

Her slow manner of choosing words struck him as the circumspection of telling half-truths. He watched her until she lifted her gaze from the ground to meet his.

"Very well, let us suppose you are telling me all you can about yesterday's accident," he said. "Why would you return to the scene of your ordeal today? I should think you would never want to see this spring again."

She turned and looked toward the pool, a visible tremor rolling down her body. He scrutinized her profile, waiting for her answer.

"Sometimes you have no choice but to face your fears." She swallowed. "You might say I came back here to undo the harm yesterday's accident did to me."

"By leaping back into the spring?" He wished he could believe her, but no sane young woman would make such a choice, especially with no escort to protect her. Of course, she might not be sane, but that possibility pleased him no better. "What if, once again, you were unable to pull yourself out?"

She shuddered and tore her gaze away from the water, instead staring off into the woods. "The thought did cross my mind."

At least she showed some fear of death—in essence, some will to live. He walked to the edge of the pool and turned his back on the water, providing a temporary barrier between her and the unthinkable. "Why did you not 'face your fears' with someone standing by to keep watch?"

She still would not look at him. "I didn't want anyone to interfere."

"To interfere with what? With your leaping into the pool?"

"Yes."

He let his shoulders slump in frustration. "I don't like this. If you are telling the truth, I want to hear the rest of the story now. I suggest starting with what brought you to the spring yesterday, followed by as full an account as possible of the accident."

"I . . . I'm not ready to relate all that." Finally she met his gaze, her eyes bright and direct. "I wish I could, I really do, but you'd never believe me. You'd think I'm crazy and have me locked away in Bedlam."

So, she showed some concern for her perceived sanity as well. Perhaps he could prod her into showing more. He steeled his features into a glare. "And what do you think will happen to you if you don't cease these attempts on your life?"

Her eyes rounded yet again. "You wouldn't! You wouldn't put me away, would you, David? I told you I wasn't trying to kill myself. I swear I wasn't."

Of course he would not consign her to an asylum, even if he knew for certain she meant to hazard her life again. But perhaps stoking up a healthy fear in her would stave off the possibility of another such attempt.

"If you continue to show a tendency toward self harm, I will have no choice," he said. "Suicide is an abomination, and if physical restraint is the only way to prevent your committing it, then you must be restrained."

She stared at him in manifest horror. When her lower lip began to quiver, he almost recanted but reminded himself her fear would serve her well.

"You are positively gothic!" she exploded, her chest heaving as her breath came in quick puffs. "Though in *this* day and age, why should that surprise me? All right, fine. I promise I won't come near this spring on my own again—or try killing myself in any other way. Are you satisfied?"

"I should think not. I shall have to keep a very close watch on you." He felt a twinge of pleasure at the prospect but immediately chided himself. "Naturally, Lord and Lady Solebury will wish to attend you as well."

"What? You're not going to tell them this nonsense about my being suicidal, are you?" She stepped forward and grasped his upper arm, her warm fingers digging into his muscles. "Please, David, don't."

"I fear they already have their own suspicions, Leah." With the scent of roses teasing his nostrils, he could not resist continuing to use her given name. How could this beautiful creature want to squander her life? He would do his best, inadequate as that may be, to prevent her. "Indeed, I did not call up the idea myself."

She let her hand slide down his arm and paced a few steps away. "This is worse than I thought. Are they thinking of having me committed? Please tell me."

He shrugged. "I am certain the marchioness wishes to help you any way she can, but she will need your compliance, you know. As for the marquess, well, I have never known him to show a great deal of empathy. If I were you, I should tread very cautiously where he is concerned."

"Oh, God." She put a hand up to her lips. "If they think I tried to kill myself yesterday, today's fiasco will only double their suspicions. And I really didn't. I definitely don't want to die yet. David, please don't tell them about finding me here today."

He could see she had begun trembling again, and he regretted the necessity of maintaining a severe stance. But the sound of twigs snapping in the woods signaled that the decision would not be his, anyway. Phoebe emerged into the clearing, dressed in dinner attire and followed closely by her maid.

"Miss Cantrell, thank God you are safe!" she exclaimed, expelling a deep sigh as she hurried forward. "When I found your chamber empty, I thought . . . but that no longer signifies. What on earth are you doing at the spring? David, are you mad, bringing her back to this place?"

He nearly laughed at her automatic assumption of his poor judgment. She had provided stable ground for prevarication on Leah's account. Should he stand upon it? One glimpse at Leah's silently pleading eyes made up his mind.

"Admittedly, not one of my wiser decisions," he said, grimacing to himself over the power Leah unknowingly held over him. "I met Miss Cantrell just outside the manor, and she asked if I would accompany her here. She hoped that facing the spring would help alleviate some of the fear she has suffered since yesterday's mishap."

Phoebe looked to Leah, her big brown eyes registering astonishment. "How brave you are, Miss Cantrell! Did your strategy help?"

She glanced at David and, receiving no further aid from him, dropped her gaze. "If it has, I can't tell yet. I still feel pretty shaken up."

"Yes, you look upset, you poor thing. Your face is as pale as the moon." Phoebe stepped closer to her and placed a hand on her shoulder. "Let us return to the manor. I have no doubt you will feel much better once you have eaten dinner."

Leah gave her a weak smile. "I have to admit I'm looking forward to eating a real meal again. My appetite was still off this afternoon, but now I'm starving."

Phoebe laughed. "Starving, are you? What a colorful manner of speech you Americans have. Well, I daresay a good appetite betokens recovery from the laudanum I gave you. Thank goodness!" She let go of Leah's shoulder and started toward the path to the drive. "Molly, could you run ahead of us and tell his lordship to meet us in the dining room? I walk rather slowly these days, and by the time we reach the house, Cook will be anxious to serve the first remove."

As the marchioness spoke, David could feel Leah's gaze fixed on him. He looked to her, and she gave him a crooked smile, silently mouthing the words, "Thank you."

Unsure he had made a wise choice in concealing the truth, he scowled back at her.

He had a notion this woman could beguile him into any number of unwise choices. His only defense might be to keep her from realizing the ability.

Chapter 5

LEAH FELT HER heart pounding, even after Lady Solebury had turned away. Thank God David hadn't told the
marchioness she'd come to the spring on her own. Did that
mean she'd convinced him she didn't want to commit suicide? Hopeful, she looked to him and mouthed an unvoiced
"Thank you."

He shot her such a glare that she almost jumped back. As
if the smallest hint of goodwill would have cracked his too-
handsome face! So much for winning his trust. She should
have known Mr. Bitterness wouldn't cut her any slack.

Disgusted, she spun around and followed Lady Solebury
up the path to the main drive. She could hear David crunching through the thicket behind her—and swore she could
feel tension prickling between them like static electricity.
She couldn't comprehend his mood swings. Only moments
ago he'd looked at her so tenderly her knees had gone weak.

The thought of how his arms had felt around her recharged the dancing ions on the nape of her neck. She shuddered with acute awareness of his nearness. If she stopped quickly enough, would he run right into her back?

Ridiculous! Not only had she gone back in time, her mind had reverted to adolescence. A peek over her shoulder gave her a glimpse of his continued scowl. She looked forward again and walked faster. This actually topped adolescent fantasy for its absurdity. The man who had her shuddering like a schoolgirl had threatened to lock her away in an asylum!

"Are you quite all right, Miss Cantrell?" Lady Solebury asked as Leah caught up with her on the drive. "Now your cheeks are flushed."

"What? Oh, yes, I'm fine." She tried to break her thoughts free from David Traymore's magnetic pull. Her constant distraction had already raised suspicions. From now on she had to focus all her energy on appearing normal. "Seeing the spring again just shook me up a little. I guess I'll need some time before I can put my accident behind me."

"Have you remembered anything more about what happened, dear?" the marchioness asked. "Of course, you mustn't feel obliged to speak about the ordeal if you don't wish. I don't want to give you any further cause for distress."

"My memory seems to be returning, little by little," Leah said, scouring her brain for some story to concoct. Never a good liar, she had to settle for stalling. "I'll tell you everything I can when we sit down to dinner."

Lady Solebury's eyebrows rose just perceptibly. "As long as the telling does not overset you. . . ."

Leah assured her she'd manage but sighed in relief when David chose that moment to step up beside them. The marchioness turned to him, asking about conditions in the gatehouse. Meanwhile, Leah's mind raced for believable answers to the questions she would face. Why had she come to Solebury House? With whom had she been traveling and to where?

By the time they reached the manor, she knew she'd never come up with a good story. She would have to stick as close to the truth as possible—without revealing she had traveled back in time, of course. Her stomach gnawed with hunger, but she dreaded the thought of going to dinner. How long would she have before the inquisition started?

"Oh, good," Lady Solebury said when they entered the drawing room where Leah had slept the night before. "Our dinner companions have arrived. Ben, Letitia, allow me to present Miss Leah Cantrell, a friend of mine visiting from America. Miss Cantrell, Lieutenant Harlowe and his wife, Mrs. Harlowe. The lieutenant fought in the Peninsula with my late father and Mr. Traymore. I suspect he would like to return to the Continent now that Bonaparte has escaped Elba, but Mrs. Harlowe will hear nothing of the sort."

"How do you do?" Leah dropped an uncertain curtsy to a stocky, thin-haired man and a plainly dressed, thirty-something brunette. The smiles they gave her seemed to indicate she'd done well enough. The marchioness had been sweet to introduce her as a friend.

"Lady Solebury will have you believe my wife holds me on leading strings," the lieutenant said, his sharp gray eyes crinkling at the corners when he laughed. "If so, I will not be the one to confess the truth."

Leah smiled in response, as Mrs. Harlowe swatted her husband on the shoulder.

"You will have Miss Cantrell think worse of *me*!"

"Ah, Harold, there you are," Lady Solebury said, looking past Leah's shoulder toward the door. "Have you greeted the

Harlowes? Yes? Well, then, at last you will have the opportunity to meet our houseguest, Miss Cantrell. Miss Cantrell,
this is my husband, Lord Solebury."

Leah turned around and couldn't stop herself from staring. Dressed in elegantly fitted black formal wear, the marquess looked exactly how she pictured his son would in
another decade or so. The father's main differences consisted of a slightly fuller build and sprinkles of gray in his
midnight hair. She remembered David's saying he didn't
know how the marchioness had wound up with his father,
but *she* understood. With looks, presence, and power in his
favor, Lord Solebury probably could get any woman he
wanted.

She curtsied deeply, smiling without having to remind
herself.

"Charmed," he said, his dark eyes twinkling as he bowed.
"We are so pleased to have you with us, Miss Cantrell. My
wife is always eager to entertain when we stay in Kent. I
hope your visit will endure for some time."

"Thank you," she said, charmed herself. Could this man
really be the monster David implied? She glanced at the son
and found him watching her.

He switched his focus to his father, lower lip curling.

He hates him, she realized. The marquess didn't acknowledge the frown, but the sparkle in his eyes dulled. She
turned away, feeling sad for them, Lord Solebury because
his own son hated him, David because his bitterness poi-
soned his whole outlook.

But why should she care about a man who threatened her
with Bedlam? She could overlook a little moodiness—what
woman didn't get dizzy on a dose of Byronic cynicism? But
romanticism had to stop somewhere. Don Juan wielded a
cape, never a straitjacket.

"Shall we move into the dining room?" Lady Solebury suggested, leading the way into the hall. "How pleased I am to have so many guests! We have entertained very little in recent weeks, you know."

She continued to chatter, asking after the Harlowes' children as she showed everyone what seats to take.

Leah found herself next to David, studiously watching a servant place soup in front of her. The herb-tinged steam made her mouth water, but she waited for everyone else to pick up their spoons before she did. Who knew what to expect from nineteenth-century manners?

Potatoes and leeks, she determined with her first taste, letting the hearty broth loll on her tongue. She swallowed, and her stomach contracted, demanding something more substantial. She'd hardly eaten in a day and a half.

"Miss Cantrell," Mrs. Harlowe said, reaching for the roll on her bread plate, "may I inquire how long you have been in England? I hope you find our country to your liking."

Leah copied the other woman's manners, tearing a ladylike chunk from her own roll. She wished she could have finished at least one course before being questioned. "I've only been here a few days. I love what I've seen of England so far, and I can't wait to see more of the country."

Instantly she sensed all eyes on her, three pairs more intent than the others.

David took up the questioning. "You and I have had little chance to speak, Miss Cantrell. I hope your voyage from the States passed smoothly—and that you had pleasant companions to help speed your time aboard ship?"

Subtly phrased, but every bit as probing as she'd expected. She forced a smile, dabbing the corners of her mouth with a stiff linen napkin. "Unfortunately, I was seasick most of the trip. I spent a lot of time alone in my cabin, feeling too terrible to care. My traveling companion, Jeanine, is an old friend but sometimes . . . impatient. I'm afraid that being trapped in close quarters with a sick person for, uh . . . weeks took a toll on her nerves."

She jammed a piece of bread in her mouth while the others absorbed the information.

"If you will pardon my saying so, this Jeanine must be rather a fair-weather friend," Lady Solebury said, her pregnancy-puffed bustline accented by obvious indignation. "Is she the same companion who left you stranded here in Kent? Has your memory improved any in that regard?"

Across the table, Mrs. Harlowe gasped. Leah ignored the sound and nodded, looking into her soup bowl. She couldn't see any alternative but for poor Jeanine to take the brunt of the blame for her predicament.

"Yes. While Jeanine and I traveled here from London, I'm afraid her nerves wore thinner and thinner. You see, I was carsick—that is, I suffered carriage sickness, too. I'm such a bad traveler! She got tired of my complaints, we argued, and, well, I actually ended up asking to be let out of the carriage. I felt so sick I couldn't stand to go on."

"And she left you behind while she traveled on?" Lady Solebury threw her napkin down on the table. "Abominable!"

"Yes, well, I should have known better than to travel with her in the first place. We've had disagreements in the past." Leah stole a peek at David and found him watching her through narrowed eyes. She guessed he didn't believe her but meant to hear out her story. "She was the only person I know who could afford to accompany me to Europe. I wanted to see the land where my ancestors lived. I have some English blood."

"How did you wind up at the spring?" David asked.

He *would* refuse to let the conversation flow away from that topic. She resisted the urge to frown. "After Jeanine drove away, I walked up the nearest drive, looking for a place to rest. Along the way, I found the spring and thought a drink of water might help settle my stomach. But when I leaned over the pool I got dizzy. I guess I fainted, because the next thing I knew I was struggling in the water, too disoriented to pull myself out of the pool."

"Good Lord!" Mrs. Harlowe exclaimed. "What a fortunate coincidence that you had wandered onto the estate of a friend. Who knows what might have befallen an unaccompanied young woman left alone and ill amidst strangers?"

"Indeed," Lady Solebury said quickly. "I don't like even to contemplate the possibilities. And, truly, let's not distress Miss Cantrell with further discussion of her accident. We are only glad you are safely installed with us now."

"Thank you, my lady," Leah said, gladly taking up her soup spoon again.

The marchioness picked hers up, too, looking to the opposite side of the table. "Tell me, Ben, what is the latest news of Bonaparte's doings? I cannot tell you how nervous I have been since his escape from Elba. Everyone says that if he invades England, he will no doubt choose Kent for his point of entry."

"Phoebe, dear, such is hardly a more pleasant topic of conversation than the last," the marquess interrupted. "Should we not fix upon a less serious subject?"

"In a moment, Harold, but first I insist on hearing the lieutenant's views. Why, our neighbors all speak of digging out priest's holes for hiding themselves and their valuables, in the event of an attack. What do you think, Ben? Should Harold and I stow our possessions away now?"

The lieutenant sat back, pushing away his empty bowl.

"Well, Boney has been biding his time in the area of Paris for several weeks. Since he has not moved one way or another, we have no notion what direction he might take when he does."

Leah scooped up the last drops of her soup, listening with interest. Her father made a hobby of Western history—had wanted, in fact, to teach the subject at one time, before the unexpected conception of his only child cut his college days short. She knew enough from what he'd taught her to realize she had landed in England smack in the middle of Napoléon's Hundred Days campaign.

"You don't offer me much comfort, Ben." The marchioness blinked unseeingly at the deliciously presented plate of lamb a servant set in front of her. "Have you no inside intelligence you can share?"

"Phoebe, there is no reason to believe Bonaparte is headed our way," David said, reaching across the table to place his hand over hers. "In your condition, you mustn't work yourself up. Wellington is a capable leader and will do all he can to keep England safe."

Her ladyship looked so upset that Leah winced. If only she could tell her the "inside intelligence" *she* had—that Napoléon would never invade England. He'd be recaptured for good within the next few months.

"Really, my lady," she said, "I'm sure David's right. Consider how slowly Napoléon's been moving since he escaped, meandering up through the south of France and dallying in Paris for weeks. At that kind of pace, he won't get anywhere. I bet he'll never even make it into Holland."

She hadn't been able to resist throwing in a clue to the location of Napoléon's ultimate defeat, and she grinned at her secret joke.

The marchioness smiled back, touching a finger to the

corner of each of her eyes. "How kind you are, Miss Cantrell. You nearly have me convinced—you speak with such conviction."

"Yes, you do," Lieutenant Harlowe said, his gray eyes fixed on her. "May I ask why you mentioned Holland, Miss Cantrell?"

"It just came to mind." She picked up her fork, pleased that she had helped calm Lady Solebury.

"I am surprised to find you so well informed of Napoléon's activities," the lieutenant added. "Young ladies generally take little interest in the details of war."

She paused, fork in midair, privately reminding herself to stick as close to the truth as possible. "My father studies Napoléon as a hobby. I've heard far more about the man than I care even to think about."

"But surely you haven't seen your father in at least a month? At that time Bonaparte had not yet reached Paris."

Her mouth dropped open. "Why, of course not. I suppose now I'll have to confess to an unladylike interest in war. Some of my father's fascination has worn off on me, and I read the papers to keep on top of the news. Sometimes, that is. I definitely can't claim a thorough knowledge of current events."

The marquess laughed, relieving some of the tension Leah sensed building. "I should think not. Meeting a young lady who reads something other than novels, the social column, and *La Belle Assemblée* is unusual enough. One does not run across many bluestockings in Kent."

"No," Lieutenant Harlowe said, though he didn't laugh. "Nor are we often up-to-date in reading the *London Gazette*. Perhaps you know more about Bonaparte's latest moves than we do, Miss Cantrell. Why don't you give us a report?"

She swallowed a mouthful of lamb and purposely

widened her eyes. "I'm afraid I don't know any more than what we've already said. He's holed up in the Paris area."

"I think we might move onto another subject," David noted, for once choosing a course Leah liked. "Her ladyship cannot be entertained with this line of conversation."

They all looked at the marchioness, who poked at her food, clearly without any appetite.

"War talk does discomfit me," she said. "I cannot stop thinking about an invasion on Kent."

"I am sure Wellington will defeat Boney before he can even think of invading Kent, my dear," the marquess said, serious again. "But I can look into digging out a priest's hole for us, if the act would lend you any comfort."

"I believe it might." She looked up, scanning all the faces around the table. "Please forgive me. How maudlin you must think I am! Let us return to our dinner. Miss Cantrell, will you pass the salt, please?"

Leah reached for the crystal saltcellar at the same time David did. She pulled back, and his gaze followed the movement of her hand into her lap.

He passed the container to Lady Solebury and turned back to Leah. "Pardon me, Miss Cantrell. I could not help noticing that you wear a diamond. Are you betrothed?"

She lifted her hand and looked at her fingers, shocked to realize she hadn't thought of the ring or the giver since she'd arrived in the past. Even during her brush with death, Kevin's face hadn't come to her, only those of her parents. This must have been the longest stretch of time in years that she'd gone without thinking of Kevin.

"Miss Cantrell?" David sat waiting for an answer.

"No, I'm not engaged," she murmured, moving her hand back into her lap. "This is a friendship ring."

"Here in England," Lady Solebury said, "such rings are

usually woven from a lock of hair. Exchanging gold rings with stones must be an American custom. Is that indeed a diamond, Miss Cantrell?"

"Only a chip," she said, preoccupied by her thoughts. How could she forget Kevin? Not that *he* often thought of *her* first—he'd just broken up with her, after all—but she'd been sure they'd be together again. Now they might never be . . . and the thought hadn't even occurred to her until now.

She barely noticed the homemade peach ice cream served for dessert, though everyone else made a fuss over the rarity. She felt too much guilt to enjoy anything. What kind of woman forgot about a three-year relationship in the middle of a life crisis? How could she possibly have passed more than a full day without longing for the comfort of Kevin's arms?

"Are you feeling unwell again?" a soft male voice beside her asked, and she looked into David's black eyes with a start. "You have barely touched your ice cream."

His tone alone had her heart racing, and she realized the answer to her question looked her right in the face. She hated herself for her own shallowness, but the fact was that David Traymore's strong presence had chased all thoughts of Kevin right out of her head.

She gave her Byronic rescuer an unsteady smile. "I'm still not quite sure of myself. I think I'd best take things slowly for a while."

What an understatement, she thought as she finally dipped into her dessert. In this bizarre parallel universe, every step she took seemed to put her on more dangerous footing.

Chapter 6

"THANK GOODNESS MISS Cantrell has begun to open up," Phoebe said to David. She looked across the drawing room, where the young woman sat with Lord Solebury and the Harlowes. "Still, I fancy there is more to her story than she willingly admits."

"Unquestionably." He watched Leah (he could only think of her by her given name now) as she laughed at something his father said. Her eyes sparkled, and Solebury grinned back, clearly entranced. David rolled his own eyes and forced his attention to Phoebe. "You, too, noticed the flaw in her story?"

"The flaw?" Her gaze darted to his. "Why, no. I only observed that she spoke in a halting manner. What did she say that you found amiss?"

"She failed to explain a rather important point. According to her story, she fell into the spring while trying to get a drink, but when I found her she was wearing only a shift. I don't know of many young ladies who travel in such a state of *deshabille,* do you?"

"Oh, David, I forgot all about that." Phoebe put a hand up over her mouth. "Good Lord, there is only one conclusion to draw. She must have been ravished. The thought is too dreadful, but it would explain everything—her disoriented state of mind, the fact that we could not find her clothing near the spring . . . even the motive behind her act of desperation. Oh, David, that poor, poor girl!"

"I don't know, Phoebe." He swallowed the sick lump that rose in his throat, despite his having already considered the same possibility. "She suffered no bruises, and her shift had not even a rent. I think that sort of a struggle would leave more physical evidence."

"Perhaps." The marchioness looked across the room again, studying Leah for a moment. "Yes, you may be right. I pray you are. A victim of ravishment would likely be more devastated than Miss Cantrell appears, would she not?"

David let his gaze drift after hers. Leah now spoke with Mrs. Harlowe, leaning forward to examine a locket the woman wore. She said something, and both of them smiled broadly. He *had* to be right. But what on earth did the true story involve?

While he pondered the mystery, Lieutenant and Mrs. Harlowe rose and announced their intent to leave. As Phoebe pressed the lady to stay the night, the husband walked over to where David stood, slightly apart from the others.

"Might I have a word with you?" he asked. "In private."

"Of course." Curious, David led him into the hall. "Is this private enough, or shall we go into the library?"

"This will do." The lieutenant glanced back into the drawing room, where the rest of the party remained talking. He turned back to David but focused his eyes on the floor. "I am not quite sure how to broach this subject."

"You had best broach it quickly," David said, made uneasy by his friend's manner. "The others are not far behind."

Harlowe nodded, gaze still averted. "Pray forgive me, but I must ask how well the marchioness knows Miss Cantrell. The young lady mentioned this is her first visit to England, so I gather their past acquaintance was limited to correspondence. Can you tell me any more about the friendship?"

David frowned, reluctant to share what little he knew about Leah. She undoubtedly needed protection from something, and until he knew from what or whom, he could not allow speculation about her to spread. "Why do you inquire?"

Harlowe rubbed one of his pork-chop sideburns, again peering toward the rest of the party, who had not yet moved. "I realize I appear to be prying, and I apologize, but I would not do so unless I felt I had cause." Finally he looked David in the eye. "Do you recall Miss Cantrell's remarks over dinner about Bonaparte's trail through France?"

"I do."

Face muscles taut, the lieutenant lowered his voice to a whisper. "And what she said about Boney being defeated before he can take Holland?"

"Yes." David had no conception where the man was leading.

"Well, I should not tell you this, Traymore, but I am confident you, above all people, can be trusted." He wet his lips. "There are top-secret intelligence reports that indicate Bonaparte's military plans do indeed lie in that direction. No one, but no one, knows this . . . except Miss Cantrell, apparently."

In spite of—or perhaps due to—his friend's gravity,

David laughed. "Oh, Ben, my stepmother's hysteria must have rubbed off on you tonight. Miss Cantrell's *insight* is surely no more than a lucky guess."

Harlowe shook his head. "Normally, I would agree, but I swear I saw a glint of amusement in her eyes when she made the comment—this while everyone else in the room fairly ached with sympathy for Lady Solebury. I thought her behavior very odd, Traymore."

This observation made him think. He, too, had seen the wry smile accompanying Leah's prediction. At the time he had shrugged off her little grin, but the timing of it definitely had been strange.

"Do you accuse her of being a French spy?" he asked.

"No. That is, I don't know. Odds are that she is a perfectly ordinary, amiable young lady, and the last thing I want to do is insult Lady Solebury with wild conjectures about her friend. But I cannot help noting that the girl is American; she has no reason to feel loyalty to the Crown. If she and the marchioness are not well acquainted—and I believe this is the case—I think you may do well to keep an eye on her."

David had to admit, ridiculous as the lieutenant's notion seemed, that this latest theory had about as much validity as any other explanation for Leah Cantrell's presence. Suicide, insanity, rape, espionage . . . what would be the next extreme attributed to this woman's life?

Harlowe awaited his response, but he had little desire to offer any. He shuffled his feet and shrugged.

The lieutenant gave him a stiff smile, likely trying to lighten the awkwardness that had descended on them. "You must agree that watching her could afford your eyes no strain. The chit is certainly not difficult to look at."

David only raised an eyebrow.

His old friend sighed. "In trying to spare Lady Solebury's

feelings, I see I have insulted you. Again, I apologize for what I acknowledge is overcaution. Military circumspection dies hard. But I wish you would at least tell me if you plan to stay on at Solebury House while she is here."

David pursed his lips, half offended for Leah's sake, half disturbed by the possibility the outlandish allegation could be true. He wanted to begrudge Harlowe an answer, wishing the man had never brought his conjecture to light. But such an antic would be childish.

"I will be at the gatehouse for the time being," he said, enlightening himself as well as Harlowe. "I don't foresee leaving any time soon."

"Then I have every faith that all will be well here." The lieutenant swept him a bow. "Tonight has been a pleasure. I hope you will excuse all I have said, as well as keep my thoughts to yourself. I should not want to add to Lady Solebury's worries about the war."

David nodded, stepping away as the rest of the party at last made their way into the hall. While the others exchanged goodbyes, he watched Leah smiling and offering pleasantries.

Could she possibly be a French spy? If so, she would uncover little information at Solebury House. But perhaps she only meant to establish herself among a prominent family and work her way into society. Situated within the local circle, she could glean details of how Kentish estates prepared for invasion. So she would indeed have intelligence to gain. He would have to watch her even more carefully than previously planned.

Gaze still fixed on her, he twisted his mouth. Ever since he had pulled her out of that damned spring, she had commandeered his thoughts, influenced his decisions. Why, a mere two days ago he could not have imagined anything inducing him to stay on his father's estate. Now he had just told Harlowe he would be here indefinitely. Leah Cantrell had too much leverage on him. He would have to get to the bottom of her story before she wasted any more of his time and energy.

When the Harlowes' carriage had started up the drive, Phoebe closed the door and leaned back against it. "Phew! I am exhausted. I fear I may have to retire soon."

"You deserve a good night's rest after such a conscientious job of hostessing," the marquess said, putting an arm around her shoulders.

Not to mention all the other tumult she has faced, David thought. Suddenly he realized that if Phoebe retired, he might be able to question Leah more closely than the marchioness would allow.

"Why don't you go upstairs now?" he suggested. "I will be happy to entertain Miss Cantrell."

She smiled at him. "Somehow, I thought I might count on you. But before I go upstairs, I need to ask you something. I saw Ben draw you aside before he left. I know I ought not intrude on a personal confidence, but I have an inkling your discussion had to do with Bonaparte. I should like to know if I am correct."

His jaw went slack for an instant before he recalled himself. "Why, of course not, Phoebe. Why would you think so? You will drive yourself mad with all these unwarranted fears."

"You never were a good liar, David. If we are in danger, I have a right to know." She placed a hand on her protruding belly. "I have an unborn child to protect. I have a large estate to help defend. Now what did Ben tell you? I don't care whether the information is classified or not."

Solebury turned his wife toward him, wrapping both arms

around her. "Now, now, love, all this anxiety cannot do the baby any good. Please try to calm yourself . . . for your sake and the child's."

The appeal to maternal instinct proved an effective approach. Phoebe leaned into his body, closing her eyes and breathing slowly.

"If you'll pardon my interrupting, my lady," Leah said, her tone gentle, "I, personally, have total confidence Napoléon will never invade England. After being defeated once, only think what a hard time he must be having getting soldiers together. Ships will probably be even harder to come by. He'll never regain enough power to launch an attack by sea."

David stared at her. She sounded more like a military strategist than a civilian woman. Unfortunately, Harlowe's spy theory looked that much more creditable.

"You have a good deal of sense, Miss Cantrell." Phoebe opened her eyes and stood straighter, still encircled by her husband's arms. She looked to David. "I am sorry for asking you to betray Ben's confidence. With this baby coming, I fear I am rather more emotional than usual."

"I am the one who should apologize." He felt terrible for heightening her fears with his plain attempt at lying. "I can tell you this much, Phoebe. Part of what Ben told me was that he knew no reason to expect an invasion on Kent. In that, I am speaking the truth."

Her eyes searched his, then she nodded. "I know you are."

Solebury bent and kissed the top of her head. "Will you be all right now, love?"

"Quite. But I must confess I am growing eager for my confinement. No doubt I shall feel more myself again once the baby has come."

"No doubt," he said. "Now, why don't we both retire? You have had a very long day."

"I shall, but you must feel free to stay up, Harold. You and David will enjoy Miss Cantrell's company."

David saw yet a better chance to quiz Leah. "Actually, I had thought to ask Miss Cantrell to join me for a walk in the gardens. A lovely spring evening should not be wasted indoors."

Leah shot him a surprised look.

Phoebe shook her head. "David, Miss Cantrell won't want to walk out alone at night with a man she scarcely knows." She turned to Leah. "Of course, if you are inclined to walk, my dear, I can assure you my stepson is a perfect gentleman—in that respect, anyway. But your reluctance is entirely understandable. Admirably prudent, in fact."

Leah glanced from the marchioness to David and back again. "No, I trust David—in that respect." She smiled. "And the fresh air will do me good. I'll go."

"You are not tired?" Phoebe asked. "Between your accident and my laudanum, you have suffered quite a trial."

"On the contrary, I'm wide awake. I slept so late today that the last thing I want to do is close my eyes again. A brisk walk may be just what I need to use up some of this energy."

"Very well, then." She looked to Solebury. "Will you join them, love, or do you have something else to occupy you?"

"I have the estate accounts to review, but I shan't be long. Once David has brought Miss Cantrell safely back to the house, I shall retire, too."

"Wonderful." She turned back to the others. "If you need anything when you return, the servants will accommodate you. And, Miss Cantrell, dear, if you should ever want me—

for any reason at all—don't hesitate to have Molly summon me. Good night to both of you."

She kissed Solebury on the cheek and began a slow ascent of the stairs. David watched her progress with a tug of compassion. At this late stage of her pregnancy, she could ill afford a mysterious houseguest and a head full of worries about war. If he could do anything at all to help, he would be happy to stay at the gatehouse.

He turned to Leah and offered her his elbow. She smiled and curled her hand around his arm. The pressure of her fingers through his shirt set his skin to tingling. *Foolishness.* He reminded himself this walk had nothing to do with pleasure.

"Don't be long," Solebury said, his eyes narrowing as he scanned David's face. "Remember that Miss Cantrell is recovering from a difficult experience."

He met his father's gaze squarely. "You have no need to worry, my lord."

The marquess nodded. "Enjoy the evening, then."

Leah thanked him, and they stepped outside into a mild night. Solebury waited until they had descended from the portico before he closed the door, shutting out the light from the hall chandelier. Without speaking, they started up the moonlit drive, attended by a chorus of crickets and countless twinkling stars.

After a long moment David heard a soft sigh from her.

"This is beautiful," she murmured, "like being in a fairy tale."

He could not think how to respond, incapable of disagreeing and unwilling to concur. The splendid evening made an unfit backdrop for an interrogation. How on earth should he begin?

She adjusted her grasp on his arm, nestling a little closer

in the process. Her body felt warm and snug against his side, and the scent of rosewater grazed his nostrils.

"When you suggested walking," she said, "I had no idea you'd had a stroke of genius."

He had thought so, but now his intellect failed him entirely. No sensible comment would come to him.

She sighed. "This place seems so magical. Funny, I never used to believe in magic. . . ."

Her voice trailed off with her last words, as though she had drifted into thought. He looked at her and saw that she stared at the sky, her expression now sober.

"Do you believe in magic now?" he asked, immediately deploring the pointless inquiry. He had so many *important* questions, yet he would waste his time with nonsense.

"Oh, yes." She pulled her gaze down from the heavens and gave him a soft smile, the sort of smile that had kept men speculating about the *Mona Lisa* for centuries. "And, for the moment, I'm not even afraid of it. The magic I feel right now is too beautiful to fear."

Too beautiful to fear. He stared into her starlit eyes and felt the weight of those words, even as he chided himself for melodrama. He had to begin his questioning, before this encounter took on all the aspect of a romantic tryst rather than an investigation. But where should he start?

A light breeze blew, wafting the scent of tulips over from Lady Solebury's private garden. Leah closed her eyes, breathing in the fragrance with a smile.

He squelched the urge to lean over and kiss her, forcing himself to think of French espionage. *She could be a French spy.* He had to ask her . . . ask her *something*!

" . . . *Parlez-vous français?*" The words emerged without forethought, but at least he had posed a question.

She laughed, a light chuckle that echoed quietly in the

trees. "I have to wonder why you're speaking French, David, but maybe a night like this calls for a romance language. Let's see. Give me a minute to remember what little I know."

While he stared at her, she looked up at the sky, then back into his eyes. "Okay, to answer your question: *Un peu, monsieur.* Wait, more is coming to me. *Je m'appelle Leah. Je suis americaine. Comment allez-vous?*"

She had the worst accent imaginable, pronouncing her French words even more flatly than her English. Of course, he had proved nothing in this exercise. She could be feigning her ineptitude. Or she might even communicate to the French in her own peculiarly bland English.

"You haven't answered my question, *monsieur,*" she said, grinning at him. *"Comment allez-vous?"*

He gazed down into her face. In the moonlight her skin looked just like cream, spilling down her lovely cheekbones, over her slim neck, and into the expanse of her bosom

"David, you started this game. Now you have to tell me how you are. And on this gorgeous night, I defy you to answer anything but *'Très bien.'* Now, come on." She tilted her head sideways. *"Comment allez-vous?"*

Her eyes glittered like the stars in the clear sky above. The sweet, lopsided way she smiled at him rendered her silly request irresistible.

"Très bien, mademoiselle," he whispered.

She grinned wider, revealing a pearly set of perfectly even teeth.

They watched each other for a long moment, David increasingly aware of the heat of her body against his. Taking a deep breath, he shifted slightly aside. She loosened her grip to allow his movement, letting her fingers slide down his arm. Somehow, they ended in holding hands.

Her fingers felt slender and warm, and he lifted them, his

dazed mind focused on kissing her hand, if not her lips. But the sudden sight of her ring halted him. He looked back up into her eyes, unconsciously twisting the gold band around her finger.

She dropped her gaze to their clasped hands, and her smile faded. With a brief glance at his face, she looked away, staring at the path ahead.

The muscles in his midsection tightened. Obviously, the ring had more significance than she had indicated. And why should that surprise him? Had she been candid about anything else whatsoever?

"I think maybe we should return to the house," she said, extracting her fingers from his. She transferred them back up to his upper arm, her touch light and cool. "Lord Solebury will wonder what's happened to us."

He acquiesced silently, turning back with her to retrace their steps. With each stride his chance to interrogate her slipped further away, but only one question loomed is his mind—and the subject had nothing to do with espionage.

"Your friendship ring is from a male friend." The question, in fact, came out more as a statement.

She hesitated only briefly. "Yes."

"And you share more than mere friendship with him?"

This time the paused lasted longer. "We *did*."

Did. Implying the relationship had ended—but she still wore the ring. Not that any of it signified! He should have abandoned the matter and moved on to something more important—but at the moment, nothing felt more important. "Did you and he talk of marrying?"

She shrugged and, he noted, failed to meet his gaze. "The topic came up, but we never got near the point of making plans. As I said earlier, he gave me the ring in friendship."

An odd sort of friendship, he reflected, his guts now

sour—he must have eaten too much rich food at the manor. Despite the discomfort in his abdomen, he fancied he could feel the cold metal of her gold band through his sleeve, where her fingers rested. And now more questions—inappropriate questions—erupted from him as of their own will.

"Do you still think of marrying him?"

She shook her head. "He is very far away."

"And if he were here?"

"Here?" The idea seemed to affect her oddly, as though she had never considered such a prospect. She bit her lip, glanced at him, and faced forward again. "Actually, if he were here now, I don't believe marrying him would be on my mind at all."

They had reached the front of the manor, and she let go of his arm, leading the way up the steps.

"Thank you for a lovely walk." She smiled but not so naturally as she had earlier. "Will I see you tomorrow?"

"You will." He thought of her earlier return to the scene of her accident and added, "Remember, you promised not to go to the spring on your own."

"I remember." She held his gaze. "You're kind to worry about me."

He stared at her a moment longer, searching his mind one last time for a question pertinent to espionage. Instead, her safety occupied his every thought.

"If you find you want to face the spring again, tell me and I will take you there myself. If you feel you must leap into the water, then I shall leap in with you."

Her eyebrows drew together, and he thought he saw her lip quiver. "You're . . . brave."

He snorted. "I am not likely to fear a few feet of water."

She looked up the dark drive, toward the woods surrounding the spring. "Are you afraid of the unknown?"

"The unknown? *You,* for example?"

She made no answer.

"My greatest fears are based in the evils I know," he said, hoping to prime her candor with some of his own. "The unknown at least offers the possibility of good, as well as evil."

She shivered, hugging herself to rub her own arms. "It offers *something.*"

"Certainly too much to throw away."

"Yes." She nodded, finally looking back to his face. "Don't worry about that. I wouldn't throw away any of this. Good night, David."

She gave him another small smile and disappeared through the door, leaving him to wonder what on earth their obscure exchange had truly signified.

He sighed and started off for the gatehouse. So much for his interrogation. Relevant questions would have to wait for another time.

Chapter 7

STARTLED AWAKE, LEAH sat up in bed. She could have sworn she'd heard someone scream—or had it been her own mind crying out for help? Now she heard only the sound of birds chirping outside the window. The orange glow of dawn lent a cheerful peachy tint to the yellow wallpaper.

A muffled moan came from somewhere outside the closed door to the hall.

Someone *had* cried out.

She kicked off the covers and scrambled out of bed. Without a thought for the robe the marchioness had lent her, she dashed out of the room in her nightgown. The sound of someone sniffling traveled up the hallway, and she hurried toward the source, her bare feet padding on the carpet.

When she rounded a turn, she nearly ran into Lady Solebury's maid. The girl slumped on a sparse wooden chair in the hall, tears streaming down her reddened cheeks.

"What's wrong, Molly?" Leah stooped down beside her, placing one hand on her arm. "Is there something I can do?"

"Oh, miss, I wish you might! Alas, my mistress has gone into labor, and the babe is coming too early." She pulled a big white handkerchief out of her apron pocket and blew her nose, nodding toward a door across the hall. "The midwife is in there now. She wanted me to go downstairs with his lordship and Mr. Traymore, but I reckoned my lady might want me."

Leah looked at the closed door and, between Molly's sniffles, heard quiet voices coming from the room. She distinguished two women, speaking in tones that sounded calm.

"Are you sure the marchioness is in labor?" she asked the maid. "Has she cried out in pain?"

"She was crying before the midwife came," Molly said, "though she's settled down since. Mayhap Mrs. Carson gave her a potion to soothe her."

Leah frowned, wondering how a "potion" might affect the unborn child. Given her own recent experience, she hoped the marchioness hadn't taken laudanum.

The door opened, and a woman who could have been Mrs. Santa Claus came into the hall. Her pure white hair formed a neat bun, and clusters of crinkles around her eyes showed that she spent a lot of her life smiling.

"I am Harriet Carson," she said to Leah while Molly pushed past her to get into the room, "the midwife. Are you a relative of her ladyship?"

"A houseguest. My name is Leah Cantrell." She bobbed a brief curtsy. "Is the marchioness in labor?"

Mrs. Carson curtsied in return, shaking her snowy head. "False alarm. My lady suffered a few pangs of pain, but they seem to have passed. I reckon she'll carry full term, providing she keeps to her bed. If you are a friend to her, you'll see that she stays put."

"I'll do anything I can."

"For the moment, you can go in and sit with her while I coax that silly maid into fetching the marquess." She glanced back toward the bed, where Molly kneeled beside Lady Solebury. "If the girl stays here, she'll only work her ladyship into a state. I'll have a long talk with her before I leave, but I'm glad the marchioness has a sensible friend like you to counter that fretting maid."

She walked back into the bedroom, but Leah paused in the doorway, reluctant to intrude.

Propped against a mound of pillows, Lady Solebury murmured a greeting as the midwife returned to her. When she noticed Leah, she stretched her neck to give her a faint smile. "Miss Cantrell, I am sorry to have disturbed your sleep. Do come in for a moment, so I can assure you all is well."

"You haven't disturbed me, my lady." Leah stepped up to the bed, still feeling uncomfortable. "I'm only glad to hear you're not in danger."

The marchioness bit her lip. "I daresay I have let my nerves get the best of me. If only I can temper my concerns about the war, I shall be perfectly fine. Mrs. Carson has insisted that I keep to my bed, however."

"A good idea, my lady." Leah glanced toward the midwife, who spoke in low tones to the anxious maid while she maneuvered the girl into the hallway. "She seems a very sensible woman."

"Indeed, she is the best midwife in the county. I only wish I could have remained on my feet a little longer." Her ladyship sighed. "I meant to make my rounds with the tenants today. Every week or so I bring the less fortunate ones baskets of fruit and bread. The gesture is small, but I like to think the children benefit from it."

"I'm sure they do."

"I suppose I shall have to send Molly in my stead, but I fear she will make a mull of it." She shook her head. "I cannot do without the girl, but whenever a situation has the air of a crisis, she falls to pieces. She will worry about me ceaselessly for the next few weeks."

"I'd be happy to take care of the baskets, my lady," Leah said. The idea of knocking at strangers' doors in a foreign country *and* a foreign time intimidated her, but the gifts she'd be bearing would probably win her a good reception. "I'd like to make myself as useful as possible while I'm staying with you."

"Would you truly not mind?" Lady Solebury's shoulders relaxed visibly, and Leah thought she saw color seep back into her cheeks. "How kind you are, Miss Cantrell. I loathe to charge you with such a time-consuming task, but I believe the goods are important to the little ones."

Leah waved off her thanks. "Consider the baskets delivered. Is there anything else I can do to help?"

"Seeing the tenants will be quite enough for now. I wonder if I should send Molly along, or if she would only prove a hindrance to you."

"Send Molly along where?" a man's voice asked behind Leah.

She whirled around and faced the marquess, his son behind him, remaining at the door. David's gaze captured hers briefly and swept down her body before he quickly looked away.

His glance reminded her she should have put on a robe, though her long silk nightgown didn't divulge much. David looked like he'd also rushed out of bed, his sleep-puffed face a little more vulnerable than usual. His sooty hair was tousled and his white shirt only halfway buttoned, revealing a hint of well-toned chest. Her thoughts flew to their late-night walk—how intimate the mood had gotten before the sight of Kevin's ring had come between them.

This morning she'd had a weird dream that the two of them were arguing about her ring—Kevin telling her to wear it, David urging her to throw it in the spring.

She peeked at David and caught his eye. Embarrassed, she dragged her attention back toward the bed.

Lord Solebury had gone to his wife's side and taken her hand. "You ought not even think about household matters, my love—though I confess that right now any plan that will take Molly out of the way sounds wise to me."

She smiled up at him. "Miss Cantrell has very kindly offered to deliver the tenant baskets for me, and I feel a good deal better knowing the job will get done. But, indeed, I am not convinced I should send Molly along in her current state. The coachman knows which tenants I usually visit. He can guide Miss Cantrell to the right cottages."

"I shall go with Miss Cantrell," David said, crossing the threshold to join them. His mouth formed a grim line, and his tone was firm. "Have Molly help the housekeeper today."

Leah looked at him in surprise, wondering about his motives. Normally, she'd think he offered out of politeness or simply to be with her, but his grimace seemed to rule out both. He must have still considered her under suicide watch, and he didn't look too happy about having to guard her.

He didn't seem to mind being with me last night, she thought, bothered by the change in him. She wanted their walk back again, with him holding her hand and speaking soft French in the dark. The memory sent a shiver down her spine.

How ridiculous could she be?

"So you have taken up an interest in helping those in need?" The marquess curled his lip in a manner reminiscent of his son's. He slid a quick glance at Leah, then back to David, who glared at him without comment.

"David has always shown a benevolent character," Lady Solebury said, tugging on her husband's sleeve until he looked to her instead of his son. "He fought nobly in the Peninsula and was a great personal help to my father as well. His offer to escort Miss Cantrell is very thoughtful. She will feel more comfortable if she has someone to accompany her, and he will do far more admirably than Molly."

"Perhaps Miss Cantrell would not agree." The marquess looked at Leah. "Do you find my son's escort acceptable?"

She turned to David, who coolly matched her gaze. She'd seen heat in those eyes when he looked at her last night—until she'd glimpsed Kevin's ring and been attacked by guilt. She'd felt she owed something to a guy she'd dated for three years—but *why*, when that same guy had broken off the relationship half a dozen times? The truth was she didn't care anymore—and she had a right not to care! Now she regretted pulling back from David and extinguishing the fire in his eyes. This man had a cauldron of emotion bubbling just beneath the surface. What if she'd lost her one chance to unleash his passion?

At least he still wanted to go with her today, even if for the wrong reasons.

"More than acceptable," she answered the marquess, still eyeing his son. "I'll be glad to have his company."

David nodded to her, expressionless, while she stirred her

own brew of emotions. Had she been right to try to preserve a sense of loyalty to Kevin—or had she foolishly ruined her chances for . . . for what? What could she expect from a romantic involvement in this time period? What little she knew about this society promised some major problems.

She glanced at the clasped hands of the marquess and marchioness, their wedding bands and her rounded belly prominent symbols of nineteenth-century love. If Leah let David know about her attraction to him and he returned it, would marriage and instant baby-making be their only option? She had always wanted children but hadn't imagined them coming until years down the line. In this era reliable family planning would no longer be an alternative—and here a woman risked her life with every pregnancy. Poor Lady Solebury! No wonder she had problems with nerves. In her place Leah would be a wreck.

Her gaze shot to David's perfect profile, grazing the straight, noble nose, and the dark lashes edging his eyes. The thought of having his baby made her shudder—but not completely because of fear. She must be insane to think about marrying and bearing the children of a man she'd met two days before! But she couldn't help wondering if his thoughts had touched on the same subject. Why else had he asked all those questions about Kevin?

No, ridiculous. She looked downward, focusing on the bare toes that peeked out under her nightgown. Her fantasies had run rampant ever since her fantastic voyage back through time. She needed to slow down, think clearly, plant her feet in reality . . . nineteenth-century reality, if she had no other choice.

"Cook will have the baskets prepared shortly after breakfast," the marchioness said. "No doubt she has already started putting them together. John Coachman will be ready to drive you around—"

"I can drive," David interrupted. "I will talk to the coachman beforehand to learn which tenants we are to visit."

"Suit yourself," her ladyship said. Suddenly she grinned, as if she'd had an amusing thought. If so, she didn't share it, subduing her smile to look to her husband. "Have one of the maids fetch Cook for me when you go downstairs, won't you, Harold? I have a few additional instructions for her."

"Gladly." He beamed down at her. "I am so pleased to see you smiling again, love. You have already recovered much of your usual glow."

Leah noted that the marquess hadn't exaggerated. His wife looked happy, even flushed with excitement.

"I have simply recalled how many good things there are in life," she said. "With all my worries about the war, I have been dwelling too much on the bad."

"Well, I intend to do all I can to lay your worries to rest." He brushed her hair back from her forehead. "You keep concentrating on the good."

Leah glanced at David, expecting to read scorn in his face for all this tenderness. Instead, she saw concern in his crunched brow, deep thought in his narrowed eyes.

"I should like to speak with you on that head, Solebury," he said. "Do you have a moment to join me in the study?"

The marquess raised an eyebrow. "Of course. Or would you rather discuss your thoughts over breakfast?"

"I should rather speak with you now, if possible." He slid a quick glance at Leah and then back to his father. "The idea is fresh at the moment."

Leah didn't hear what the marquess replied, too stunned by the latest emotion she'd discerned in David . . . distrust, dropping like a veil over his eyes when his gaze had met hers.

Considering all she'd been hiding from him, she really had no reason to feel surprise.

Chapter 8

"WELL DONE, DAVID." Solebury dropped two lumps of sugar into his tea and stirred the steaming cup. "I had no idea the gatehouse concealed a secret tunnel."

David swallowed a bite of croissant. Somehow he had wound up eating breakfast with his father after all—not that he cared, since Leah had not joined them, and his chief concern had been to keep her from hearing his plan.

"If *you* never discovered or heard about the entrance, I doubt anyone else has." He paused to sip his orange juice. "Even if someone does know, using the tunnel will provide more security than digging out a priest's hole. Such a project would require a number of laborers."

"And all would know the location." The marquess added a dollop of cream to his cup. "In any case, once we store whatever valuables Phoebe thinks we ought, we can seal off the entrance thoroughly enough to confound a casual thief.

As for Boney's troops, I don't actually expect them to invade, but if they do, they shall have no clue to the tunnel's existence."

"True," David said, "but retaining as much secrecy as possible can only afford an advantage. I suggest keeping your activities from the servants and even from neighbors and friends—Miss Cantrell, for example. What good can come of spreading the information?"

Solebury nodded. "I shall swear Phoebe to secrecy, perhaps not even tell her where the tunnel is. You have a good head on your shoulders, boy."

David's gaze leaped to his father's face, but he refused to match the marquess's tentative smile. Instead, he looked back to his plate, picking up a knife to spread marmalade over a second croissant.

"Would that your brother had inherited half the sense you have," Solebury added, his tone lower, as if he thought aloud.

David looked at him again and saw that his brow had creased with lines of worry.

"Further tales from London?" he could not resist asking.

"Only more of the same." The marquess gulped his tea and stared into the cup. "William has written to ask for yet another advance on his quarterly allowance. I can tell you he is already drawn well into next year, and I suspect another stipend will do little to ease the debts he has amassed. This time I shall deny him. He has to learn responsibility eventually."

Did he indeed? David might have laughed but settled for smirking as he bit into his roll. William had never had to fend for himself, and, with a title and a large estate coming his way, he never would. Creditors would make exceptions. Solebury would capitulate and cover his heir's debts. Young men of William's prospects never wanted much of anything for long.

"Good morning," a cheerful feminine voice addressed them from the arched entrance to the breakfast room. Leah stepped inside, dressed in a white muslin gown adorned with pink sprigs. David could still picture her in the sleek nightrail she had worn earlier, her hair wonderfully disarrayed by sleep. Since then, she had pinned the long locks up in a loose knot. He wished he could reach out and free them again but clenched his fists against his longing.

Annoyed by the course of his thoughts, he dragged himself to his feet and nodded a greeting. Solebury had already sprung up to pull out a chair for her.

She sat down, tendering her thanks with a grin that turned wry when she glanced down the table to acknowledge David's scant welcome. "Molly brought tea and toast to my room earlier, but I think I'll have some of those strawberries. I always try to eat some fruit at breakfast."

"Do you have the same fruits in Philadelphia as we do here, Miss Cantrell?" Solebury asked with a broad smile that rankled David. He surmised that his father had used the same radiating charm to win Phoebe. Could he not let up a bit, now that he already had a wife half his age—or nearly so?

"Oh . . . yes, pretty much." She spooned several large berries into her dish. "Strawberries . . . apples, cherries. Of course, everyone knows the story of Washington and the cherry tree."

"Do we?" Solebury laughed, eyes twinkling, while David pushed his plate away, no longer hungry.

She stopped with her spoon in midair. "Oh, I guess you wouldn't hear moral tales about George Washington here in

England, would you? Never mind. This one is only a little legend told to children to teach them the value of honesty."

"And did *you* learn honesty from it, Miss Cantrell?" David cut into their prattle, watching for her reaction.

A muscle in her cheek twitched, but she smiled and met his gaze. "In the story Washington is a boy and confronted by his father about whether he chopped down a certain cherry tree he shouldn't have. He replies, 'I cannot tell a lie' and admits he did. If someone confronted me with a similar charge, then yes, I'd answer just as honestly."

"But you won't reveal anything beyond what you are asked."

For an instant her eyebrows tilted with apparent regret. He got the impression she wanted to confide her story but could not. But why not? Because she served as a spy for France? Or because she feared someone from her past? A stab of compassion prevented him from probing further. Besides, he reasoned, such questions ought to wait until they spoke in private. The mere fact that she kept personal information to herself did not warrant alarming the whole household.

Solebury leaned back in his chair, clearly free of any unusual curiosity. "Unfortunately, the current crop of English royals are unlikely to inspire moral tales in our people. I don't suppose you, being an American, think much of our monarchy, do you, Miss Cantrell?"

"I have to admit I'm glad *we* don't have one." Other women would have answered lightly, but she spoke seriously, obviously weighing her words. "There's no question that equality is a worthy ideal. No offense intended, but I can't support making birth the determining factor in choosing who leads the world and who gets trampled on."

David bristled, ever conscious of his own birth, but all her attention appeared to rest with Solebury.

"No offense taken." The marquess dabbed a napkin to his lips. "After all that has happened in France, one wonders how much longer the English nobility can continue."

She smiled. "I'd bet anything the system lasts at least another two hundred years."

"You sound so confident," David noted. He had never met a woman who spoke on political issues with such assurance.

"I wish *I* felt the same," Solebury said, "but even if the nobility endures, I fear my title shan't. I expect the estate will be run to the ground within a decade of my demise, with the way my son squanders money."

Leah's gaze traveled to David.

"Not I," he scoffed. "The *heir*."

She studied him for a long moment, her forehead furrowing. At last he grew so uncomfortable, he threw down his napkin and stood to leave the room.

"You're finished?" she asked, abandoning her frown and rising. "If so, I think we should go. The sooner we deliver the baskets, the better Lady Solebury will rest. Are you ready?"

He looked into her expectant eyes, ruing his decision to accompany her. Every second he spent with her felt like a struggle . . . against losing his wits in her beauty, against losing his dignity in her scrutiny.

But he could hardly allow her to go alone, free to glean intelligence for the French . . . or to leap into the spring again, if her objective lay there. He grimaced. "Let's go."

When they emerged from the house, they found Solebury's barouche packed with nearly a dozen baskets. The sun shone bright and warm, so they elected to ride outside on the box. At the last minute a groom warned them not to visit one of the houses, due to a case of smallpox. Then they set off.

David fixed his attention straight ahead as he directed the horses up the drive. He knew he should take the opportunity to question Leah more thoroughly now that he had her alone, but he first needed to gather his thoughts. His ill-judged attempt at speaking French to her had proved the folly of rushing an endeavor as serious as interrogation.

"You know, you shouldn't let your birth bother you so much," she said suddenly, shattering his thoughts. "I know it's none of my business, but you'd feel much better if you could let go of your bitterness."

He stared at her. In his entire adult experience, no one had ever dared broach the subject of his birth with him. But Leah Cantrell always managed to fall beyond the pale.

"You are right in one respect," he said finally, turning away from her to urge the horses into a trot. "You have no concern in the matter. Next time confine your advice to matters you understand."

"But I do understand, in a way. You see, I was conceived out of wedlock, too."

Again, he shot a look at her.

She met his gaze calmly, as though her statement had been no more outrageous than a remark about the weather. "Of course, my experience has been a lot different from yours. My parents did marry before I was born—only six months before, though."

He could think of no response. Would a time ever come when this woman could no longer shock him? Might shocking him even be her intention? Or did she mean to win him over by confiding some wild, contrived tale designed to gain his sympathy?

"Unfortunately, my father has always resented the marriage—and me—for being foisted on him." She looked down at her lap, fiddling with her well-manicured fingernails. "He doesn't come out and say so, of course, but sometimes his resentment shows. He did nothing to help me get through college, for example—actually impeded my progress in some ways. And I really think it was because *I* cut *his* education short, just by existing."

"What do you mean 'get you through college'?" he asked. "What sort of college could you have attended?"

She hesitated. "I went to . . . school. You must realize our education system is different from yours. I probably am more educated than most women you know, but that's beside the point. What I'm saying is, at least your father doesn't resent you. You know, fathers are never perfect anyway. Down deep, I know my father loves me, and I'm sure Lord Solebury loves you. I can see it in the way he looks at you. Have you noticed that he watches you all the time?"

Did Solebury truly pay him inordinate attention? David shrugged off the reflection and guided the horses down a dirt lane. "This is the Browns' cottage. Our first stop."

He jumped off the box and retrieved one of the baskets from inside the barouche. By the time he circled the vehicle to help Leah, she had already climbed down on her own.

"*This* is where they live?" she asked, gaping at the cottage.

He glanced at the tiny shack, which appeared ordinary in every way, except, perhaps, that the roof had been thatched more recently than most tenants' homes. "Yes."

A woman came to the door, a babe in her arms and two smaller children at her apron strings.

"Mrs. Brown?" Leah stepped forward and offered her hand, an unexpected courtesy that David respected. "I'm Leah Cantrell. I've offered to deliver Lady Solebury's food baskets for her today, so she can have some time to rest."

"Goodness, I hope her ladyship is well." The woman curt-

sied to Leah's outstretched hand. "The babe ain't comin'
yet, is it?"

"No, not yet." Leah hunched down to smile at Mrs.
Brown's youngest, who gurgled in return. "She's precious.
She *is* a girl, right?"

David looked on with interest. Whatever doubts he held
about Leah, he had none about her professed belief in equality. He liked the easy familiarity she showed to this poor
family—to *him,* for that matter. She had known about his
birth from their first meeting and never demonstrated a hint
of disdain. Even if she had told the truth about her parents,
she had still been born legitimately. He had not.

"Yes, she's a girl, ma'am. A handful, though." Mrs.
Brown cited some of the difficulties she had caring for her
other children with her newborn crying whenever set down.

David listened to Leah express her sympathy with a complete lack of reserve. His admiration heightened as she
turned to tying shoelaces, wiping noses, and prodding the
older children to the well, where she helped them wash their
hands and faces before sitting them down with a luncheon of
bread and cheese.

When they returned to the barouche, he told her, "You
certainly exceeded your duty to the Browns. One does not
often see an elegant young lady tending the rather inelegant
needs of poor children."

"They're no different from any other children," she said
with a dismissing wave of her hand. "And ten minutes of my
time is nothing compared to the lifetime that woman will
spend running after those kids."

He shook his head. "Your views are so unusual. American
society must be rather more extraordinary than I imagined."

"I do come from a different world. Not that the society
I'm from doesn't have some major wrinkles in need of iron-

ing out, but I hope the wrongs are slowly being righted. And I think you personally might find some advantages there."

As he stopped in front of the next cottage on their route, he assumed she meant his birth would be better accepted in her country, and he supposed she had a point. In a land where titles meant nothing, missing out on one would have little consequence. He would still be illegitimate, of course, but with his family thousands of miles away, who would know or care?

Over the course of the next few stops they made, the idea of emigrating to America began to take root in his mind. As he watched Leah chat openly with tenants, he found himself intrigued by the concept of a land where all were regarded equal. He wondered why he had never before considered that he might find greater acceptance overseas.

Furthermore, if Leah represented the typical American, he had to admire the self-reliance of the people. He stood amazed at cottage after cottage as she voiced strong, sensible opinions. At one sickbed she forcefully discouraged the practice of bloodletting—a view he shared, after witnessing too many soldiers die from the procedure. At another house she prescribed oranges, lemons, or limes for prevention of scurvy, an idea new to him, but somehow one he trusted when expressed so confidently. At another stop she penned a letter in crisp handwriting, more lucid than any he had ever before seen, for an illiterate woman with a brother fighting on the Continent.

By the time he brought the last two baskets up on the box of the barouche, his mind whirled. He made an effort to concentrate on the task at hand, consulting a list that Phoebe had given him. "We seem to be finished. The only house left is the Banfields, and they are the family with smallpox. The other basket must be a spare."

"There's a note on the handle." Leah plucked off a folded paper and opened the message. She grinned and said, "This one is for you and me. Lady Solebury urges us to picnic at the grove beyond Oxhead Stone. Do you know where she means?"

"Yes, she refers to a secluded creekside clearing that is a favorite of the marquess's." David's stomach rumbled at the thought of eating, and he privately commended Phoebe for providing extra food. "The creek is not far past the Banfields. Would you like to stop?"

"I'd love to." She sighed and looked up at the clear blue sky. "The weather is perfect. But about the Banfields—I can still deliver their basket. I've been exposed to smallpox before, and I can't catch the disease."

This show of courage topped all the other strengths she had demonstrated already. Naturally, he could not agree to her suggestion. "Your courage is commendable, Leah, but just because you escaped infection once does not prove you immune. This time you could be less fortunate."

"Actually, in a way, I *have* been infected." She lifted one of the short, puffy sleeves of her dress and revealed a star-like scar on her shapely upper arm. "This is a pock mark."

"That cannot be," he said, affording the scar a mere glance. "Survivors of smallpox are always severely disfigured."

"This is the only mark I have, but I know I am immune."

He looked at her with skepticism. Surely, she did not believe that single mark represented survival of smallpox. Did she have a death wish? His mind flew back to the suicide theory.

"I cannot allow you to risk your life," he said. "If you won't think of yourself, think of Phoebe and the baby. If you fell ill, you could infect them. In any case, I recall that one of Solebury's grooms has had the disease. He can deliver the basket."

"Okay," she said. He recognized the strange term as a concession. "That would probably be best."

They rode past the Banfields and on to the grove. After they had spread out a cloth they found in the basket, they pulled out the picnic fare. Phoebe had supplied fresh-baked breads, cheeses, fruits, and wine. They attacked the feast, eventually settling back to enjoy the peacefulness of nature. To David's astonishment, Leah had no scruples in stretching out on the ground like a young lad might. Her resemblance to a boy ended with the sensual curves accentuated by such a posture.

He wrenched his gaze from the rise of her hips, reminding himself that he had pertinent questions for her. Still, he could not seem to think about espionage. Instead, his mind kept returning to the admiration he had felt for her all morning.

"You were marvelous today." His own words sounded alien in his ears. He had sometimes commended soldiers on their conduct but never a woman. "Are all Americans so self-reliant?"

"You'd consider me self-reliant?" She propped herself up on one elbow, her raised eyebrows registering wonder.

"Decidedly," he told her, surprised by her surprise. "You are confident in your opinions—and rightly so, for your judgment is very sound. To speak as frankly as you do, you are by far the most self-assured woman I know."

"Are you serious?" A smile alighted on her lips. "I've always considered myself meek. But, you know what, I'm resolved to live up to the strength you give me credit for. The events of the last few days have made me take a look at several areas of my life that I've left stagnant for too long. If I ever get back to . . . back home, there are some major changes I plan to make."

"You are not certain you will return?" he asked with a sinking in his gut. Surely, he hadn't been thinking he might visit her in America—had he? He must have simply hoped she would share his new enthusiasm for her country.

"No." She sighed and mustered a smile. "But if I don't return, my life is already changed, isn't it?"

"I don't know. You reveal so little about your life."

She pursed her lips. "I have my reasons."

"What atrocities can you possibly need to hide from me?" Once again forced to ponder her involvement in espionage, he sat up. "What could you have to fear from me?"

She sat up, too, rubbing her temples. "You did once threaten to lock me up in Bedlam."

He winced at the smallness of her usually confident voice. Reaching forward, he lifted her chin to look into her eyes. "I only said that to prevent you from trying to leap into the spring again. I never truly intended to commit you to an asylum."

"If not, you still might, after I tell you everything." She moved free of his grasp and began packing up the leftover food, plates, and utensils. Only when she had folded the cloth and returned it to the basket did she look at him again. "If I confide something that sounds crazy to you, can you promise to keep it to yourself?"

"Of course." He tried not to show the excitement that surged in him.

She pressed her lips together, studying his face. "I'm really at your mercy, David. If your family throws me out of the house, I have nowhere else to go."

"I promise," he said, his mind racing, "as long as what you tell me entails no harm to them."

"I would never harm such nice people." She stood and took several steps away before turning back to face him. "I'm from the future."

Her abrupt statement made no sense, but the gravity of her expression unnerved him. "I don't understand."

"I don't really understand, either. I'm not even sure how to attempt an explanation." She chewed her lower lip. "Before you found me at the spring, I lived in the future—at the end of the twentieth century. One afternoon I took a tour of Solebury House that ended with a visit to the spring. I found that gold coin . . . well, the details don't even matter. In short, I fell into the little pool but felt as though I'd been sucked into an abyss. I thought I was going to drown. Then you pulled me out, and suddenly it was 1815 . . . almost two hundred years in *my* past."

He stared at her, clinging to a thread of hope that her solemn face might dissolve into laughter, revealing the story for a jest. As seconds ticked by with no change in her expression, nausea began gnawing at him.

"Just before I fell in the water, I had tossed a coin into the spring—a coin from *this* time period. I think that's what instigated my transport." She frowned when he didn't respond, her voice quavering. "I know the story sounds crazy."

Crazed, indeed, but she showed no other signs of madness. On the contrary, she appeared all sense and intellect. Was she lying then? Only the worst sort of fabricator could come up with a tale so fantastic. And for what purpose? To hide spying activities? To conceal her identity because of some crime in her past? He turned away from her, thinking, for a minute, that he actually might be sick.

"I can tell you all about the future, if you want to know," she said quietly. "Maybe if I reveal enough, you'll realize I couldn't have made everything up. I'd have to have a very active imagination to—"

"Enough!" he erupted. He took a minute to breathe deeply, quelling his sickening chagrin by exchanging it for rage. How stupid could she think him? He stalked toward the barouche, tossing back over his shoulder, "If you want a ride back to Solebury House, you had best step lively."

"David, wait!"

He could hear her snap the basket lid shut, then her foot-falls as she ran up behind him.

"I know this is hard to believe, but I think I can convince you if you'll give me a chance."

"Have you not insulted my intelligence enough?" He could not bear to look at her. Turning away, he opened the carriage door. "You can ride inside."

For a moment, she stood still, then he listened to her climb into the carriage.

When she spoke again, her tone sounded high-pitched and urgent. "When you calm down a little, I want to talk to you, David. Please."

He let the door bang shut and climbed onto the box. On the way back to Solebury House, the horses could not gallop fast enough for him. He passed the whole ride agonizing for the moment he could rid himself of his deceitful passenger.

Unfortunately, he could only avoid her for so long. She could scarcely be trusted enough to leave her on her own.

Chapter 9

"THANK YOU AGAIN for delivering the baskets, Miss Cantrell," Lady Solebury said, enveloped in a pile of pillows. Eyes clear and cheeks tinged with pink, she looked reassuringly healthy after her day in bed. "And thanks, too, for coming up to chat with me about the tenants. I cannot tell you how much I have enjoyed our little coze."

"My pleasure." Leah shifted her position in a well-stuffed armchair beside the bed, thinking just how much a pleasure it had been to escape to her ladyship's room. If a barreling ride home inside the carriage hadn't been enough to make her regret trying to explain the truth to David, his constant glares during dinner certainly had. She still didn't know what to expect from him ultimately. This very moment he might be telling his father that he thought she should be committed.

She shuddered and tried not to expect the worst, refocusing her attention on Lady Solebury. "I'm happy to be of use to you. I feel bad for imposing on your hospitality so much, but for the time being, I'm afraid I don't have anywhere else to go."

The marchioness smiled. "You are welcome here for as long as you like, dear. Now that I am confined to this bed-chamber, I am doubly pleased to have company—not that I want you to feel you must pass all your time with me. Indeed, tonight you have entertained me far longer than you should have done. I ought not to have kept you from the gentlemen."

"I've enjoyed our talk," Leah assured her. Her ladyship's accounts of nineteenth-century life had been fascinating—and she hadn't missed David's stony looks one bit. "Besides, I think your stepson had his fill of me this afternoon."

Lady Solebury gave her a crooked smile. "I rather doubt that. My husband told me David brooded all through dinner, but you must not imagine his sulking is directed at you. As bright a young woman as you are, you cannot have missed the tension between him and his father."

This evening all the tension had been between him and *her*, but Leah chose not to enlighten her on that point.

"I've noticed it, all right," she said, "and I think David's bitterness is a shame. He really should try to lighten up. I told him as much this morning."

"Did you, indeed?" Her ladyship pulled herself up into a sitting position, stuffing pillows behind her back. "I don't imagine he accepted your counsel graciously."

She let out a short laugh. "Not at all. He told me to mind my own business. I suppose I should have."

"On the contrary, I believe your words may already have had an effect on him. David has spent this entire evening with his father, an event I have unsuccessfully tried to orchestrate since marrying into the family. In fact, last night was the first time since his childhood that he has sat down to dinner with his father. Until this current visit, David has confined all his calls to an hour at most."

"Really?" Leah was surprised but didn't delude herself about her powers of influence. If David's staying longer this time had anything to do with her, it was only because he wanted to keep an eye on her. Still, if his distrust forced him to deal with his father, maybe her presence did some good. Bringing the two men together might even be her "purpose" here in the nineteenth century—if she had one.

"Really." Lady Solebury grinned. "I suspect the two of them have even concocted some kind of conspiracy between them."

Leah couldn't share her amusement. She could only see David colluding with Lord Solebury if he had a very good reason . . . to protect Phoebe from an insane houseguest, for example.

"What makes you think they are conspiring?" she asked, every muscle in her body tense.

With a glance toward the open hall door, the marchioness lowered her voice. "When I remarked to Harold about David's unusual willingness to spend time with him, he told me they had specific business to discuss. I asked what sort of business, but he put me off, claiming it didn't signify. Now, if the matter weren't important, I am certain David would not tolerate his father's company. Clearly, they are scheming together."

Leah's anxiety rose to panic level. They had to be discussing her. What other matter would concern them both so deeply? Right now David was probably relating everything she'd told him, recommending that she be locked away forever.

She looked at the doorway, half-expecting the men to charge through and grab her, dragging her out of the house. But they wouldn't want to upset her ladyship, especially after last night's scare. They would wait at least until Leah left the marchioness's room. Did that leave her a chance to save herself somehow—to come up with a better story? Or maybe run away?

"I think I comprehend their game," Lady Solebury continued, her lips curving upward. "They are plotting to construct a priest's hole. Do you remember David's mentioning he wanted to speak with Harold this morning?"

"Yes," Leah managed to utter. She could feel her pulse throbbing in her throat. "But why would they hide their plans from you? The priest's hole was your idea in the first place."

She shrugged. "They likely don't wish to trouble me any further on the subject. Harold has instructed me not to think about the war at all—as if I might simply halt my concerns. You know how men's minds work."

"I wish I knew better," Leah murmured, not convinced. More likely, the subject they thought would worry her was her houseguest's impending commitment. She eyed the doorway again, wondering if they'd be waiting in her room, ready to haul her away to some filthy cell. Or would they hold off until morning?

The marchioness laughed at her comment. "Don't we all? And after spending the day with David, you must be more confused about men than ever. Pray do not judge them all by his quirks. He is hardly typical of his gender."

"No," she answered absently. "He's a hard nut to crack."

"An apt character summation. But consider this: Perhaps the 'nuts' with the most difficult shells are the ones who yield the most tantalizing fruit. I have known David for years, and I can tell you he is truly a remarkable man. Beneath the hard exterior, he is quite sensitive to the needs of others. His own needs are the ones he tends to neglect."

"I know." Leah had seen enough evidence of his concern for her to agree. Even now, if he did mean to put her away, she knew he only wanted to protect his family from a crazy woman—or even to protect *her* from her supposed suicide attempts. Was there any chance he'd come up with a solution other than Bedlam? Not much. *She* couldn't even think of one to suggest to him.

Watching her face, Lady Solebury frowned. "You seem troubled, dear. Are you certain you don't want to talk about your difficulties? Often, matters don't look as bleak once you have expressed them openly."

"I appreciate your concern. Unfortunately, I haven't had much luck when I've tried discussing this particular matter." Unable to hide her growing anxiety, Leah decided she might as well face whatever awaited her in her room. She took a deep breath and stood. "I think I'll go to bed now. Thank you, my lady, for everything you've done for me."

Lady Solebury extended her hand. "And thank you for all your efforts on my part. I wonder, Miss Cantrell, if I might call you by your given name? I should like very much for you to call me Phoebe."

"I'd like it very much, too, Phoebe," Leah said, giving her hand a squeeze. She wondered how the men would explain her disappearance to the marchioness once they took her away. She supposed they would say she'd run away. Phoebe would have no reason to doubt them. She probably already thought Leah had run away from home. "We haven't known each other long, but you've been a good friend to me."

"And you to me, Leah. Good night."

"Good night."

She stepped out of the room with her heart pounding. No one was waiting for her in the hallway. Determined not to lose her nerve, she walked to her room quickly and found that empty as well. She entered and locked the door but still felt insecure. The marquess would have a key. If she had any hope of saving herself, she'd have to act before he came after her.

Moonlight peeked through the open drapes of her window, and she went to lean on the wide sill, checking the distance to the ground. The drop looked too steep for jumping, but a large oak tree grew close enough that she might be able to step out onto one of the thicker branches and climb down. Then where would she go? She'd have no choice but to try the spring. The thought of drowning terrified her but, at this point, trying to live in the nineteenth century seemed equally dangerous.

She fetched the sundress she'd worn on the day of her time transport, stripped off her borrowed costume, and threw on her modern clothes. She'd lost her own shoes in the water, so she put on the halfboots Phoebe had given her for walking. Snatching the only coin she owned from a cloth purse also supplied by the marchioness, she opened the window. A breeze fanned her face, cooling the mist of perspiration on her forehead.

Hesitating would only allow time for her fear to build. She swallowed and climbed out onto a narrow ledge. The wind gusted, adhering her dress to her legs much like she glued her back to the cold stone wall. Ignoring the chill of the air, she held onto the window frame with one hand and stretched the other arm to grab an overhead branch. She caught hold and swung onto a larger limb below, immediately inching toward the trunk. The old tree had lots of thick branches, making the rest of her descent relatively easy.

She dropped onto the ground and scanned her surroundings. There was no sign of anyone around. Nevertheless, she darted her way to the drive, crouching behind one tree, then the next. On reaching the gravel, she ran until she met with the path to the spring. There, a canopy of leaves blocked the light of the moon, and she had to tread more carefully. She fought the urge to fly through the unseen brambles. She could feel terror chasing her—gaining fast—its cold breath whipping up her spine.

A twig snapped somewhere behind her, and she froze, breathing hard from fear and exertion.

"Is someone there?" she asked, her voice carried away on another surge of wind.

She held her breath to listen, goose bumps rising on her sweat-dampened body. Shivering, she rubbed her bare arms. If the spring didn't take her forward in time, she would be left wet, cold, and helpless—but she would worry about that when the time came. Dismissing the feeling that someone followed her, she trudged ahead to the clearing where the springhouse stood. Here the moonlight shined through the trees, glittering on the breeze-rippled pool.

Not nearly enough time had passed to dull the memory of her near-drowning, and the sight of the water made her knees weak. But she hadn't drowned, she reminded herself, and now that she knew the nature of the transport, she wouldn't need to struggle against the water. In a few minutes she could be home again—in time, if not space.

She slipped off Phoebe's halfboots and stepped up to the pool, the moss beneath her bare soles cold and clammy. Staring into the water, she wondered if she'd fulfilled a purpose here or not. She had no way of knowing, but her presence had forced David to spend time with his father—and she'd learned a lot about herself over the past two days.

The memory of David calling her self-reliant made her smile, despite all her fears. She *could* rely on herself and looked forward to demonstrating her power when she got home. Why had she thought she needed Kevin's unstable companionship to be whole? Why had she thought she needed her father's blessing to finish school? From now on, she would move ahead on her own—and she would stop expecting her father to be something other than what he was. Seeing the way David's bitterness for his father ate at him had made her realize she had to let go of her own resentment toward her parents.

"So many reasons to go ahead and prove myself," she said aloud, staring into the water. Part of her felt excited about taking on the future . . . but part longed for something else. More precisely, *someone* else. "Only one reason to stay behind—and not a very logical one."

She tried to will away the thought of David, but his brief presence in her life had meant too much. She could almost feel him near her now—though in another minute, he might well be two hundred years away, never to be seen again.

Choking on a sob, she drew the shiny George III coin out of her pocket.

"I wish I were back in the future," she mumbled. She flipped the gold disk into the pool. The coin sank into darkness, and she watched the circular ripples expand and fade—just like they would in any ordinary puddle.

It's not going to work, she thought. The George III coin was from *this* time period. Somehow she knew it wasn't the right currency to pay for a ride to the future. Of course, she still had to make sure, especially since she didn't have a coin from her own era.

She stepped into the perimeter of the pool with a gasp at

the coldness of the water. Her feet sank into the muddy bottom, and she wrinkled her nose at the ooze between her toes.

Nothing happened.

Clenching her teeth, she hiked up her dress and eased closer to the center of the pool. Icy water washed up over her knees, and her right foot settled on something gnarled and slimy—a tree root, she realized. Before she had quite gained a foothold, the touch of something cold on her left toes startled her and made her lose her balance. She splashed rear-first into the shallow pool. Freezing water drenched most of her dress before she could spring to her feet again.

Still, no magic exploded around her.

With an odd mixture of frustration and relief, she sloshed out of the pool, shivering violently in her dripping sundress. Now what could she do? Run somewhere else—or leave herself to David's mercy?

Twigs crackled in the woods, and David himself stepped out from behind a tree, answering the dilemma for her. His dark eyes were round with shock rather than narrowed in rage, as she would have expected. She counted herself lucky and waited for him to walk up to her.

He stopped directly in front of her. "Well, you have convinced me you are utterly mad."

What little hope she'd clung to fell away, leaving her dizzy with fear. She stared up into his face, her teeth chattering. "So, you'll put me in Bedlam?"

"Oh, Leah." His voice softened, and he shook his head. "I told you I would not. What I will do, I don't know, but I would not wish the horrors of Bedlam upon anyone."

She looked into his eyes, and his steady gaze told her he spoke the truth. Relief flooded her body, priming two big tears to roll down her cheeks. She saw his jaw muscles tighten before she hid her face in her hands.

"You must be freezing." His voice trembled slightly, and she heard his clothing rustle with movement. The next second he wrapped his jacket around her shoulders. As the warmth of the garment engulfed her, he pulled her against his chest.

She leaned into his body, savoring the security of his arms, too emotional to say anything without sobbing.

He stroked her hair and spoke softly. "Since you clearly believe this wishing-well story of yours, I can only wonder about your accident again. I know you claim you escaped injury, but please reconsider whether you might have sustained a head injury. Such trauma has been known to cause delusion. I, personally, have witnessed similar cases in soldiers."

She looked up at him sadly, knowing she would never persuade him to believe the truth. Unwilling to lie, she remained silent.

"Think about it, Leah." He lifted her chin with his fingertips, gazing into her eyes. "You are a rational woman. You don't really believe in wishing wells, do you? Especially after this episode here?"

"I . . . I don't know." She closed her eyes and pulled him tightly against her.

He hugged her back, his arms strong and warm. "Come. Let's return to the gatehouse. You can dry yourself before I take you back to the manor. Allow me to help you with your shoes."

She held on to his shoulder while he stooped to slip her feet into Phoebe's halfboots. He stood again, and she sank against his body, letting him guide her back to the drive. Her mind spun with a jumble of emotions. Remaining here with David filled her with happiness, but just below the surface a hint of despair pricked at her. If she couldn't convince him of the truth, she would never be able to share her history with him, never be able to relate all the experiences that made her who she was. In short, he would never really know her, and right now knowing him meant more to her than anything.

She dammed up a fresh threat of tears, burying her face against his chest. Captivated by the warmth of his body and the faint, starchy scent of his shirt, she almost believed living with him would be enough . . . even if she'd be living a lie.

Chapter 10

DAVID GUIDED LEAH ahead of him through the rear door of the gatehouse, his hand light on the small of her back. Beneath the hem of the jacket he had wrapped around her, her shift clung to her thighs. The wet fabric ended at the back of her knees, baring a shocking expanse of calf. He yanked his gaze away and glanced out over the moonlit garden. Then he stepped inside and shut out the rest of the world.

He turned in to face the kitchen and cleared his throat. "Her ladyship's servants stoke up the sitting room fire before they retire to the manor house. The door is ahead to the right—the one where you see the glow."

As they walked through the hall, dimly lit by a single oil lamp, a sharp awareness of her sparked through his body. Since he had refused any overnight help, he and Leah had the entire cottage to themselves—a notion that quickened his blood.

"This is lovely," she said as they entered the sitting room. Many would have thought the room small, but he had always loved the cozy setting. She walked to the hearth, holding her palms out to the embers.

He stepped up beside her and stooped to rekindle the fire. As flames licked at the new wood, he resisted a sting of conscience, telling himself he had good reason to bring her here. He could not have allowed her to walk all the way back to the manor drenched and shivering. And while their isolation in the gatehouse might tempt him, he would never take advantage of the situation.

After a moment of warming her hands, she began to pluck at the wet cloth that adhered to her legs. He did his best to avoid watching.

"My dress is soaked."

"Let me find a robe for you to wear." He felt his face flush with heat—and not because of the building blaze in the hearth. He could only hope the lack of lighting would mask his embarrassment. "Now that the fire is burning, your clothes should dry quickly."

He strode from the room, bounding upstairs to his chamber. When he returned a moment later, she had removed his jacket and stood before the flames in only her shift. The light of the fire created a silhouette of her body on the thin fabric, delineating her slender waist and the gentle curves of her hips and thighs.

Looking away, he handed her his dressing robe and a wool blanket, then turned to leave the room.

"Please don't go again. I don't want to be alone."

He swung around in surprise, inadvertently sweeping his gaze down her body before he fixed on her face. She must have noticed, but to save himself from mortification, he tried to believe she had not. "You need time to change."

She moistened her lips and avoided looking at him. "Will you come back quickly?"

"Of course. I shall return in a moment . . . with brandy to help warm you."

Without offering her an opportunity to object, he rushed off to the study, trying not to dwell on the mental image of her disrobing. He fetched a decanter and two snifters, filling one of the glasses and gulping a burning mouthful. He had quaffed the entire drink before he went back to the sitting room.

When he did, he found Leah curled up on a settee in front of the fire. She sat watching the flames, his robe voluminous on her petite frame. The firelight lent a soft glow to her complexion and gold-like glints to her hair. She had draped the blanket over her lower limbs, but their bare beauty was freshly etched in his mind.

He handed her a glass of brandy and pulled up a chair. "Are you feeling better now?"

"Warmer, though you can imagine I still have a few things on my mind." She sipped at her drink, wincing when she swallowed the fiery liquid. After blinking several times, she took another sip and fared better. "Will Lord Solebury be looking for me?"

"I see no reason why he would, unless someone other than I also witnessed your descent in the oak tree—and I don't believe so. You frightened the hell out of me with that escapade, Leah. I would have called out to stop you, but I feared startling you into losing your balance."

He thought she blushed, but she quickly recovered her composure. "Phoebe said your father told her you two had business to discuss. Did that business involve me?"

He hesitated. Though he no longer suspected she had connections with the French, he considered a vague answer his best choice. "I have some ideas for preparing for Boney."

"Not ideas for dealing with me?" She held her snifter with both hands, elbows squeezed against her body. "I mean, did you tell him what I told you this afternoon?"

He shook his head, noting her lack of interest in his reference to Napoléon. "None of it."

"Thank you."

He drew his chair closer to the settee. "Regarding your story, Leah, have you had time to consider what I suggested during our walk from the spring? Even if you did not strike your head the other day, the shock of nearly drowning could be enough to cause you some . . . some confusion."

"Do we have to talk about this?" She swallowed a mouthful of brandy and pulled her legs up on the settee, huddling her knees to her chest. Drawing the blanket more tightly around her, she said, "I'm so cold."

"If we discuss it, we may be able to discover what truly happened to you. You said yourself that you don't understand how you could have traveled through time. Let us start with that. Tell me, what is your last memory before you fell into the spring?"

She shuddered, the last of her brandy nearly splashing out of the snifter. Through chattering teeth, she said, "I can't seem to shake off this chill."

He got up and sat beside her, wrapping an arm around her shoulders before he realized he had upped the intimacy of the situation. Disengaging his hold again, he pried her glass from her fingers. "Let me get you another drink."

While he poured more brandy for both of them, he focused his thoughts on her reluctance to discuss her mental state. She seemed to have no desire to learn the truth, and he believed he knew why. Fantasy had displaced her true memories, so she had no idea what might actually lay in her past. No wonder the prospect of remembering made her shake like a leaf.

He turned back toward the settee and handed Leah her glass. Sitting back down, he made sure to leave several inches of space between her body and his.

To his dismay, she slumped against him, tucking her head under his chin. Instinct told him to get away, but her trembling body begged for comforting. Almost without his volition, his arm dropped back around her.

She sighed. "Thanks for coming over to warm me up."

He still suspected the move had been a mistake. So close to her, and in such seclusion, he lost all ability to refrain from thoughts of lovemaking.

"I feel better already. I don't think I'll need any more brandy." She leaned forward and set her snifter down on the hearth stones. With a glance over her shoulder, she gestured toward his drink. "Do you want that?"

He handed it to her, scarcely able to think. As she took the glass and placed it beside hers, he struggled to recapture his common sense. "Leah, we must talk. It is important."

"I know it is, David, but I'm cold and tired, and I'm all talked out." She nestled back against his chest, likely able to hear his pounding heart right through his shirt and waistcoat. Yawning, she asked, "Can't it wait till morning?"

Her body felt dangerously tantalizing, and her sleepy comment brought to mind how good it would be to snuggle up beside her for the night. If she'd had her wits about her, she would have realized the dangers of her behavior. Since she did not, he needed to watch out for her.

But her hair smelled like rosewater, and the flecks of light within the red mesmerized him. He lifted a lock and ran his fingers through the silken strands.

"As shiny as candy," he murmured.

"My friend Jeanine compared the color to cinnamon," she said, gazing into the fire.

"Two temptations." His mind seemed to go off on its own pointless path. "Which one is it?"

She gave a quiet laugh. "Why don't you taste it and see?"

His mouth fell open, and he stiffened. He felt a stirring in his breeches and tried in vain to contain his wild thoughts.

She lifted her head and looked into his eyes, their lips only inches apart. Raising one hand, she grazed the side of his head, so his hair tickled his neck. "What flavor is yours? Such a deep, rich black could only be licorice, I suppose."

His breath came quick, despite his knowing he ought to steer her in a more serious direction. But the temptation to return her teasing was irresistible.

"Why don't you taste it and see?" he asked.

Her eyes rounded but only fleetingly. Then she lifted a lock of his hair, the back of her hand brushing his earlobe. She paused, then leaned in close, as though she truly meant to taste his hair!

Then . . . she did. Or she must have, also sampling his flesh, because he felt the tip of her tongue, warm and moist, just behind his ear. For a moment she remained pressed close to him, and he thought, hoped, feared she would kiss his neck. But she pulled back and looked into his eyes, emerald-tinted flames reflected in her own.

"Licorice?" he uttered, his breath rushing out. He had not realized he was holding it.

"Much more delectable. But you haven't tried mine." She tilted her head back and to one side, a gesture that proffered her neck rather more than her hair.

He knew she lacked lucidity of mind, knew he had to protect her from her own precarious mental state. But he *needed* to taste her, now, while he could. Shameful or not, a starving man had to feed.

Closing eyes that felt like they would burn under her gaze, he bent and brushed his lips over the soft skin under her jawline. The scent of roses captivated him, and he pressed his mouth hard into her flesh, sowing downward to the curve of her shoulder. He pulled her body to his, savoring the softness of her breasts against his chest. He longed to plunge kisses downward, deep within the yielding neckline of her robe, but he checked himself. He would have her mouth instead. He had to have her mouth just this once, before this marvelous dream ended.

He glimpsed green fire in her eyes before leaning in to savor her lips. She fed on his mouth in turn, hungrily answering his kiss. She parted her lips to offer her tongue, faintly sweet with the taste of brandy—and ten times more intoxicating.

Intoxicating—nay, toxic, because the stupor descending on his brain prevented him from protecting her from herself—indeed, from him. He fought his reeling senses and pulled away from her lips, holding her head between his hands to stare into her eyes. He could feel her chest heaving against his.

"Leah," he whispered. "Good Lord, Leah, you have no notion what you are doing to me."

She reached up and ran her fingers down his cheek. "Only kissing you, David."

"We must stop. We must stop now." He summoned all his willpower and extricated himself from her arms. How in heaven's name had he allowed circumstances to go this far—nearly too far to turn back?

"We . . . don't really have to stop," she said quietly. "There's no harm in kissing."

"No?" He looked away from her, covering his lower face with his hand. Perhaps his base birth did tell, after all. A true gentleman never would have exposed a vulnerable woman to such an ignoble display of lust. He was a cur indeed. "My behavior is shameful. If your mind were entirely sound right now, you would not even be sitting here with me."

"My mind is sound."

He leaped up from the settee, pacing the length of the hearth. "Your judgment is impaired. I know that, and I have behaved reprehensibly. I never should have brought you here in the first place. I am afraid I must escort you back to the manor house this instant. If your shift has not dried, you can keep the robe. Indeed, you must keep it regardless."

She rose slowly, pulling the wrap closer around her body. "I appreciate your concern for me, David, especially considering the lack of concern I'm used to receiving. But I want you to know that *I* don't believe my being here with you is the least bit reprehensible. I wish you felt the same."

He stopped in his tracks, shaking his head. "Leah, you must try to think clearly. Surely, you can see how perilous our being alone here is."

"Okay." She pressed her palms together in front of her, as if about to deliver a speech. "We'll *both* think clearly. Now, first of all, let's establish just what is perilous here. What would that be, David?"

He pressed his lips together tightly. "No matter what delusions you may entertain, Leah, I know you have enough sense to realize your virtue is in jeopardy here. If someone were to happen upon us now—let alone several minutes ago—you would be thoroughly compromised."

She put her hand up over her mouth, only half-concealing a smile.

He threw his hands up in frustration. "You show no anxiety whatsoever over your reputation! Your recklessness is downright frightening! Now, you said you would try to think clearly. Do you truly not perceive any danger here?"

Her expression sobered, and she studied his face for a moment. Bending down to retrieve their drinks, she handed him a snifter. "Did you ever consider that the world might be a better place if an adult man and woman could choose to be alone together if they wanted? Now I'm urging *you* to think."

"I fear I cannot think at all at the moment." He swigged down a gulp of brandy.

"Don't you think we ought to be able to sit here together if we want?"

He froze with his glass in midair. "The world does not go on that way!"

"No . . ." She looked into her drink, swirling the amber liquid onto the sides of the snifter. "Not yet."

He frowned at her apparent reference to the "future" she had fabricated in her head. "What, precisely, are you saying?"

"Nothing." She walked to the chair where her shift hung and turned the garment so the opposite side faced the fire.

"Leah, how far does this future-time fantasy of yours go?" He wondered whether he wanted to hear her answer, suspecting that the deeper her delusion went, the more difficulty she would have casting it off. "Do you actually have 'memories' of life in another time period?"

She sat back down, again gazing into her brandy. "I see no reason to tell you, since you're so sure it's all fantasy."

"I am only trying to gauge the nature of your problem. Do you have memories or none at all?"

"I have memories." Her focus remained fixed in her glass.

"And the events you recall cannot conceivably have taken place in this century?"

She met his gaze, eyes narrowed, but gave no response.

He gathered that her subconscious mind had actually invented ideas about her life in the future. "What makes you believe they occurred in another time?"

Her shoulders sagged, and she set her glass down on the floor. "I think I should go, David. This isn't getting us anywhere."

"Why are you unwilling to discuss your memories? I told you I would never send you to Bedlam. Do you not believe me?"

"I believe you. I just don't want to talk about it. Hand me my dress, please."

He watched her a moment longer, noticing her expression had gone sad. Suddenly a new thought came to him: Perhaps she refused to try to work on understanding her problems because she had reason to avoid the truth. Perhaps she had created a fantasy background for herself because her true past was too painful to retain. If so, he might do best to indulge her for the time being. When she grew ready to remember, she would remember.

Placing his brandy on the mantel, he fetched her shift from the chair. The feminine softness of the garment absorbed him. As he tested the material for dryness, he observed the fabric felt too fine for cotton, yet lacked the shine of silk. He had opened his mouth to ask about the material when he noticed a label of some sort sewn into the back of the neckline—perhaps a name tag. Curious, he tilted the little piece of cloth toward the firelight and read 100% RAYON,

DRY CLEAN ONLY. The letters appeared uniformly printed, as they would in a book or newspaper.

"What is this?" he asked.

"The tag," she said, her gaze anchored on his eyes. "Mass-produced clothing is labeled like that."

He resisted inquiring what the term *mass-produced* signified. Though he had decided to indulge her fantasy, he had no intention of encouraging further delusion.

"Look at the seams," she said. "Have you ever seen sewing like that?"

He turned the neckline inside out, revealing an intricate pattern of looped, twisted and interlaced stitches, all amazingly equal in size and spacing. He could scarcely fathom why a seamstress would choose such an elaborate pattern for the inside of a garment. "This must have taken an extraordinary amount of time to produce."

"On the contrary, the work is done very quickly . . . by a machine." She continued to regard his face. "By machine, I mean a tool constructed of multiple, moving parts, the way a clock is. A sewing machine can whip out those seams in seconds."

He glanced down at the labyrinth of stitches and the peculiar printed label. Gooseflesh rose on his arms.

But her explanation could only be nonsense. The brandy, the flickering enchantment of firelight, the spell her lips and body had cast upon him—all these factors had clouded the line between reality and the fantastic until he could no longer trust his own judgment.

His fingers tightened on the fabric as anger welled up inside of him. If he could have shaken sense into her, he would have tried, but mindless action would do no good in a case as complex as this.

"Put this on," he said through clenched teeth, tossing her the shift. "We shall leave in five minutes."

He marched from the room and went to the study, slamming the door behind him. The empty shelf where the brandy decanter usually stood glared at him, reminding him he should have brought his glass with him. He could have used another drink to help settle the whirl of emotion agitating his mind and body—though mere alcohol would hardly blank out the disorder Leah Cantrell had brought into his world.

If the confusion of sorting out her life did no more than leave him with a predilection for spirits, he would be fortunate. If he proved less fortunate, he might come out of the experience a madman.

Chapter 11

LEAH WOKE UP in a flood of sunlight, realizing she must have slept late. Between her failed attempt to return to the future and the so sweet, so brief romantic encounter with David, she'd had plenty to keep her up most of the night.

She stretched her arms above her head, wondering if she'd ever get home. Worrying about it would only make her crazy. If she were meant to return, she would find the way. Meanwhile, she had resolved that whether her time in the nineteenth century would be long or short, she wanted to spend as much of it as possible with David. She also realized that to get close to him, she couldn't live a lie. Somehow, she would have to convince him of her story—a task that wouldn't prove easy.

She climbed out of the high bed and washed her face with tepid water from a pitcher on the vanity. A small mirror above the basin reflected the evidence of too-little rest: a paleness to her already light complexion and faint circles under her bloodshot eyes. She would have done just about anything for a tube of concealer.

As she turned from the mirror, she almost tripped on a pile of clothes lying on the floor from the night before. She stooped to pick up her sundress, thinking she really should have been more careful with the only evidence she had of her origins—the one physical remnant of her life in the twentieth century.

Something from her own time period.

An idea popped into her head, and she gave the heap of fabric a second look. Perhaps the fountain required an offering from her own time period.

As she stood, shaking out the wrinkled rayon, something fell out of the pocket and thumped on the carpet. She looked down and, sure enough, the George III coin lay at her feet.

"The proverbial bad penny," she muttered, bending down to pick up the piece. "Only this one is a little too eerie for me."

She shuddered and stowed it away in the cloth purse she'd heard Phoebe call a "reticule." Why did the damn coin end up back with her every time she tossed it in the spring? If some greater power intended her to use it some other way, then how? She remembered wondering about the original wish-maker when she first found the piece. Was she supposed to return it to that person, whomever he or she might be?

Whatever. She put the purse in a drawer and hung her dress in the wardrobe, deciding she would think about both matters later. Her problems had stolen away her peace long enough. Right now her stomach demanded attention, rumbling a desire for Cook's flaky croissants and delicious marmalade. If she could throw on one of Phoebe's gowns quickly enough, she might still be able to get served.

Within ten minutes she reached the entrance to the breakfast room, pausing at the door when she found she wasn't the only one eating late. David and his father sat together at the table, plates pushed aside to make room for a batch of papers spread in front of them. Neither noticed her, their nearly identical mops of hair bent over their work. In such proximity she saw that David's locks were a purer black than even the darkest of the marquess's salt-and-pepper blend.

Blacker than licorice, she thought, warmth flooding her body at the memory of "tasting" his hair, his skin, his mouth . . .

He turned and said something to his father, giving her a better view of his profile: the unmistakably noble nose and sensual curve of his mouth. She liked the way his lower lip jutted forward just a little, somehow promising a talent for kissing—or maybe her new personal knowledge had suggested that interpretation.

His gaze flitted to meet hers, and she realized she'd been staring. Now he stared back at her, slowly getting up as she gathered her wits and stepped into the room.

The marquess looked up when his son stood, following the line of David's gaze to the entrance way. He smiled and jumped to pull out another chair at the table. "Good morning, Miss Cantrell. I shall ring for more tea. This pot has gone cold, and David and I need fresh cups as well."

The mention of David's name unlocked the son's gaze from hers to glance at his father. When he looked back at her again, he gave her a stiff nod. "Good morning."

"Good morning." She let Lord Solebury help her with her chair, smiling up at him. "Thank you, my lord."

While she answered her host's polite inquiries into her rest, servants bustled in with hot tea, wonderfully aromatic croissants, and big, crimson strawberries.

"I'm sorry I interrupted your meeting," she said to her companions, noticing David had begun scooping papers into a leather portfolio. She spooned what she hoped might pass for a ladylike portion of fruit onto her plate. "Please don't let me keep you from your discussion."

"We have discussed enough for one morning." Lord Solebury poured himself a cup of tea, then pulled out a pocket watch and flipped open the hinged cover. "By Jove, time passes quickly when one is engaged usefully. My son is teaching me to employ my wits, Miss Cantrell. Who would have suspected planning and preparation might offer so much entertainment?"

"Even when you're planning how you can keep Napoléon at bay?" she asked, treating herself to a dash of cream on her strawberries.

In her peripheral vision, she saw the marquess look at his son with raised eyebrows. David gave him a barely perceptible shake of the head.

She grinned. "I see. I'm only a woman and not privy to complicated male pursuits like military strategy. Well, no thanks, anyway. As far as I'm concerned, war is one male-dominated arena we women shouldn't bother infiltrating." Recalling David had served in the military, she sent him an apologetic look. "No offense intended."

He shrugged. "I have my own compunctions about war—doubtlessly outnumbering yours. That is one reason I sold out of my commission."

His father took her remarks more lightly, peering over the brim of his teacup with carefree eyes. "Tell me, Miss Cantrell, what male pursuits would you like to infiltrate?

Politics? Or a more recreational area, like men's clubs? Believe me, my dear, you ladies are missing little in being excluded from such activities."

"How about property ownership?" She smiled to soften her words, pushing a strawberry into her mouth.

"Women may own property," he said, "though I suspect you speak of making the occurrence commonplace."

She nodded.

He looked to his son, grinning. "What a place America must be, with all this free thinking bandied about, eh, David? I think I should like to visit the States myself sometime."

"I had the very same thought." David eyed Leah so intensely that for a second she forgot to chew.

The marquess leaned back in his chair. "So, what do you young people have in store for today? I don't believe my wife has assigned you any additional tasks, so your time is all your own. Perhaps you might drive over to see the ruins of the old abbey. The building is little more than a shell these days, but the locale affords a lovely view of the Channel."

"Sounds wonderful," Leah said, excited by the prospect of going anywhere with David, let alone a picturesque old abbey. "I love the idea of exploring ruins. Where I come from, we don't have many, you know."

Instead of smiling at her little joke, David frowned and looked to his father. "The abbey is also entirely deserted, isolated from everything and everyone. Would Miss Cantrell not require a chaperon for such an excursion?"

"Would she?" Lord Solebury laughed. "As her prospective escort, perhaps you are better equipped to say, but I should think a young gentleman and lady might fare well enough alone on such a short journey and in an open carriage."

David glanced at her and looked away again, an action that made his reluctance clear. "An open carriage might not be a good idea today. I believe we can expect rain this afternoon."

"But the sun is shining," she said, confused by his excuse-making. Then she remembered his concern for her "virtue" and realized he must not trust himself alone with her—or maybe her with him. She felt insulted until she reminded herself he was a product of another society. Couples in this age didn't just "hook up"—though she had no idea how their courting rituals went. People probably didn't even kiss until they got engaged.

Well, she wasn't about to sit back and wait for that, a remote possibility at best.

She tilted her head to one side and cooed, "I've never visited a ruin before. It must be fascinating to look at the remnants of an ancient building and imagine its original glory . . . to wonder about the people who worked on its construction and who once lived within its walls."

His stoic expression showed he didn't share her enthusiasm. He swallowed. "Perhaps another day. I feel a change of weather coming. An old injury in my leg grieves me whenever a storm is approaching."

She looked to the windows lining the far wall and saw that a few clouds had gathered in the last half-hour. A meteorologist might have predicted otherwise, but, in her estimation, the chance of precipitation remained slim.

"You may be able to do some exploring before the storm comes," Lord Solebury said. "I would judge that you have quite awhile before rain clouds set in."

"I am sure Miss Cantrell would not want to chance getting caught in a downpour." David looked into his cup, reached for the teapot, and poured himself another serving. "The abbey is too dilapidated to afford shelter against the elements."

"You are free to take my barouche again." The marquess watched his son with the intent gaze that ran in the family. "You can ride on the box while the weather holds and take shelter inside later, if need be."

"A barouche is not the ideal place to be trapped in the middle of a storm, either." The quickness of David's answer announced he had no intention of reconsidering.

"Depends on whom one is trapped with." Lord Solebury grinned, but his amusement faded when he looked to Leah. "Forgive me, Miss Cantrell. I simply cannot understand why my son resists such a charming scheme."

She waved off his apology and decided to show David some mercy, too. "Never mind. We can go another day, when his leg isn't bothering him. Then we'll be able to explore the ruins more thoroughly."

The marquess looked disappointed for her, but if he meant to argue further, the arrival of the butler prevented him.

The stately, gray-haired servant stopped just within the doorway, bowing deeply to his employer. "I beg pardon, your lordship, but Viscount Langston and his lady have stopped to call on their way to London. His lordship apologizes for the early hour of his visit. He says he will wait on you another time, if you are occupied at the moment."

"Langston and his wife are here?" Lord Solebury broke into a broad smile. "What a pleasant surprise. I shall go to them directly, Domfrey. Have you shown them to the drawing room?"

"Indeed, sir."

"Have some refreshments brought in, and tell them I shall be there in but a moment." The marquess looked to David.

"Do you remember Lord Langston, David? I believe you met him once or twice many years ago."

David nodded slowly, his expressive lower lip curling. "He is William's godfather."

Lord Solebury made a face. "So he is, but I should like him to see I have one son with a good head on his shoulders. You will come and greet him with me, I hope?"

The V-like slant of David's eyebrows smoothed into an arch of surprise. He darted a look at Leah.

She smiled, nodding her encouragement.

"I hope you will join us as well, Miss Cantrell," the marquess added. "Clearly, my wife cannot act as hostess, and I should like your assistance."

"I'd be honored." She got up, compelling the men to follow suit—a bit of chivalry she had already grown to like. No cause for finding such manners sexist, she reasoned, as a woman could show a man the same courtesy. As a matter of fact, she would do so herself at the next opportunity.

She took the arm the marquess proffered, turning to give his son a hopeful smile. He didn't smile back, but he followed their lead through the hall to the drawing room.

Viscount Langston looked a little older than his friend, in his mid-fifties, maybe, with thinning light brown hair and a slight paunch. His wife must have been about ten years younger, with short-cropped, tawny curls and a matronly build. Leah decided she liked both of them as soon as she saw how friendly they were when the marquess reintroduced them to David. They greeted her with just as much warmth, adding to the good impression.

After a flurry of inquiries into various people's health, most notably Phoebe's, everyone settled down with England's omnipresent tea.

"What a lovely surprise your calling is," the marquess

said, reclining in a stuffed armchair. "Solebury House is a bit off the route between your country seat and London."

"Not at all. What is a few miles of added travel where friends are concerned?" Lord Langston paused, his smile ebbing into sober lines. He glanced at the faces around the room, setting down his cup and saucer. "Actually, I have a specific matter I wish to discuss with you, Harold. But perhaps you would like to speak in private?"

"What sort of matter?" The marquess leaned forward, resting his elbows on his knees. "A business concern?"

His friend fidgeted, sitting up straighter on the settee he and his wife shared. "I wished to talk to you about William."

"Ah, I see." Lord Solebury sighed. "Well, you may as well speak freely. David knows what trouble his brother is, and the ladies are likely to learn sooner or later . . . unless of course, the boy has done something unfit for their ears."

"No, nothing quite so dreadful." Lord Langston took a deep breath. "Relatively minor, perhaps, and I hate to bear tales, but he is my godson, so I feel a certain responsibility to try to promote his welfare."

"Rightly so," the marquess said, while Leah's curiosity grew. She glanced at David, who wound his pocket watch with an absorption she thought feigned. He didn't normally hide his resentment for his half brother quite so well.

"Well, firstly, I happened upon William at Tattersall's the other week," Lord Langston said, looking his friend in the eye. "The last time I spoke to you, you mentioned his straitened finances, so you can imagine my surprise upon learning he had purchased a prime team of grays."

Lord Solebury's jaw dropped visibly. "A *team* of grays?"

Langston nodded. "I thought you might be unaware of the acquisition."

"Indeed." The marquess stood and went to the window,

his slumping shoulders leading Leah to wish she hadn't been allowed to witness the conversation after all. She sympathized with Lord Solebury, with one son who resented him bitterly and another who showed him no respect.

After staring outside for a long moment, he turned back to the others. "Well, you were right to inform me of this, John. The boy has no business making that sort of purchase in his circumstances. And I don't suppose he has sold off any of the other blood he has purchased in the past year?"

The viscount rose as well, joining him by the window. "No, and I fear there is more to the story. The very next day, news of a certain carriage race spread quickly in the clubs."

"So he means to race now?" The marquess threw his hands up in the air. "And why should that surprise me? Any pursuit that provides an opportunity for gaming is likely to attract the young jackanapes."

The viscount pressed his palms together, placing his thumbs against his chin. "This particular race had already taken place, I am afraid. Now, let me assure you William is unharmed, but I am sorry to say he had an accident, in which he overturned his carriage. The grays did not fare as well as the driver. Two horses had to be destroyed."

Lord Solebury's face went ashen, then reddened in manifest rage. When he spoke again, his voice cracked. "Those poor, hapless animals. The boy demonstrates a complete lack of responsibility at every turn! Well, I suppose there is nothing else for it: I shall have to go to London."

Silence fell over the group, as everyone stared blindly at different points around the room.

At last David cleared his throat, stating quietly, "Lady Solebury will be highly upset. She won't want you to leave her at this time."

"True." His father ran a hand through his hair. "But I can

see no other way to deal with William. I will leave immediately and make the trip as brief as possible, returning as soon as I can drag William's wretched carcass home with me. Phoebe does not expect to be confined for another month yet."

But Leah knew his going could upset Phoebe enough to endanger her and her baby. She looked around at all the grim faces and could tell everyone else thought the same. David, in particular, looked agitated, shifting in his chair and tapping his foot on the highly polished wooden floor.

Finally he glanced at Leah, then stood and stepped toward his father. "I shall go in your stead."

"You will?" Every line of worry on the marquess's face transformed to show astonishment.

"You cannot possibly leave Phoebe now. You know how your going would affect her. Of course, I don't know how much I can accomplish with William, but I daresay I may proceed as well as you would have done."

"Oh, yes. Indeed, David." His father actually looked hopeful. "You are his older brother, after all, and nearly a decade his senior. Older brothers incur a good deal of respect, often more than a father."

"I doubt that holds true in my case. All I can promise is to make the effort." His gaze traveled to Leah again, this time adhering to hers. He twisted his mouth. "I will return within a day or two. I will try to . . . I wish I did not have to . . ."

He stopped in midsentence and glanced about the room, obviously thinking twice about expressing his thoughts in front of the others. But stopping only incited a flurry of speculative looks—the visiting couple exchanging glances and the marquess studying his son closely.

Leah felt sure they would all conclude she and David were carrying on some sort of courtship. She smiled at the thought, not sure whether their conjecture had any validity or not. A single kiss, unfortunately, did not constitute a courtship—especially when one participant seemed determined to avoid a second one.

Then again, she had different ideas.

"Why don't you take Miss Cantrell with you?" the marquess suggested. "With Phoebe abed and you away, she will have little to entertain her here."

David's eyes rounded in an expression that looked more apprehensive than surprised. "My lord, this journey will require at least one overnight stay, perhaps more. We are no longer speaking of an hour's drive to see a local abbey. Proper chaperonage would be necessary."

"I can provide that," Lady Langston chimed in. Her sly grin confirmed that she suspected budding romance. "If you two travel with us, all will be perfectly unexceptional. In fact, if you choose to remain in London, we should be happy to have you stay with us. Would we not, John?"

"Certainly," Lord Langston said. "For as long as you like."

"Then everything is settled." The marquess smiled at Leah. "Should you like to go to town, dear?"

She looked at David, who watched her with a dour face. Obviously, he didn't want her to go. But the alternative meant sitting in Solebury House for who-knew-how-many days, probably not even allowed out alone for so much as a walk.

"I'd love to," she said. She grinned at David. "Shall I begin packing?"

Chapter 12

"I AM PERFECTLY fine here on the box." David drew the reins into one hand and wiped a droplet of rain from the bridge of his nose. "Now, for heaven's sake, pull your head inside the carriage and close the window. If the Langstons look back and see your antics, they will conclude you belong in Bedlam."

His choice of words had been unfortunate, but Leah showed no ill reaction. "This rain is cold, David. Why don't you let the tiger take over driving? He's dressed for the weather."

He sniffled, beginning to suffer the effects of the damp air. But he intended to avoid any *tête-à-tête* encounter with her that he could. The indiscretion at the gatehouse had shown how little he could trust himself with her. "Perhaps later. I don't mind a bit of drizzle."

"Oh, come on. What are you afraid I'll do—bite you?"

She giggled, and he marveled that she could possibly find their situation amusing. But then, she had exhibited none of the mortification he had expected to see after she'd had time to reflect on the previous night's imprudence. Lord, he hoped she soon regained not only her memories but her common sense. He severely doubted he possessed enough for both of them.

"Okay," she said when he failed to respond to her quizzing. "If you're determined to catch pneumonia, I guess I can't stop you. But I think you're foolish . . . doubly so, considering there won't be any penicillin to treat you."

After that bit of gammon, she pulled herself inside, leaving him alone with his worries. He had done all he could to avoid bringing her with him, even applied to poor Phoebe with arguments about propriety. But the marchioness saw nothing untoward in their following the Langstons on an overnight journey. She even speculated that seeing London might help Leah revive some of her lost memories, since she had been there directly before her accident. If so, he would be the happiest of anyone. But would Phoebe still have favored Leah's traveling with him if she knew how close he had come to ruining the girl? Hardly.

He pulled a handkerchief out of his pocket and blew his nose. Next time, preventing such a disaster might not prove as easy, especially since their chaperon showed a disposition for matchmaking. During their stop for lunch, Lady Langston had made sure he and Leah sat together, even concocted excuses to leave them alone while she "helped" her husband oversee a carriage repair. Solebury's eagerness to include Leah on the trip must have misled the viscountess to believe that he, David, had permission to press his suit. Her ladyship would feel quite differently if she realized Leah's father knew nothing of her whereabouts.

Leah's father. What would *he* think if he could see his daughter now, practically left alone to the devices of a baseborn scoundrel? David cringed at the self-chosen slur, but his behavior at the gatehouse had proved he could not even feign good breeding. The bone-chilling rain that dripped down on his head served him right, fit recrimination for a man incapable of cooling the fires of his ill-begotten blood.

"Looks as though they've found an inn," Leah called from the back. A peek over his shoulder revealed her leaning out of the barouche again.

After a glance heavenward, he looked forward and saw the Langstons' tiger motioning their intention to stop. Ahead on the road a small country inn appeared in the mist. A grove of trees provided a charming backdrop for an otherwise unremarkable establishment. The garden had fallen to overgrowth, and a shutter flapped loose on a front window. But wisps of white smoke rose from the chimneys, marking warm fires within. At the moment, the prospect of a cozy hearth appealed to him more than sumptuous quarters.

He pulled up behind the lead carriage and handed a few coins to a boy who stood ready to take their bags. After escorting Leah inside and depositing her by a fireplace in the dining hall, he returned to join Lord Langston in the foyer.

"I have secured a meal in a private parlor, as well as rooms for the night," his lordship informed him. "We were fortunate enough to acquire the last chambers available. The servants will share, of course."

"Thank you for tending to the arrangements." David dug into his pocket for money, but Lord Langston reached out to stop him.

"No, no, put your purse away. Your father gave me funds to cover accommodations for you and Miss Cantrell."

The usual surge of resentment rose in his gut. But before he could insist on paying his own shot, the viscount placed a soothing hand on his shoulder.

"Your father knew you would not accept money from him, but you *are* making this journey on his behalf." When David said nothing, his lordship lifted his eyebrows. "Even you must admit that visiting William will hold no pleasure for you."

He snorted, an involuntary acknowledgment of Lord Langston's point. But on further consideration, he saw no reason to argue. He would not take his pride to unreasonable lengths. After all, the funds gained from selling his army commission would not last forever, and his importing investments had not yet begun to turn a profit.

"Whatever suits Solebury," he said.

The viscount clapped him on the back. "Let us collect the ladies, then, and escort them upstairs to dress for dinner."

David agreed, eager to cast off his rain-drenched apparel—and the awkward encounter. He would have been better prepared to deal with animosity than with the compassion of his father's friend. Somehow, it left him defenseless.

When he had helped the viscount see the ladies settled, he retired to his own quarters and peeled off his clammy linen shirt and buckskin breeches. The fire in the room had not yet been lit, and the chilly air prompted him to towel dry quickly and scamper into fresh clothes. He had just squeezed a foot back into one of his sodden Hessian boots when a knock sounded at the door. He hoped it signaled the arrival of a servant with wood.

"Yes?" he called, balancing on one leg while he struggled to pull on the other boot.

"Is that you, David?" Leah's voice carried in from the hall. "Can I come in?"

The mere thought of her entering his chamber pitched him forward so he had to brace himself with both hands on the scarred wooden floor. Under no circumstances could she come into his room and retain respectability—but especially not with him in his shirtsleeves and stocking feet.

"I am . . . not presentable at the moment."

He thought he heard a muffled giggle—and, certainly, he would not put the impropriety past her. Jamming his foot into the second boot, he inched closer to the door.

"What in creation brings you here?" he hissed through the crack between door and frame. He hastened to tuck in his shirt, as if she might actually be able see his state of *deshabille* through the wood. "Unless you have some urgent matter to discuss, you ought to be dressing for dinner. Now, please return to your own quarters."

"I'm finished dressing," came her muted response. "And my room is so cold, I couldn't stand it. I threw on my dinner dress and got out of there as fast as I could."

"Well, you will have to return." He feared she would refuse to heed him and snatched his waistcoat from the bed, shrugging into the garment. "When I am presentable, I will fetch you and accompany you down to the dining hall."

She hesitated. "How long will you be?"

He ran a hand through his damp hair, stepping aside to glimpse his reflection in a glass hanging above the small dressing table. He did not dare ask for a reasonable amount of time. "Allow me five minutes."

"Okay, but meet me downstairs, anyway. That big fire in the dining hall is calling to me. See you in a few minutes."

"Leah, you cannot go downstairs alone!" He fumbled with the latch and opened the door, but she had already gone. Poking his head into the hall, he spied her turning into the staircase.

"Devil take it!" He pulled back into his chamber. Thanks to her, he would have to appear below with wet hair and a hastily tied cravat.

He mastered a simple knot for the latter and snatched his jacket from the single wooden chair in the room. He finished his rushed toilette while hurrying through the hall and down to the ground floor.

Leah sat with the innkeeper's wife on a bench before the fire, a smile on her face and a steaming tin cup in her hands. She spotted him approaching the hearth and stood, holding out her drink toward him.

"Oh, David," she uttered in a tone of rapture. "Just wait until you try this mulled wine! I couldn't have asked for a better drink to warm me up. Here, try some."

Her artlessness disarmed him, and he took the cup without thinking. She nodded her encouragement for him to sample the wine. He could not seem to look away from her sparkling eyes as he lifted the cup, wondering if her lips had grazed the same spot his own would.

Cinnamon- and clove-scented steam wafted from the drink, and his mouth watered even before the sweet, apple-tinged wine washed over his tongue. His body seemed to fill with warmth, spurred by the luscious drink, the blazing fire, and the flickering flames in Leah's eyes.

"Heavenly," he heard himself say.

She beamed and turned to the landlady. "Can we have another one, Mrs. King? Make that *two more*. This one is going quickly."

The grandmotherly woman smiled and scurried toward

the kitchen. David held Leah's wine back out to her, but she shook her head.

"Drink some more. I've already had half a cup." She reseated herself on the bench, patting the spot beside her. "Isn't this inn charming? I love this big, stone fireplace and the wizened old wood of the furniture. How old do you suppose the place is?"

He sat down, taking another sip of the spicy confection. The features she indicated could not be called unusual, but with his feet warming by the fire and a beautiful woman beside him, he, too, felt the allure of the country setting. "Several hundred years, I daresay. But you may not find the building quite so delightful when you are confined to your chamber again tonight. Old inns are notorious for drafts."

"But the servants will light fires in our rooms before we go to bed, won't they?" She shivered and leaned closer to the flames. "If not, I may have to sleep down here."

"I shall make a point to address the innkeeper on the matter," he said, praying she only jested about bedding down in the dining hall.

Suddenly she looked at him with mischief dancing in her eyes. "Wouldn't it be wonderful if a whole building could be heated by a single, powerful machine, centrally located, say, in the cellar?"

He stiffened, recognizing the hypothesis for one of her fantasies about a future world. For some foolish reason, he elected to debate her. "How could enough heat for an entire construction possibly be generated in one area? The building itself would catch on fire."

"A fuel, similar to . . . lamp oil, could be burned to produce heat, while a self-powered fan would propel the hot air through ducts running to all the rooms." She took his cup and sipped the mulled wine, watching his face with a grin.

"Nonsense," he said. "How would the fan power itself?"

"With electricity, like the lightning you see during a thunderstorm." She handed him back the wine. "You have the rest. There's only a sip left."

He took the cup absently. "And how would one harness the energy of a lightning bolt?"

She shrugged. "I believe a lightning bolt itself is too volatile to control. The electricity comes from various other sources, too complicated for me to explain—or even understand. What am I—an engineer?"

"You are a young woman with an active imagination and a bump somewhere on her head," he said. He could only hope Phoebe proved right in venturing that a London visit might help uncloud Leah's mind. "Even if you have no visible evidence of injury, I am certain you have one."

"Then we make a fine pair: I with an invisible bump on my head and you with an invisible chip on your shoulder." She paired her observation with a smile. "Here comes the landlady with more mulled wine. Finish that one up."

The Langstons chose that moment to appear as well, so he and Leah carried their wine with them into the private dining parlor the viscount had reserved. Furnished with only a crude trestle table and benches, the room afforded little comfort. A good-sized blaze burned in the hearth, but the air was too chilly for it to have been lit long.

"I apologize for the inferior accommodations," Lord Langston said as they settled at the table. "With the rain coming so steadily, my wife and I thought we should stop here rather than go on to the inn where we usually stay. I had not realized quite how little this establishment has to offer."

"Whatever the inn lacks in luxury is made up for in character," Leah said, once again seated beside David. She gazed up at the cobwebbed beams supporting the ceiling, then around at the rather small windows currently pelted by rain. "Everything is so quaint. And if the food is anywhere near as good as the mulled wine, we're in for a treat."

As though on cue, the landlady entered with a stoneware pitcher of the steaming drink. Leah urged the Langstons to fill their cups and had David pouring himself a third serving scarcely before he had finished the second. Her enthusiasm led them all to down several cups before any food came to the table. As a result, they grew quite a merry party.

When serving girls brought out freshly baked sourdough bread, Leah declared she had never tasted better. And during dinner, she praised each course, entranced by offerings as simple as Yorkshire pudding. Lord and Lady Langston laughed over her appreciation, clearly as taken with Leah as she appeared with the food. Indeed, her enjoyment had a contagious quality, and David found himself savoring the simple fare—as well as the warm company—greater than he had at any dinner party he recalled.

When the viscount and his wife got up to retire, he felt as though he had been doused with cold water.

"So early?" he asked, standing automatically. An instant of dizziness surprised him. The wine had affected him more than he realized. "Will you not stay for one more drink?"

"If you check your watch, you will find the hour is not so early, at least not when one is scheduled to travel in the morning," Lord Langston said. He and his wife exchanged amused looks. "But you young people have more stamina than we. Feel free to linger over your wine."

Brilliant. Now the viscount had taken up matchmaking as well. David stole a glance at Leah, who smiled in return, her eyes and hair glittering in the firelight.

"We had best retire as well, Le—er, Miss Cantrell," he said. "We, too, must rise early in the morning."

"Can we stay for just one more drink?" she asked with an irrepressible smile.

But he could not stay—not without longing, painfully, to repeat the previous night's shame. "I have had too much already. Come. I will escort you to your chamber."

Thus the party filed upstairs together. The Langstons bade a quick good night and disappeared into their rooms, leaving David and Leah alone in the hall. He unlocked her door for her, glanced inside to ensure the absence of intruders, then handed her the key.

She looked up at him, still smiling, her eyes focused tightly on his. His gaze dropped to her lips, beautifully formed and ripe for kissing. Could he not simply bestow one brief good night kiss on those lips?

No. He knew he could not without demanding more. And he had no right to even a single kiss.

He turned away, tossing over his shoulder, "Good night. Lock your door behind you."

Without looking back, he went to his chamber.

Ten minutes later he lay wide-eyed in the dark. A small fire burned, but the room retained a chill, and the narrow single bed made his back ache. The room also contained a second bunk, but it appeared as lumpy as the one he had chosen.

A soft knock sounded at the door. Stunned, he froze in place.

The knock repeated, this time followed by a whisper.

"David, it's me. Are you awake?"

Good Lord! She *was* ready for Bedlam. If anyone saw her outside his door at this hour . . .

He tossed off the covers and threw on his dressing gown.

Hastily unlatching the door, he scanned the empty corridor and pulled her inside by the arm. He tried to rein in his panic, closing the door quickly but quietly. Only then did he allow himself to look at her, draped only in her nightrail and wrapper. The lantern she held cast alluring shadows over her body.

"What is the meaning of this?" he hissed. "Are you well and truly mad?"

She winced. "I know. I know I shouldn't be here. But, David, the ceiling in my room leaks—not in one spot but several! The worst leak is dripping right on the bed, and the mattress is soaked through."

He could only stare.

"Honestly, David, I was going to try to sleep on the floor instead, but that's wet, too, and the room is freezing. I've never seen such a measly fire." She walked toward the small blaze in his hearth and held her palms out to it. "Mine's not even as good as this one."

There could be no doubt of her distress and, he admitted, she had cause to be disturbed. He tried to think what to do, his wine-addled mind churning slowly. He would have to offer her his room—but then where would he sleep? He had a choice of taking over her cold, wet room or sleeping with the servants, probably in the same bed with one. Not a pleasing prospect.

"I shall take your room, and you can have mine," he said. Truly, he saw no alternative. "If anyone notices, we can explain. I believe we have good cause for the switch."

"You can't sleep in there." She turned around, keeping her back close to the fireplace. "Even if you find a dry spot on the floor, the puddles are bound to spread into it by morning. The rain still isn't letting up."

He frowned, rubbing his chin in thought. No new alternatives came to him.

"Look, there are two beds here," she said, pointing to the empty bunk. "It's not like we have to sleep in the same one."

He blinked at her. "I should think not."

She sighed, shaking her head. "If only you understood how different things are . . . where I come from."

Naturally, she meant not *where* but *when*. He crossed his arms over his chest.

"What would be so wrong about my staying here? What would be wrong, even if we . . ." She trailed off, leaving him to fill in the blank with a dozen tantalizing thoughts.

What would be wrong? Everything . . . or not a thing in the world. He let his gaze wander down over her silk-encased body, remembering how slender and pliant she had felt in his arms. Heat rose up his own body and haze over his mind.

"Never mind," she said, just when his will had begun to crumble. "I respect your point of view. You can have your side of the room, and I will stick to mine."

She walked to the spare bed, pulled down the covers, and fluffed up the pillow. "I promise not to do anything to compromise your virtue."

"*My* virtue?"

"I will sneak back to my room first thing in the morning. No one will know I was here."

He opened his mouth but closed it again, no longer certain whether he wanted to protest her staying or her staying in a separate bed. Unaccustomed to extricating himself from one muddle after another, he found the task exhausting. He weighed his options. He could sleep in a freezing, water-soaked room. He could sleep in the same bed with a poxy servant. He could apply to Lord and Lady Langston like a damned pest. He could ravish the young woman left in his charge.

The least troublesome choice seemed to be accepting the arrangements as they stood. If she failed to rise early and steal back to her chamber, he would go to the other room himself. He felt sure he would wake early, in fact doubted he would rest at all, knowing she lay only a few feet away.

"Very well." He went to the door and turned the key in the lock, checking twice to ensure the latch had caught. Refusing to look at her, he climbed into bed in his dressing gown and turned his face to the wall.

"Good night," he said.

Even in his agitated state of mind, he made one resolution: Chaperon or no chaperon, he and Leah would make no overnight stops on the way back from London. They would have to travel from the crack of dawn until midnight to do so, but that hardly mattered.

The sleep he would sacrifice would amount to no more than what he would lose tonight.

Chapter 13

DAVID MUST HAVE woken half a dozen times before the thin light of dawn finally filtered through his chamber window. A draft blew through a cracked pane and chilled his face—no doubt still flushed from dreams of the woman sharing his room. All night his subconscious mind had pulled Leah out of her bed and into his . . . until he'd wake again and peer through the dark to spy her sleeping form, still across the room.

He wanted her now in reality—wanted to wake her gently, carry her to his bed, and damn the consequences. She would come willingly this very moment, he thought, if only he asked her. Would he ask her? He didn't know, but he rolled over to watch her sleep as he considered giving in to temptation.

Her bed stood empty.

The sheets and counterpane had been neatly made up, the

pillow fluffed to obliterate all hints of use. He scanned the floor space next to the bed, searching for . . . what? A dropped hairpin, perhaps—any sign that she truly had slept only a few paces away from him. He looked to the closed door, then got up and laid his palm on the mattress of her bed. All warmth from her body had dissipated.

A shiver jarred him. How cold the room had grown during the night! And how dull his senses felt, likely still sodden with mulled wine. He should have been relieved that Leah had escaped his chamber undetected. Instead, he felt numb, strangely lifeless. The wine had indeed plundered his sensibilities . . . all the better ones, anyway.

He went to the dressing table and splashed water on his face, but his mind strayed during the whole time he shaved and dressed. Once he had made himself presentable, breakfast seemed a reasonable—if not quite desired aim, so he wandered out into the hall.

As he neared Leah's door, he slowed his pace while his heartbeat quickened. Surely, he ought to confirm she had reached her chamber safely. With a glance down both ends of the empty corridor, he tapped on the door.

"Who is it?" her voice sounded through the wood.

He cleared his throat. "David. Are you dre—are you ready for breakfast?"

The door opened and she stood before him, clear-eyed, smiling, and dressed for travel. Behind her, the morning sun broke through the clouds and streamed through the window to grant her a halo-like glow. The clouds in his head lifted as well, and life surged into his senses.

"Good morning." Her smile tilted, taking on an impish air. "Did you sleep well?"

He meant to offer her the reprove she deserved for teasing

him but could not resist returning her grin. "Minx. Can I escort you downstairs?"

"Please." She joined him in the hall, closing and locking the door. But as they began walking, she stopped again. "Wait. I want to take care of something while we're alone."

She reached into her reticule and removed a gold guinea, holding the coin out to him. "Please put this toward the bill for the inn. I'm sorry I can't give you more. Unfortunately, this is all the money I have."

He frowned. "I cannot take that coin. First of all, a guinea far exceeds your reckoning for the inn. Truly, you ought to familiarize yourself with English money. Secondly, Solebury has provided financing for us, since we've undertaken this journey in his stead."

"Oh." She looked at the guinea and back at him. "Well, would you be willing to hold this for me? I, uh . . . don't quite feel safe traveling with money on my person."

He judged her proposal a wise one, given her lack of understanding for the monetary system. "Certainly. Shall I write you a note of receipt?"

She broke into a grin, waving off his offer. "Just take the damned thing so we can go to breakfast."

Her swearing surprised him. But as he accepted the coin, he recalled how oddly she had behaved when Phoebe returned the guinea they'd found in her pocket—this same guinea, no doubt. He glanced at it, frowning. "Why does this coin upset you?"

The grin on her face faded, replaced by a wary look. "It's the one I told you about—the one I threw into the spring."

"The what?" He thought back and grimaced when he remembered what she had said. "The one you claim you used to make your 'inadvertent wish'?"

She looked down at the floor. "Yes."

"Your story makes no sense, Leah. If you threw this into the spring, how could you still have it to give to me?"

"I did throw it in, twice. Once right before my transport and again the other night when I tried to go back. Both times, the coin ended up in my pocket again."

An eerie feeling shuddered through him, along with a stray thought. He had tossed a guinea like this one into the spring the same day she had arrived. Of course, he hadn't made a wish . . . well, not really. He had been thinking about aspects of his life he wished could be different, and had thrown the coin in the water on a whim. And, naturally, the action had wrought no magic.

He shook his head. "The truth is obvious to me. You never threw this coin in the water. You dreamed the whole episode—imagined traveling through time."

"*And* dreamed up a whole lifetime of experiences?" she asked, eyebrows raised. "David, the things I could tell you about—"

"I don't want to hear them."

She stared at him, lips parted slightly, as though she was deliberating whether to continue arguing. At last she spoke, her voice quiet. "You won't even listen to me?"

He felt his resolve weaken dangerously, but he refused to encourage her. Fixing a glare on her, he said, "No, I will not listen to nonsense."

Her lower lip quivered, forcing his gaze to her mouth. Again, his will faltered. Privately, he longed to still that lip with kisses, to hold her body against his and tell her she had no need for false memories. He wanted to assure her he would protect her from whatever had hurt her in her true past.

But what kind of protection could he give her? He lacked the financial means to offer her marriage. *Marriage!* How dare he even think of entering that blessed state with her? Wedding a bastard would only open up a whole new realm of problems for her.

He clenched his fists, infuriated by his own inadequacies. "Are you coming to breakfast with me or not?"

She jumped, and he regretted how sharply he had spoken. But before he could even think to apologize, she rallied and lifted her chin.

"Nice of you to offer to escort someone full of nonsense. But, thank you all the same, I prefer to find my own way." She turned away from him and stalked down the hall.

Her show of vexation startled him. Did she actually expect him to acknowledge her Banbury tales? If so, he had made no progress in convincing her to face reality.

Spirits sinking, he walked downstairs to the dining hall and found her already seated with the viscount and his wife. He joined them, receiving a warm welcome from Lord and Lady Langston and a mere nod from Leah. Throughout the meal, she barely spoke a word to him, favoring the Langstons with all her conversation, except when a direct question forced her to respond to David.

When they left the inn, the weather had turned fine, but she declined his invitation to ride with him on the box. All during the seemingly endless journey, he waited for her to poke her head out the window and quiz him about the scenery or his driving. Instead, she remained properly inside up to the moment they reached the Langstons' town house.

As the viscount and viscountess allotted tasks to the army of servants waiting in the front hall, David watched Leah climb the grand staircase behind a footman who carried her portmanteau.

When she disappeared above, he shrugged to himself and turned away from the stairs. As soon as his hosts had finished addressing the staff, he stepped up and informed them he intended to seek out William.

"So soon?" Her ladyship's eyebrows sprang upward. "You might at least take the time to change out of those dusty traveling clothes. We are in no hurry to be rid of you, you know, dear. Quite the contrary."

An unaccustomed warmth suffused his face. Throughout his adult life, he had avoided contact with friends of his father's, never dreaming to gain acceptance from society's exalted ranks. The kindness of the Langstons astonished him.

"Thank you, my lady," he sputtered, "but I may as well have done with the confrontation."

Lord Langston's brow furrowed. "Perhaps the meeting need not be a confrontation, son. A diplomatic approach could do much to aid your case."

"Solebury's case, you mean." He tried to smile but suspected he only achieved a smirk. "And I fear I am not much of a diplomat." His dealings with Leah proved that.

Lady Langston rested an index finger against her chin, apparently devising her own strategy. She looked to her husband and asked, "Why don't we invite William to dinner this evening? Rather than David's striding into the boy's quarters as though hunting him down, we shall treat him as a guest. Once we have softened him up with food and wine, we may be able to convince him to return to Solebury House of his own accord."

The viscount nodded. "Yes. Let his father take on the task of reforming him. We need only get him home."

"A splendid idea," David said, "and I appreciate your effort to save me an unpleasant duty. But from what I have heard, William keeps a full social calendar. Even if he is free, he is unlikely to accept an invitation to see me."

"He has not visited his godparents in quite some time, either, dear." Lady Langston smiled. "Allow me to issue the invitation. How can he turn down the opportunity to dine with his godparents and his brother?"

"*Half* brother." David remained unconvinced, but he lacked any will to argue for visiting William on his own. "But you may try if you like."

She beamed at him, immediately setting about dispatching a footman to William's bachelor quarters. To David's amazement, the servant returned with an affirmative reply. William had previous plans for the evening but could easily postpone them until after dinner. He would be pleased to attend his godparents and his brother.

"Viscount Traymore," the butler at Langston House announced, bowing his way out of the drawing room as Lord William strode through the open double doors.

The young lord brushed an invisible speck from his well-tailored coat, somehow tilting his aquiline nose upward even as he looked down at the impeccable blue superfine.

Peacock, David thought, scarcely able to credit they shared paternal lineage. Certainly, if he had desired evidence of their kinship, he would have had to look beyond the lad's baby blue eyes and straw-colored locks. But he made no such search. During childhood, William had impressed him as a brat, and by all accounts, he had never outgrown the label.

Though the viscount had not occupied a room with his half brother for years, he took in David with the same ricocheting glance he afforded the furniture. Indeed, for a moment, a plush recamier positioned off to the side won the majority of his notice. He flopped down on the seat, peering out an adjacent window at the street below. "My godparents are still making their toilette, I presume?"

David remained sitting across the room, undecided how much courtesy he wanted to extend his ill-mannered sibling. As he watched Lord William stretch one long leg across the cushions of the recamier, he curled his lip. "You presume correctly. Kind of you to accept Lady Langston's dinner invitation."

"Not much else to do this time of the evening, and her ladyship contends I am overdue for a call. I must say I was deuced surprised to learn you were staying here." He continued watching out the window, his wonder apparently not sufficient enough to warrant eye contact with his brother.

David made no answer and silence loomed between the two men till the sound of approaching footsteps echoed in the hall. Both looked toward the doors as a youthful parlor maid entered and curtsied deeply.

"Beg pardon, sirs," she said in a voice that squeaked with timidity. "Is there anything you require?"

Lord William swept an assessing leer over her trim figure, ending with a grin and a wink. "I can think of several intriguing possibilities. But, for now, a good measure of Langston's brandy would not go amiss. And bring one for my esteemed brother, will you, love?"

Her cheeks flushed and she dropped her gaze. "Certainly, my lord." She bobbed a second curtsy and scurried to the doors, bumping into the jamb in her haste to exit.

William laughed. "Grace as well as beauty!"

The maid flushed and lowered her head, ducking quickly out of the room.

"Well done," David said in a low tone. "Count yourself fortunate if she returns with your brandy at all."

"Seemed to me she hopped to do my bidding." Heedless of his brother's glower, the viscount reached into his coat and pulled out an enameled snuffbox. He held the trinket out in David's general direction, lifting his eyebrows in a mute question.

When David only glared, he shrugged, took a pinch, and put away the box. "I understand you have been rusticating at Solebury House this past sennight."

The youth's insouciance outstripped even David's scant expectations for him. He restrained an urge to grab the little rogue by the high points of his collar and shake him. "I stayed at the gatehouse, not at the manor, and only for a few nights."

"A day or two with the *newlyweds* is enough for anyone." William scratched at one of his long sideburns, gazing back out the window. "Wise of you to escape quickly, what with our lovely stepmama nearing confinement. A squalling babe should add charm to the household. You won't be returning soon, I gather?"

Though the young man avoided looking his way, a certain heightening of his tone led David to believe him more interested than he cared to reveal.

"Actually, I will likely set off for Solebury House again tomorrow."

At last he had the viscount's full attention, even eliciting a narrowing of William's childlike eyes. "Finally decided the old man's worth something to you, eh? Well, if your pockets are to let as badly as mine, I cannot fault you. I may have to make a visit to Kent soon myself."

"I seek no money from the marquess. You may rest easy on that score."

William now eyed him with open curiosity. "Then what could possibly keep you at Solebury House?"

The sound of footsteps in the hall again drew their notice toward the doors. But instead of the little parlor maid, Leah stepped over the threshold, resplendent in an emerald green gown that magnificently complemented her hair and eyes. Her gaze went straight to David, and she crossed her arms over her chest, unwittingly accentuating a revealing *décolletage*.

"David." She pursed her lips, apparently not noticing William at his post by the window. "Well, I guess sooner or later we had to be alone together again. Should we risk trying to hold a conversation, or would we do better without words?"

The saucy pout she gave him made him wonder if she offered kissing as an alternative to conversing.

A low whistle sounded from the recamier, perhaps indicating the same thought had crossed William's mind. Before David could think how to respond, his brother rose, sauntering to the center of the drawing room.

"Allow me to save you the inconvenience of any *tête-à-tête* you don't desire, madam."

Leah started, letting her arms drop to her sides.

David got up, dragging himself forth for the hapless task of introducing her to the knave. "Miss Cantrell, allow me to present Viscount Traymore. Lord William, Miss Leah Cantrell."

"A pleasure indeed." He scooped up her hand, bowing low to brush his lips over her knuckles—a gesture that made David ball his fists. "How is it I have never met you before, Miss Cantrell? And you and my brother are on such intimate terms. I noticed you employed his given name."

David realized he should have offered background in the introductions, but he found himself loathe to reveal the least detail about Leah to his half brother. He had no desire to share the acquaintance with the jackanapes. Since *some* explanation seemed in order, he said, "Miss Cantrell has been staying at Solebury House."

"Ah, at Solebury House. I *see*." William slid him a cunning grin, then looked back to Leah. "I was just telling my brother I mean to visit Solebury soon."

"Really?" She darted a wondrous glance at David and looked back to the viscount with added sparkle in her eyes. "What a surprise. I mean, I'm sure your father will be pleased."

"You flatter me, Miss Cantrell." He flashed her a brilliant smile, the one attribute in which he most closely resembled his father. "Will you be returning to Kent with my brother?"

"I expect so." She glanced at David as though she thought he might contradict her, but he simply returned her gaze.

"Indeed?" William's grin widened. "How merry you must all be with such a party staying at the estate. I shall have to make arrangements to join you as soon as possible. Perhaps I may even be able to reschedule a few appointments and depart with you tomorrow."

David clenched his teeth, noting that the viscount's concern about the coming babe had vanished quickly once Leah entered the picture. If William wanted to join them, his only reason could be a hope of insinuating himself with her. As many qualms as David had about being on the road alone with her, the thought of his brother infiltrating the party enraged him.

He glanced at Leah, acknowledging she looked lovelier than ever dressed in her formal regalia. The twinkle in her eyes indicated her mood had lightened, and he felt a stab of pure jealousy that William's presence had lifted the spirits he, David, had blackened earlier. The thought of his brother's courting her made him ill—especially when he gauged how eligible a suitor the handsome young heir might be considered.

"We leave at dawn," he said through a rigid jaw. If he

could discourage William from traveling with them, that would keep him away for a few extra days. When the viscount did arrive at Solebury House, David could only hope his father's anger still stood. A disgraced son at home would not hold so much appeal for Leah as the London dandy making up to her here.

"At dawn?" The viscount appeared astounded. "Can I not persuade you to delay your departure to a less ungodly hour? I shouldn't think you would be quite so anxious to see our dear father again."

"We must make the journey in a single day," David said. "Lady Langston traveled here with us, but since she will remain in London, Miss Cantrell no longer has a chaperon."

"Indeed?" William looked to Leah and rubbed his chin. "Well, isn't that . . . a pity. I cannot tell you how much I wish I might add to your security with my escort, Miss Cantrell. Unfortunately, I have obligations this evening that are like to keep me out past dawn."

"I understand," she said with a hint of a smile that added to David's resentment of his brother.

"Her security is well assured," he snapped, then felt a wave of guilt as he recalled how close he had come to trying to lure her into his bed that morning. If he truly wanted to protect her, he would do well to guard her against himself. Maintaining a certain detachment between them would be the kindest service he could do for her.

The sound of voices in the hall announced the approach of their hosts. While the Langstons welcomed their godson with polite reserve, the parlor maid entered and slipped the two brothers their brandy. David surmised she had delayed her return until her employers' entrance provided a diversion for William. He sympathized with the girl, but she dashed away before he could even thank her for the drink.

After the Langstons and William had exchanged greetings, the party moved into the dining room. David found himself seated in his usual place beside Leah, William across from them and their hosts at either end.

"I hope you don't mind our dining *en famille*," the viscountess said. "The nice thing about sitting down with such a small group is that any conversation must include everyone at the table."

"Much preferable to a large party." William leaned back to allow a servant to place soup before him. "For instance, in a larger group, I could not quiz Miss Cantrell about her accent, as I am not seated next to her. But here I am free to speak to anyone. May I ask where you acquired such unique articulation, Miss Cantrell?"

"She is an American," David said, irritated by his brother's simpering smile.

"Truly?" William's gaze never left her face, as though she rather than his brother had answered. "I have never met an American before! Pray, tell me all about life in the States."

She laughed, though David willed she might sneer at the stale question.

"*All* about it? Well, let me see if I can sum up the American experience in a few words. We speak the same language you do, only we try to pronounce every syllable very carefully. We drink coffee instead of tea. We're very casual, whereas you're more formal. And our sense of humor isn't so dry—nor so witty, *I* think."

"You think us clever?" William shot his brother an expression of exaggerated surprise. "Do you hear that, David? We shall have to be very amusing during dinner tonight. We would not want to disabuse Miss Cantrell of her flattering estimation of our countrymen."

He bristled, only too aware he had no talent for social

banter. Perhaps William had intended to point out that fact. He tried to think of a poignant retort, but nothing came to him. Not since the tauntings of his early schooldays had he felt so inadequate to meet a challenge.

While he sat dumb, William turned his charms on his hosts, complimenting everything from the soup to Lady Langston's gown to a carriage Lord Langston had recently purchased. The praise had no evident effect on his godparents, as they continued to treat him with civility but no appearance of partiality. Perhaps sensing his lack of headway, William refocused his attention on Leah.

"Tell me, Miss Cantrell," he asked as the servants collected soup plates, "how long will you be visiting Solebury House?"

"I really can't say." She dabbed at her lips with a napkin. "Probably as long as the marchioness will have me."

"Then you must be enjoying yourself." His gaze stole toward David and flitted back to her. "But surely you are impatient to get back to your *betrothed*? I hope you will pardon my asking, but I could not help but notice your ring."

As on the first occasion she had been quizzed on the subject, she looked at her hand with something like surprise. But her ensuing reply differed greatly from before.

"Oh, this? This isn't an engagement ring. Not at all. In fact, I've been meaning to get rid of it. You're not the first one to mistake its significance, and I don't want people thinking I'm unavailable."

David shot a stunned look at her, while the others chuckled, William, in particular, tickled by her remark.

"Sell it," he recommended. "Get a few shillings for the gold, and you can buy yourself some hair ribbons."

"Not a bad idea. But, actually, I have another plan in mind." To David's shock, she removed the ring and dropped it into the pocket of her dress. "For now, this will do. I may as well get used to the feeling of a bare finger."

"Don't bother," Lord Langston said. "I have a notion your finger is not likely to remain bare for long."

David stared unseeingly at the plate of beef a servant set before him. If his lordship's reference to an impending betrothal related to *him,* the man would find himself quite mistaken. Leah had not taken her ring off when *he* asked about it. Quite to the contrary, she had told him about her American suitor and implied the ring still held meaning for her.

He peered to the side to watch her stab a fork into her dinner. Clearly, the trinket had lost significance now that William appeared to court her! He had known she hid many things from him, but he had never before suspected her for an adventuress. But how else could one explain a clever young woman falling for such transparent charisma—especially when she knew very well of the viscount's failings.

He barely touched the rest of his meal and made no attempt to compete with William in his efforts to charm the party with prattle. Easily carrying the conversation, William held the advantage over him in that field every bit as surely as in the quest for Leah's hand—a pursuit completely closed to David.

With no right to woo her himself, he could only pray she came to her senses regarding William. He even debated pulling her aside to warn her off the posturing boor.

But if he did so, he would betray his own unworthy feelings for her. He hoped that, when the viscount returned to Solebury House and faced disgrace, she would realize how unequal a match William would make for her. Then she could go on to find someone else for a husband—anyone but *him.*

By the time she found that other man, David planned to be far removed from her life . . . starting his own over in America.

Chapter 14

"LEAH. LEAH, LOVE, wake up."

The whisper penetrated her subconscious mind, and she fluttered her eyes open, squinting against a spot of light in the darkness. The light floated—a lantern, she realized, held by David at the door of the carriage. Had he just called her "love," or had she dreamed it? Her drowsiness started to clear, and she remembered he'd behaved miserably toward her all day. She must have dreamed the endearment.

"We are here," he said, his tone tender.

She pushed up into a sitting position, kneading a kink in the back of her neck. His mood must have improved while she'd slept. He certainly hadn't shown her much tenderness earlier. Even when they stopped to eat lunch and dinner, he'd barely spoken to her.

"Come into the house with me, Leah." He held out his

free hand. "You will be far more comfortable in your chamber."

"We're at Solebury House?" She stood up, bumping her head on the roof of the carriage. "Ow! What time is it?"

"Nearly midnight." He took her arm and helped her down onto the drive. "A footman has already taken your portmanteau upstairs. Allow me to escort you inside."

"I slept a long time." A cool breeze blew her hair across her face but helped to clear her mind. As the short walk across the gravel revived her, she remembered how his moodiness had ruined what could have been an enjoyable trip. She turned to him and frowned. "If I'd had a more pleasant companion, I might have traveled on the box and managed to stay awake."

He didn't defend himself, guiding her up the front steps in silence—and annoying her even more.

When they reached the door, she pulled her arm out of his hold and edged in front of him. She walked inside, fully intending to stomp upstairs without a look back.

Then she saw the front hall.

He collided into her back, quickly grabbing her elbows to keep her from falling. "Forgive me!"

She barely heard him, dizzy with disorientation. Annoyance forgotten, she reached out for him, clenching his coat in her fists.

"Leah, are you unwell?" He stepped up beside her and put his arm around her shoulders. Then she felt his body stiffen, and she knew he'd seen the hall. They both stared at the remnants of what used to be an elegant foyer.

The normally lavish corridor had been stripped of every last painting, every decorative sconce, every ornamental vase that had given the entrance grace. Only a few empty pedestals and stands were left, along with the overhead chandelier, presumably too difficult to remove.

His arm dropped from her shoulders. "What the devil . . ."

Down the hall, the marquess stepped out of an open door. But instead of mirroring their shocked expressions, he smiled. "David, Miss Cantrell, welcome back! No need for distress, let me assure you. We have not been burgled. I have simply put our anti-ransacking plan into effect."

"You what?" David extricated himself from Leah's clutch and walked forward, gaping at the walls.

She still couldn't move. Despite Lord Solebury's explanation, she was left with a sense of foreboding. The hall looked too much like she remembered it from the twentieth century. For a moment, she'd actually thought she'd returned.

David reached his father's side and shook his head. "You must have been well occupied these past few days, my lord. How many of your possessions have you placed in hiding?"

"Nearly everything of any value from the ground floor—family portraits, gilded frames, all that *chinoiserie* your late grandmother collected." Lord Solebury leaned back against the door frame, crossing one long leg over the other. "The upstairs still needs to be cleared, but Phoebe already feels a great deal of relief."

Relief? Leah took a step backwards, filled with quite the opposite feeling. *They had made a mistake.* Instinctively she knew they had. She sensed that the house wouldn't recover from this plunder. For some reason, the beautiful home would decline, eventually evolving into the shabby shell she had toured in the twentieth century.

"What is it, Miss Cantrell?" The marquess came to her

and took her hand. "You look as though you have seen a ghost."

"I . . . nothing. I just . . ." What could she say? That she was afraid the family had seen the last of their most treasured possessions? She felt sure they had . . . unless she had been sent back in time to prevent the loss. Could that be her real purpose here in the past?

"Get her a drink, David." Lord Solebury grabbed her by the arm and pulled her into his study. Looking over his shoulder at his son, he added, "You will find a bottle of sherry in the cabinet by the clock."

He led her to a large, leatherbound armchair, easing her down onto the cushions.

David rushed to her side and held a glass to her lips. "Do you need smelling salts, Leah? Shall I burn feathers?"

She shook her head, taking the glass from him. As she sipped the sweet liqueur, she wondered whether to tell them what she feared. Maybe with a word of warning, they could prevent some catastrophe about to happen. But no, David would only take her intuition for another symptom of her "problem," and his father would probably think she was hysterical.

"She must be weakened from travel," Lord Solebury said above her head. "Are you certain you are not faint, dear?"

"I'll be fine in a minute." She took another gulp of the saccharin drink, probing her mind for answers. What would happen to the family's valuables? She knew Napoléon's troops would never reach them. Would Lord William somehow get hold of the treasures and squander them, like he did with his quarterly allowance? If so, could she possibly stop him?

"Shall I fetch a maid for you, Leah?" David asked, stooping beside the chair. "I can call for Molly."

"No. Really." At the moment Molly's fussing would only make things worse. "I'm all right."

"I shouldn't have pressed for making our journey in one day." His eyes gleamed with worry. "You did so well on the way to London that I forgot your inclination for carriage sickness."

"My wha—?" She stopped, remembering the story she'd first told the family about her arrival at the spring. Apparently, David chose to believe that fiction over the truth. "I don't have motion sickness."

"There must be something I can do for you." He glanced around the room, fixing on the back wall, where a row of windows offered a view of the garden. "How about some fresh air?"

Before she could answer, he had thrown open one of the windows. A breeze swept inside, tinged with the fragrance of roses. The scent reminded her of the late-night walk when he'd spoken French to her.

The urge to get outside overwhelmed her.

"I think fresh air might be just the thing for me." She braced herself on the arms of the chair, pushing herself up to stand. "Why don't we go for a walk?"

"Are you certain you ought to get up, Miss Cantrell?" the marquess asked, slipping a hand under her elbow. "Perhaps you should rest awhile longer."

"I need to get outside." The more she thought, the more she wanted out of the house. The barren interior upset her. "I love the grounds here at night."

David studied her face for a moment, his expression unreadable. He nodded.

"Son—" Lord Solebury started.

"No cautions are needed." David put his arm around her

waist, his touch light—reserved. "I shan't take her farther than the rose garden."

She didn't really need his support, but she leaned into him, calmed by the solid warmth of his body. She hoped once they got outside, he would agree to walk farther.

"Very well." The marquess rushed ahead and opened the study door wider for them. "But don't be long. The night air may not be good for Miss Cantrell. Moreover, I have something important I want to discuss with you."

"William has agreed to come home," David said, leading Leah past his father into the hall. "You can expect him as soon as tomorrow, I should think."

"Indeed?" Lord Solebury sounded surprised. He moved ahead of them again and unlocked the front door. "I must say I am impressed with your efforts. But I have another matter I want to discuss with you in private as soon as possible—news I hope will please you."

David stopped at the door and gave him a long look but didn't ask about his news. "We shan't be long. I am certain Miss Cantrell will wish to retire shortly."

She wondered if he really thought she would or only said so to try to plant the idea in her head. The thought of being holed up in her room, probably not able to sleep after that long nap, didn't appeal to her one bit. But she kept her thoughts to herself. Maybe once she had David walking, she could coax him into staying out. The garden had several stone and wooden benches where they could stop and enjoy the evening . . . if only he didn't slip back into one of his moods.

He led her onto the portico and down the steps, hesitating at the bottom to give her a worried look. By this time she didn't feel as anxious as she had, but she paused to gulp in the breeze.

"Would you like to stop here?" he asked, his words soft over the backdrop of chirping crickets.

She looked up into his face and smiled to lessen his worry. "No. Let's walk the way we did last time."

They stepped onto the drive without talking, while Leah let the tranquility of midnight wash over her. She snuggled closer to him, and he put his arm around her, apparently dropping his guard in his concern for her. She looked up at the sky and marveled at the number of stars—so many more than she had ever been able to see through the light pollution that shrouded modern Philadelphia.

"Perhaps you should slow your pace, Leah. You would do well not to overexert yourself."

She smiled at him again, gently removing his arm from her shoulders so she could take his hand. The scent of roses got stronger as they walked. She wanted to say something silly in French but resisted, afraid he'd put up a wall if she tried to get playful.

He stared into her eyes. "You look more yourself now. Are you feeling better?"

When he watched her that way, like no one else in the world existed, she felt . . . oh, as though no one else did exist. She wanted to kiss him but told herself to wait. Let the beauty of the night enchant him first, then she could try adding whatever charms she had to the spell.

"The fresh air helps." She made herself look away from him, fixing on the path ahead. They had unintentionally set off toward the spring. Somehow, the course seemed natural. Now she felt eager to see the pool again, a sixth sense telling her she might find a form of guidance there. After all, the spring did wield some kind of magic.

"What exactly happened back at the house?" he asked. "Was it indeed the carriage ride that made you unwell?"

She kept her gaze focused ahead. "I guess it must have been. That, combined with the shock of seeing Solebury House ransacked."

"But the house had not been ransacked, and when you learned that your fit of vapors persisted."

"Vapors?" She couldn't help flashing a grin at him. "Well, I suppose we all succumb to vapors once in a while."

The concern clouding his eyes didn't clear. "Are you certain there is nothing more upsetting you?"

"What else would there be?" They reached the path leading to the spring, and she motioned in that direction. "Come on, let's visit my favorite spot."

"What?" He resisted the tug she gave him. "You cannot possibly want to return to the spring again, especially not now. You have just calmed yourself from one disturbance. Why subject yourself to more distress?"

"Don't worry. I have no desire to jump in the pool tonight." Suddenly she remembered the plan she had formed in London when Lord William asked about her ring. She had decided to throw it into the spring, just as Jeanine had advised her. "I have something else in mind."

He wouldn't budge, holding her back by the hand. "Whatever your idea is, I cannot think the notion a good one. Why don't we return to the manor? You heard my—Solebury say he wishes to speak to me."

She caught his slip of the tongue and grinned, pleased to know he wanted to speak to his *father.* "We'll go back in a minute, but first I have something I want to do. And I'd really like you to be there while I do it."

He frowned but gave a grim nod. "Very well. But I refuse to let go of you throughout this entire visit."

"That suits me fine." She laughed and led him off the drive and down the trail to the spring.

The pool of water looked especially peaceful this evening, glittering with a rippled reflection of the moon and stars. She brought David right up to the edge, surprised she didn't feel any fear of the time portal. Maybe she had grown to accept her trip to the past, trusting that she had some mission in store for her. Whatever her role here might be, her strange calling had lent her focus, assured her that her life had meaning. She couldn't wait to throw away Kevin's damned *friendship* ring. The cheap trinket had come to symbolize the aimlessness of her old life.

"Must you stand so close?" David asked. "This moss is damp and slick, and you could slide into the pool."

She fished the ring out of her pocket and grinned at him. "Afraid of a few feet of water?"

He snorted. "Certainly not. I simply don't want you to dunk yourself again."

"Aren't you even wondering why we're here?" She held up the ring to show him. "I'm going to get rid of this, like I should have done long ago . . . years ago, in fact."

To her disappointment, his face didn't light up with enthusiasm. His mouth, in fact, took on its habitual twist of cynicism. "I presume this is the plan you mentioned when William asked you about your ring. Does this mean you have dismissed your old suitor?"

"Definitely." She watched for his reaction.

Still, he frowned. "Rather a quick turnaround from the sentiments you betrayed a few days ago."

"A lot has happened in the past few days." She felt a painful stab that he didn't realize what he'd become to her—that their encounter in the gatehouse seemed to mean less to him than to her. "I thought you'd be happy."

He gave her what could only be called a scowl. "Why would *I* be happy?"

She snatched her hand away from him, hurt but determined to go through with her gesture of independence for her own sake. "Well, if that's how you feel, you can stop pretending to protect me from this stupid pool. You don't believe there's any danger here, anyway."

She turned and stared into the spring, ceremoniously suspending the ring above the water.

"Leah, you have been fortunate so far, but if you get soaked again, you are quite likely to catch cold, perhaps even worse." He took her elbow in his hand. "You ought to be more mindful of your well-being."

"I don't need *you* to look after my well-being." She wriggled her arm to try to break free. "I don't need anyone for that anymore. I only wish I could have the chance to tell Kevin as much."

"Leah, please, stop this nonsense." He tightened his grip and tried to pull her away from the pool, but she twisted harder and yanked free. Unfortunately, the movement threw off her balance and she lost her footing. She slid into the pool, wincing in an icy splash.

The ring slipped from her fingers as her body dropped— no, her body plunged! In a lightning stroke of terror, she realized the time portal had opened.

Panic shot adrenaline through her blood vessels, and she flung out her arms to try to clutch on to anything solid. She smacked into David's arm and grasped frantically, but her fingers slid down to his wrist. He grabbed her hand, and, for a moment, she thought he might be able to save her. But the spring raged and sucked harder. His hold loosened, and she spiraled downward, clamping her mouth shut against a scream.

It won't last. It won't last, she repeated in her mind, trying to ignore the muffled roar of the cold cauldron's brew and the bubbles accosting her skin. *In another minute, I'll be able to breathe again. I'll be . . .* Where? Back in the twentieth century? Or in yet another time period?

She curled into a ball, squeezing her eyes shut to try to blot out the teeming abyss. Surprisingly, the tactic seemed to work. The bubbles felt as though they grew softer against her body. Could they actually be subsiding? Her rear end settled on the bottom of the pool at the same time her head and shoulders emerged above the surface.

A jolt of daylight blinded her, but she forced her eyes to adjust, anxious to orient herself. She rose in the thigh-deep water, slowly distinguishing her bright surroundings. The springhouse stood in ruins again. The great oak tree cramped the little clearing, dwarfing the pool with its huge roots. When she spotted her purse on the grass near the edge of the water, there could be no further question of what era she'd reached.

She sloshed out of the pool, too numb to feel chilled by the air. Mindlessly she leaned over and began to wring out her skirt. But when she looked at the burgundy fabric between her fingers, she stopped. Phoebe had lent her this gown for her trip to London. A minute ago the dress had been a minor detail in an intriguing world. Now, the gown was the only thing left of that life. The rest of the world was gone, everyone who had lived there, dead.

David was lost to her forever.

She stared at the fabric, forgetting her efforts to squeeze the water out. Suddenly she clutched the skirt against her chest and dropped down onto the ground. Immersed in yards of soaked sarcenet, she sobbed like a lost child.

Chapter 15

DAVID LUNGED TOWARD the whirlpool that stormed
and swelled around Leah. He grasped for her outstretched
arms as the water engulfed her. An instant before the spring
could swallow her, she caught his forearm with one hand.
Her grip skidded down his skin, but he managed to capture
her fingers.

Afraid the pool would drag him in as well, he hooked his
foot around the trunk of a tree. He pulled with all his
strength, praying he would not wrench her arm. She flailed
and he grabbed for her other arm but missed getting hold.
Then the fingers he'd already had in his grasp slipped free.

The maelstrom devoured her.

"Leah!"

He dropped flat on his abdomen and sliced his arms
through the water. Around his head and shoulders, the surge
tempered into a gurgling, and his hands struck mud at the

bottom. As he probed the roots and rocks on the floor of the pool, the bubbling diminished into ripples. The tantrum had subsided.

Pale moonlight penetrated the water, outlining dark natural formations but no trace of Leah. He refused to accept the evidence and tumbled headfirst into the spring, splashing madly. As he righted himself, his limbs scraped on stone and bark but met with nothing akin to human flesh.

She was gone.

He clenched his fists and balled up his body, ducking below the surface and opening his eyes. The blackness around him only grew quieter, and cool night air skimmed the top of his head. The depth of the pool did not even cover him.

Frustrated, he sprang back up, dousing the surrounding area with a huge splash. He lost his balance on the rutted floor and fell forward, elbows thudding into the bank.

Half draped on the ground and half submerged, he buried his face in the crook of his elbow. She was gone, irretrievably swept from his life. She had tried to tell him the truth, and he had refused to believe her. Her story had been outlandish, but he might have at least listened. Eventually she would have told him enough to prove her case. Now the future had reclaimed her and thrown her two hundred years away from him—a distance he had no means of spanning.

He clasped his fingers behind his neck and squeezed his head between his arms. Not since his mother's death had he felt so bereft. He wondered why Leah's departure should affect him on the same scale as such a personal loss. Had he actually harbored some hope of bridging the social gap between them?

Yes. For the first time, he realized that her easy acceptance of his birth had indeed given him hope. Foolish or not, he had secretly longed to win her in the end. He had dreamed he might accompany her back to the States to reunite with her family. There, where the efforts a man made counted more than the station of his birth, he would have worked to build his own success. He would have sweat blood to prove himself worthy of her—to convince her to become his wife.

Instead, Fate thwarted him again. As with every other important aspect of his life, his efforts would amount to nothing. All of his abilities, his exertions, any scheme he could devise . . . none of it would bring her back. Preternatural powers had brought her to him and ripped her away again. Divine or demonic, such forces loomed beyond the realm of his influence. Disgusted, he collapsed, his arms spread out across the ground.

Something warm brushed his fingertips, and he jerked back. A metallic gleam, half hidden in the grass, cut through the darkness. He reached forward and picked up Leah's guinea, apparently fallen from his pocket during the struggle to save her. Oddly enough, the gold still retained his body heat.

As he gripped the coin, he imagined the metal grew warmer. The gold began to feel almost hot. And the water around his legs started bubbling. He remembered that Leah had credited the guinea as a catalyst for her original transport, the means by which she'd wished herself back in time.

The metal flared hotter, and the waters of the pool increased in turbulence. Apparently, this strange spring accepted trinkets in turn for granting wishes, though it hadn't when he'd thrown in his guinea. Or had it? His life had indeed changed since that day. Perhaps this coin actually was the one he'd sacrificed. In any case, he sensed the spring wanted it back now.

Did he dare ask for a return?

"I do want to be with her," he whispered.

The water surged to his waist, and the heat of the coin intensified. The metal burned into his palm, forcing his hand open. The gold dropped into the water with a hissing wisp of steam. Then the ground fell out from beneath him, and his body plummeted into rumbling blackness.

He closed his eyes against the brew and stretched his arms above his head. Already, the water topped his reach. The pool no longer had a surface or a bottom, only endless rioting currents reverberating around his body.

By rights, he should have said his prayers then. He should have pleaded forgiveness for all his sins and prepared to meet his Maker—or the nothingness he often feared might comprise the next world. *But Leah had survived the same experience.* She had braved this trial, and he would, too. He felt more excitement than fear, more freedom than loss of control.

He soared, weightless, through the void, likening the effervescence around him to years bubbling past. The moment his lungs began to ache for air, his feet touched down on the bottom of the pool, and he burst through the surface, gasping.

The glare of afternoon sun blinded him, and he shielded his eyes, blinking to adapt to daylight. He had traveled through time! Gradually he made out details in the surrounding scene: a huge oak crowding the pool, the springhouse in a wretched state of repair . . . and Leah, sitting before him in the grass. Soaked, bedraggled, her face swollen with tears, she gaped at him as though she had witnessed a ghost materializing.

To him, she couldn't have looked more beautiful.

He sloshed out of the water, offering her an unsteady

smile that she failed to return. A trace of doubt flickered through his mind. What if she didn't want him in her world?

She sat frozen as he approached, her gaze never straying from his face. Only when he stood directly in front of her, looking down into her eyes, did the set of her features melt. Her brows tilted upward and her lower lip quivered. He had to bite his own to keep from responding in kind.

At last she leaped to her feet and threw her arms around him. She let out a sob and squeezed his body against hers, pressing her hands high on his back, low, then in the middle, perhaps testing his corporeality.

"You really are here," she choked out. "I thought I'd never see you again."

His throat tightened as he returned her embrace. "I thought the same."

"Incredible." She gazed into his eyes, shaking her head. "How did it happen? I know you tried to pull me out of the spring, but you didn't fall in with me, did you? I've already been here for . . . oh, I don't know—five, ten minutes. It seemed like a lifetime."

"I gave your guinea back to the spring." He stroked her hair to calm her, swallowing his own emotions.

"*You* made a wish with the coin? I wonder . . . Check your pockets to see if you still have the guinea."

He gave his pockets a quick patting. "Empty."

"But the coin always came back to *me*." She looked up into his eyes. "Why would it be gone now?"

"Perhaps the guinea's task is complete."

"But who made the original wish? Where did the guinea come from in the first place?"

He broke away from her gaze and stared at the pool. "I believe it was the same coin I threw in the spring earlier that day."

"*You* are the original wisher?"

He could feel her watching him closely.

"But of course you are. Then I only need to know one more thing. Did you get your wish?"

"*That* one? Well, I wanted certain parts of my life changed, and I've indeed experienced changes." Finally he looked down at her. "And *this* time I wished to be with you."

The interest in her expression dissolved into anguish. "Oh, David, I'm sorry. I know what it's like being thrown into a world where you're an outsider. And you'll probably have even more problems adjusting to this time than I did with yours. There's so much for you to learn. And the coin is gone now! What will you do if you can't get back?"

He stared down at her hair. The prospect of living in a future world scarcely frightened him, as long as the world were *hers*. "I suppose I will do what I have always done. I have never quite belonged and perhaps never will, but I shall work hard to make a place for myself."

"But life today is so complicated. There are nuclear weapons, biological weapons, HIV . . ." She looked up at him, her brow creasing. "Military horrors and insidious disease. Evils that could wipe out the human race."

"We faced the same sort of evils in the nineteenth century," he said. Though her distress showed she cared about him, her feelings must not have run deep, or she would not mention these abstract concerns. Of course he would have to adapt to this era. He knew he would have to acclimate himself to changes in speech and manners, but he had expected to do as much when he removed to America, anyway. There would be history to learn, but only two centuries' worth—little in comparison to the span back to classical times. Clothing styles would have changed, and perhaps a better carriage spring had been invented or a quicker horse bred. He anticipated those differences with pleasure.

"But the evils of your time don't seem quite *so* evil." She bowed her head, clenching his shirt so tightly water squeezed between her fingers. "Oh, David, you shouldn't have come."

Her words hurt. He wanted her to be glad about his arrival—no, *more* than glad, overjoyed. But he reminded himself he would prove his worth to her. He had that chance now.

"I regret that my presence should distress you," he said, keeping his manner stiff. "I assure you I will bide my time here usefully and, I hope, happily. I don't ask for your guidance, though some counsel would naturally be helpful. I hope you will at least consent to maintaining our acquaintance."

"Of course I will!" Once more, she embraced him. "Oh, David, you haven't got a clue, have you?"

"A clue to what?" To life in the this new century? But he did have many clues, provided through his knowledge of her. If other people of this time shared her spirit, her independence, and her fair-mindedness, he looked forward to living amongst them.

"Never mind." She detached herself from him and bent to pick up a small satchel from the ground. She slipped the bag over one shoulder and stretched her other arm around his waist. "Come on. I think we've arrived back on the same afternoon I first came to the spring. If I'm right, we may still be able to catch the bus back to London. Our tour guide is pretty laid-back. I think he'll let you hitch a ride."

A hint of apprehension tingled through his body. Her confusing words represented only the first of a world of matters he would not comprehend. He inhaled deeply. The sooner he started, the sooner he would learn. "As you wish."

Brambles and trees had overtaken the path to the drive, so they wove their way through the woods. As they emerged onto the drive, David saw that a wooden fence had been erected along the side, and the approach itself sported new gravel. No, not new. Like the splintered fence rail they stepped over, the white pebbles showed evidence of neglect. The stones had scattered into the wayside, and tufts of grass sprouted through in spots. Clearly, the present owner employed a groundskeeper far less proficient than his father's man.

His father. He stopped, staring down at a rut in the ground. Until that moment, he hadn't thought about Solebury and Phoebe being gone. They would be dead—no, he would not think of them as such! They were simply on the other side of the abyss he had crossed. Perhaps they were lost to him or perhaps one day he would find himself restored to their time. For now, he had to concentrate on more urgent matters.

A strange sound, somewhat akin to the rumble of thunder, drew his notice to an astounding sight at the end of the drive. Some sort of enclosed carriage, gleaming like a polished onyx, sped toward them . . . with no horses leading it! The conveyance glided closer and halted abruptly beside them.

He marveled as a window, fashioned in crystalline curved glass, slid into the side of the carriage toward the rear. An elderly man, his white hair long and unruly, stared at him with eyes nearly as wild as his coiffure.

"Good Lord! Son, is that you?" He shot a glance to someone seated beside him. "I swear, Isabella, it is Davy. I *knew* he hadn't drowned. What have I said all these years? Not such a swimmer as he!"

Leah leaned close to David's ear, whispering, "He must be the current marquess, and I think he's mistaken you for his son. I saw the viscount's portrait, and you do resemble him. If you remember, I also thought you were him when I first saw you."

The current marquess? David studied the man's features, but wizened skin obscured any resemblance he may once have borne to the Traymores of the nineteenth century. Could the man truly be their descendant—*his father's descendant*?

A mature woman leaned in front of the man, her snowy hair pulled into a bun. On meeting David's gaze, her eyebrows rose in high arches. As she examined his features, the arches sank and drew together. She scanned his wet person from head to toe, eyes narrowing.

"Good afternoon, sir, miss." Her thin lips formed a rigid ruby line. "I gather you've met with a mishap of some sort, though I can't imagine why you've been wandering the grounds in costume. May I inquire what business you have at Solebury House?"

"Isabella, it's Davy! Don't you recognize your own nephew?" The old gentleman tapped a cane on a divider separating him from another man in the front of the carriage. "Gerald, help me out of the car. I must see my son."

David exchanged a look with Leah while the second man emerged. Dressed in an all-black costume marked by long trousers, Gerald moved with a certain efficiency that branded him a servant. He spared but a glance for the strangers, then moved to open the rear doors of the carriage.

"Davy, why are you drenched in water?" the old man asked as he struggled to quit the conveyance. He wore an ensemble similar to his coachman, except in a dull blue decorated with fine vertical stripes. On attaining his balance, he stopped, his pale gray eyes rounding. "Not the waters of the Mediterranean! Isabella, are we seeing an apparition? Lord help us! Do you see him as well?"

"I do, Jonathan, and he appears entirely earthbound to me." The woman called Isabella joined them on the gravel, revealing spindly ankles beneath a flower-adorned dress cut to a brevity that startled David. She continued to observe him with fixed hazel eyes. "Sir, pray assure my brother you are not an apparition."

He shook his head, happy to be able to assure his inquisitors *something*. "I am not."

"Then you are alive. Praise be!" The old man began to shake alarmingly, prompting his sister and the servant to steady him by the elbows.

Isabella pursed her lips. "Jon, this young man cannot be your son. He does favor the boy, but his hair and eyes are both considerably darker. Besides, David would have celebrated his fortieth birthday this year. This gentleman can only be thirty at most."

"But of course he is Davy." He tried to slip away from his helpers, but they held him fast. "Tell your aunt, son. Her eyesight must be failing her."

David glanced at Leah, but she only gave him a weak shrug. He turned back to the elderly man. "I fear you have mistaken me for another, sir. I am called David, but I am not the David you know. My name is David Traymore."

"Exactly, boy. You are Viscount Traymore, and I am your father, Lord Solebury." For the first time, the man's wrinkled brow puckered. "Don't you recognize me? Isabella, he must be suffering amnesia. That explains why he has made his way back to us only now, after all these years. Where have you been, Davy? Lost somewhere in the jungles of Africa, I daresay."

"Mr. Traymore, do you have some form of identification with you?" the woman called Isabella asked.

Leah stepped forward. "I'm afraid he doesn't, ma'am. Your brother is partly correct, you see. My friend here does have amnesia. He can't remember anything but his name."

"Does he also forget how to dress? And what about you?" Isabella's gaze swept over Leah's apparel. "Why are you wearing a costume—*a wet one at that*?"

She looked down as though she'd forgotten what she wore. "We, uh . . . we dressed like this for a historical tour of local houses. The guide believes that wearing period costumes adds to the experience. Unfortunately, we fell in your spring while walking the grounds. You see, I noticed your family had the same name as David and wondered if you were related. I thought if he'd been here before, seeing the estate again might jog his memory."

"Or you thought you might fool an old man into believing his lost heir has returned." Isabella lifted her chin to look down her nose at them. "Well, if you're seeking to gain your fortune here, you've chosen poorly. The estate is rapidly nearing bankruptcy. Even if my brother were to mistake you for his son, you'd inherit nothing but debts."

"Madam, indeed, you wrong us. I lay no claim to your brother's estate." David looked to the old gentleman. "I am sorry, sir, but I have not the honor of being your son. I most certainly am not the viscount."

The marquess only stared, apparently unwilling to credit the truth. His sister eyed David as well, but her expression softened, her chin no longer jutting forth.

"We'd best be on our way, David," Leah said. "We wouldn't want to miss the tour bus."

"One minute, miss." Isabella scrutinized David's eyes, the wrinkles between her eyebrows deepening. Her gaze slid down the length of his body and back to his face. "You do bear a resemblance to my nephew, Mr. Traymore. Do you remember anything at all about your family or your home?"

He swallowed, reluctant to lie but acknowledging he had no other recourse. "No, madam."

"And has Solebury House 'jogged your memory,' as your friend here hoped?"

He paused, then shook his head.

"If you had claimed it did, I'd suspect you of trying to impersonate my nephew, and I'm still not certain you didn't intend to." She stepped around him, inspecting him from all angles. "You most assuredly are not my brother's son, but the likeness is such that I daresay you could be a relative. I'd like you to have dinner with us. I think we can find some dry things for you to wear up at the house."

Leah exchanged another glance with him, her eyes growing wide. She wet her lips and addressed Isabella. "Thank you, ma'am, but our bus will be leaving the parking lot any minute. We have to go."

The marquess banged his cane on the ground. "No, Davy, I'll not let you leave again so soon. I don't have another ten years left to wait for your return."

His sister frowned and looked to David. "Sir, I'd like you to go over the family tree with me. Perhaps we can determine who you really are."

Leah shifted from one foot to the other. "A friend of mine is waiting for us at the bus. She's expecting us to return to London with her."

Isabella raised an eyebrow. "Do you have any reason to

believe Mr. Traymore may recover his memory more read-
ily in London?"

"Well, no . . ."

"Then I must insist you come with me. If you truly want
to help this young man, Miss . . . Miss—I'm sorry. I didn't
catch your name. I, by the way, am Lady Isabella Traymore."

"How do you do, my lady?" Leah curtsied. "My name is
Leah Cantrell."

"Leah Cantrell?" Her brow furrowed. "Why is your name
so familiar? Do I know you, Miss Cantrell?"

"No, ma'am."

Lady Isabella contemplated her for a moment, then
shook her head. "I'm certain I've heard your name before,
but I don't recognize your face. In any case, I insist you stay
for dinner. Take a later coach to London."

"Really, my lady, we don't want to trouble you." Leah
looked to David, but he held up a hand to stop her.

"I should like to join them," he said. He had his apprehensions, but these strangers *were* his family, after all. What
better place to begin his introduction to the twentieth century? "I believe I may have much to learn here. Would it be
too much trouble to delay our journey?"

She glanced up the drive, pressing her lips together. At
last, she turned back to the others. "No, it's no trouble. I
won't be continuing with the tour, anyway. But I'll need to
let my friend know I'm staying behind."

"We'll send someone out to the parking lot with a message," Lady Isabella said. "Now, let's get in the car before
you two catch cold."

David eyed the remarkable conveyance. "You wish us to
ride with you?"

"Yes. Don't worry about getting the seats wet. The upholstery is old." Her ladyship gestured for her guests to enter first.

"Thank you, my lady." With a rush of excitement, David helped Leah inside and climbed in behind her, settling into a seat that yielded like a plush armchair. The coachman assisted Lord Solebury and Lady Isabella into the carriage and returned to the front.

David stared as the driver adjusted knobs and levers, situated at both his hands and feet. Suddenly the carriage rolled forward, gliding faster than he had ever imagined possible. He felt like a bird in flight as he watched trees tear past the windows at a tremendous rate of speed. They must have traveled at twice the rate of any horse-drawn carriage—perhaps some thirty miles an hour!

Near the house they pulled onto a flat, even, black surface, and the ride grew smoother yet. The vehicle came to a stop before the manor doors, the glorious trip over far too quickly.

As the rest of the party climbed out onto the drive, David sat, grinning to himself. A better carriage spring, indeed! What other surprises did this new world have in store?

Chapter 16

LEAH FOLLOWED A gray-haired housekeeper into the upstairs hall, all too conscious of the tattered wallpaper and worn carpet. With the knowledge that David had made the original wish, and evidently been granted it, she'd gotten her own aimless wish. But she couldn't help feeling her time transport could have been used for a more meaningful purpose: namely, to save Solebury House. She couldn't shake off the sense that she'd failed the Traymores. According to Lady Isabella, they were at the brink of bankruptcy. That meant they'd have to sell the estate, and not many prospective buyers would have a stack of ready cash for repairs. Would a bank end up owning the place? What if the house had to be torn down?

She stopped to wait for David, who lingered on the stairs, looking at the walls with a grim face. A chill shivered through her, and not because of her damp clothing. She was afraid for him. The ruined house was only the first culture shock of many he'd have to deal with.

When he reached her side, she took his hand and leaned close to his ear. "I'm sorry you have to see the manor this way. I'd hoped I could do something in the past that might prevent this. Unfortunately, I didn't have time to try."

"Your pity is unnecessary." A gruffness in his voice undermined the stoicism of his statement. "This never was my home. I am no more attached to this building than you are."

She slipped an arm around his waist and rested her head on his shoulder. "If you're trying to say you don't care about the ruin here, don't compare your feelings to mine. I've grown very attached to Solebury House."

A few seconds passed, then he placed his hand on her back. The small gesture told her a lot. In his way he had accepted her sympathy.

The housekeeper led them into a section of the house closed off from the tour route. She stopped in front of the first door they reached. "Lord Solebury insisted you be shown here." She watched David over the top of her wire-framed glasses, as though she expected some sort of reaction from him.

When he didn't show one, she opened the door and motioned for the guests to enter ahead of her. "This room belonged to the viscount."

David stepped inside and surveyed the antiquated but well-maintained decor. He ran his hand over the surface of an old writing desk and leaned down to inspect something carved into a windowsill. Walking to the side of the bed, he took one post in his hand and stared down at the gold velvet bedspread. Leah had never seen the room before, but she got the impression he had.

"Everything has been kept exactly the way you—or Viscount Traymore, rather—had it." The housekeeper gave him a sidelong glance. "I've lain out dry clothes for both of you. They're a bit . . . vintage, shall we say? I hope they'll do, however. Miss, if you'd like a room of your own for dressing, I can show you to another."

Leah shook her head. "I'll be fine here."

"Very well, then." The housekeeper didn't seem to notice David's eyes had ballooned open, then narrowed to fix on Leah. "There's a lavatory through that door. Dinner will be served at six. Anything else I can do for you?"

"No, thank you." Leah avoided meeting the glare she felt coming from him. She'd obviously shocked him by agreeing to change in the same room. Now he was mad, but she had to hide a grin. Maybe she shouldn't laugh, but in this case she wasn't worried about him. His naïveté wouldn't last long.

"Very good. Ring if you think of anything else you need." The housekeeper left, closing the door behind her.

Pretending she noticed nothing wrong, Leah crossed the room and picked up a carriage clock from the dresser. "Five o'clock. We have an hour to get ready."

David stood statue still, probably stewing.

"Did you see the odd way the housekeeper looked at you?" She stooped down and untied her halfboots. "Lord Solebury isn't the only one who believes you could be the long-lost viscount."

"Leah, why did you agree to that woman's outrageous assumption that we would dress in the same room?"

"Why put our hosts to any extra trouble?" She glanced up at him, feigning innocence as she pulled off a boot. "Besides, we really should spend this time talking. We should make sure we've got our story straight."

He threw his hands up in the air. "A woman's reputation

always outweighs all other concerns. You know that. Let us hope you have not just done irreparable damage to yours— and *mine,* for that matter."

She yanked off the other boot and wriggled her toes. "Oh, I'm pretty sure we'll both be able to withstand the scandal."

"Leah, we are already on dubious footing here. What on earth will Lady Isabella think of us now?"

"Lady Isabella probably *told* the housekeeper to put us in here together." She peeled off a wet stocking, sliding him a grin. "Welcome to the twentieth century, Sweet Pea."

He stared at her, the set of his features slowly mutating from exasperation to skepticism. "Are you quite serious?"

"Totally." She stood and walked to the bed, picking up the dress the housekeeper had laid out for her. Made of navy blue linen, the simple style had a shin-length, straight skirt. Above a fitted bodice, lace faintly yellowed with age trimmed a square-cut neckline. She couldn't wait to get out of her wet clothes and put on the elegant old garment.

She reached behind her neck to unzip herself before she remembered she still wore a Regency-era gown with a dozen tiny hooks running down the back. She looked over her shoulder at her companion. "Undo me, David, will you?"

There was a pause before he answered.

"No, I don't believe I will, actually."

She stifled a smile. The poor guy would definitely need some adjusting before he'd feel comfortable with modern ways. "Look, I'll get changed in the bathroom, behind a closed door, but I do need help with these hooks. This type of thing isn't a big deal nowadays. I'm only asking for your help. Please."

Lifting her hair, she turned her back to him. After a long moment, she heard him move closer. The light scent of sandalwood teased her nose. His fingers brushed the nape of her neck, and a shudder rolled down her spine. Apparently, modern women weren't quite as immune to casual touching as she'd implied—not when the right person did the touching.

"There are some things I shall need time to get used to," he said softly from behind her ear. His fingers grazed her back as the hooks came apart one by one. The light pressure made her skin tingle, and goose bumps rose on her arms.

She reached back and grabbed his hand, warm in her chilled fingers. "I know. It's not really as easy as I made it out to be. There are fewer rules, and that makes it difficult to know exactly what's right—even for those of us who are used to it."

He cleared his throat, letting her turn his hand to hold it. "I simply want to avoid having Lady Isabella throw us out on our ears. She and the marquess are my family, however far removed, and I shouldn't like them to think badly of me. Is that terribly daft of me?"

"Not daft at all."

"I am pleased you agree. Now, let me tend to these hooks." He slipped his hand from hers and skimmed down her back until the dress fell open, leading her to tremble again. "There you are. All finished."

He stepped away and shrugged off his jacket, hanging the garment on a chair.

She stood motionless, still tantalized by the experience of his undressing her. She wanted him to finish the job.

"Have I forgotten something?" he asked, untying the scarflike neckpiece she'd heard called a cravat. "Do I not make a good lady's maid then?"

She studied his partly averted face, admiring the contours of his forehead, lashes, and nose. Her focus stuck at the curve of his lips, perfect for kissing. "I suspect your talents lie in other areas."

Without acknowledging her gaze, he stripped off his jacket. The clinging shirt beneath outlined muscle that made her suck in her breath. An urge to go and take him in her arms pulsed through her. Not used to a woman initiating physical contact, he'd be caught off guard. She felt confident she'd get a glimpse of passions he normally hid too well.

But did she really want to ambush him?

No. For now, at least, she'd be good.

She released a ragged sigh. "I'll get changed now, okay? In the bathroom, I mean. Oh, the bathroom. Wait until you see this, David. Hot and cold running water, and no more disgusting chamber pots. But, no, we really should get out of these wet clothes first, shouldn't we? I'll show you the bathroom when I come back out."

He shot her a look over his shoulder, eyebrows raised at her barrage of words. As he unbuttoned his shirt, he smiled. "Go and get dressed, will you?"

The rare smile made her grin back. She turned toward the bathroom, then stopped again. Turning around, she said, "I'm really glad you're here. We're going to have so much fun. I have so much to show you. I can't wait."

He laughed, surprising her again. "Dress yourself, and you won't have to."

She grinned and backed into the bathroom, closing the door. Funny how being thrust two hundred years away from what he knew didn't even seem to faze him. No, in fact, he seemed more carefree than ever before. A very different response from the one she'd had!

As she shimmied out of her gown, she hoped his attitude would last. She had no idea how to help him start fitting into the modern world. He would have to support himself somehow, and he didn't have so much as a birth certificate, let alone a current education or knowledge of today's jobs. But she had jumped ahead of herself. For all she knew, the spring could take him back in another week, the way it had with her.

She blanked out the thought, grabbing a towel from a pile on a white wicker etagere. She wouldn't think about his leaving. He was here with her now, and, if she could keep him beside her, she would gladly support him herself for as long as Fate allowed.

She took a brush out of her purse and stared into the mirror as she struggled to tame her wet hair. Her reflected eyes looked big, the pupils dilated with apprehension and excitement. She would concentrate on the excitement. For now, she had David with her, and she intended to enjoy his company to the fullest. As his only close acquaintance, she virtually had him to herself. And she'd have the privilege of showing him a whole new world.

With a burst of anticipation, she sat on the side of the tub and pulled on the blue tights Lady Isabella had provided for her. One foot propped on the toilet seat, she stretched the nylon up each leg. As she stood to finish the job, she eyed the toilet with a new light of interest.

She couldn't wait to demonstrate a flush for David.

"I don't see any other Davids here." Seated at a heavy oak table stacked with ledgers, journals and packets of papers— as well as leftovers from dinner—Lady Isabella ran a finger up and down a family tree. "Of course, we don't have complete records for some of the more distant cousins. One of them could be your father."

Leah leaned over to offer pretend assistance, reading from the outside branches. "Bernard and Elizabeth, Arthur and

Barbara, Randall and Frederica . . . Do any of these names ring a bell, David?"

He shook his head.

Her ladyship continued scanning the peripheral areas of the tree. "I believe I've already mentioned the rest of these names without your recognizing them. I'm afraid we've come up empty-handed. Any other ideas how we might help you?"

He rubbed his chin in thought. "I wonder, Lady Isabella, if you could tell me some of the family history. If we have common ancestors, the tales may be familiar to me. Are there any unique stories that have passed down through the generations?"

"Indeed, we have our share of skeletons." She sat back in her chair and gave him a wan smile. "But are family disgraces the sort of thing you want to remember?"

"Anything you can tell me might be useful."

Her ladyship tapped a finger on her lower lip. But before she came up with anything, her brother spoke up.

"Tell him about the family curse." The marquess sat in an armchair in front of the fire, ablaze in spite of the warm weather. "The story always fascinated him as a lad."

Leah shot the sister a curious look, but Isabella gave an irritated frown.

"Jonathan, we didn't know this young man as a lad. Anyway, I refuse to spread that foolishness. I'll never understand what possesses you to bring up such nonsense."

"Nonsense, Isabella?" He fussed with the blanket that covered his thin legs. "This family was once among the wealthiest in England. Now, we're up to our eyeballs in debt. I'd say the curse is damned close to doing us in completely."

His sister glanced at David. "I'm sure this isn't what you had in mind, Mr. Traymore." To her brother, she said, "If one is to believe those old tales, one might also argue that the curse has ended. After all, the spring is flowing again."

Leah exchanged a look with David and turned back to hear more.

"The spring's drying up was only a symptom of our blight. The curse began when the sixth marquess spurned his mistress, leaving her alone to bear his illegitimate son." His lordship held up an index finger as he made his point. "All that has happened since makes it clear that boy should have inherited. The line of descent went awry, and each subsequent generation has suffered the consequences."

Leah watched the color drain from David's face, confirming her guess that his father had been sixth marquess. She tried to divert attention away from his reaction, asking, "What does all this have to do with the spring?"

"The lad disappeared in the spring." Lord Solebury shook his head to himself. "He vanished the very night his father intended to try to make amends. The legal heir was a wastrel, you see, so the father changed his will so every unentailed piece of property would go to his by-blow—a fellow who had distinguished himself as far more worthy. Unhappily, the gesture came too late. Before he could even tell his son about the decision, that spring out there sucked the lad away and instantly dried up. A gamekeeper witnessed the whole thing."

Leah's mind whirled with the dizzying revelations. David's poor father—losing the son he had only just come to appreciate! Would David share any of the grief his father must have felt over what might have been? She watched him and saw the muscles in his temples tense as he clenched his jaw.

Lady Isabella snorted. "Jonathan, that absurd gamekeeper clearly fabricated that little fantasy. You neglected to mention that a young woman disappeared with the son. Obviously, the spring had nothing to do with their vanishing. Any fool can deduce that the two of them eloped."

"Yes, a *romantic* fool might deduce that. Those who accept the hard evidence know otherwise. That girl's shawl was found in the desiccated spring."

Leah looked down at her hands. She had worn a shawl out to the woods, hadn't she? How odd to hear herself discussed in the third person and be forced to hide the unbelievable truth. How eerie to find herself included in the legends of an aristocratic English family.

Her ladyship crossed her arms and turned to David. "Have you heard quite enough of our so-called family history?" As she looked into his face, she frowned. "What is it, Mr. Traymore? You don't look at all well."

His normally warm complexion had gone so white that his lips looked bluish. Leah shook off her own discomposure and went to his side, putting an arm around him.

"The story is familiar to you, isn't it?" Lady Isabella asked him.

He nodded without meeting her gaze.

"Take a little at a time, David," Leah said before their hostess could pose more questions. "You don't have to *remember* everything at once."

He looked up at her, his eyes murky.

She placed one finger over his mouth. "Shhh. It's okay."

"Do you remember us now, David?" the marquess asked, leaning forward in his chair. "Do you remember me—your father?"

Lady Isabella winced but chose to ignore him, keeping her gaze fixed on David. "*Do* you recall anything more about your origins, Mr. Traymore?"

He shook his head, his face practically green. Leah

pressed a hand on his forehead, half expecting him to feel feverish. He looked so sick.

"Isabella, tell him more about the curse of the sixth marquess," Lord Solebury urged. "The story is spurring his memory."

Her ladyship pursed her lips. "I think he's heard enough for one day, Jonathan. We can talk more tomorrow." To David, she said, "I should like you to stay with us for a few days. We are likely related in some way, and, until you regain your memory, you belong here."

He stared into space but managed to recover enough to speak. "I would like to stay, if you don't mind."

"Of course you'll stay," Lord Solebury said. "Where else would you go?"

A phone rang in the hall, stopping after two rings. The next moment a male servant entered the room carrying a cordless receiver. "Person-to-person call for Leah Cantrell from Jeanine Whitaker."

Her shoulders slumped. Jeanine would be raging mad.

"Leah Cantrell," Lady Isabella murmured.

Leah looked her way and her ladyship snapped to meet her gaze. The older woman's eyes narrowed, and she watched Leah sharply as the servant handed her the phone.

"Hello."

"Leah!" The shrill voice nearly pierced her eardrum. "Thank God you really are at Solebury House—and safe! I didn't know if that note you sent out to the bus was for real or not. I almost got off and went to look for you, but if someone had kidnapped you or something, I was afraid they'd get me, too. What the hell are you doing? I was frantic for the whole ride back to London!"

"I'll have to explain some other time." Leah tried to ignore Lady Isabella's stare; she'd find out what that was about later. David gaped at her as well, but she knew his reasons. She hadn't yet had a chance to introduce him to the telephone. "I met some people. There's a lot to tell."

"You met people—in the fifteen minutes between when I left you and the time you sent the note?"

Leah looked at the others, still watching her. "Yes."

"Who? No, never mind, I made this call on my phone card, and I'm sure it's costing me a fortune. You can explain when you get here. Just tell me when you're coming in. We're leaving for Paris early tomorrow. You'd better not miss *that* bus."

"Actually, I *will* be missing that bus." She braced herself for another outburst. "I'm staying here in England."

There was a second of pure silence, then earsplitting tones of disbelief. "*What?* By yourself?"

"With a friend."

"Who?"

"His name is David." She glanced at him when she said his name. He was still eyeing her but had composed his expression into one of mild interest. *Damned if he didn't adapt quickly.* "Maybe when your tour gets back to London in two weeks, you can meet him before flying home."

"*My* tour? Leah, what about *your* tour? You're giving up Paris and Rome for some guy you met a couple hours ago? When I told you to go for other men, I didn't mean to lose your head! Now, get on the next bus for London, so you can come to Paris with us in the morning. *Paris,* Leah, for Pete's sake."

Leah gave her audience a forced smile and turned her back to them. "Paris and Rome have been there a long time and aren't likely to go away soon. I'll see them another time."

"But you *paid* to see them now! You're going to throw away two weeks' worth of travel, hotels, and food?"

She stifled a laugh. "Don't worry about that. I'm getting my money's worth out of this trip."

"This is insane! If you don't agree to get on the next bus and meet me here, I'll have no choice but to call your parents. I'm tired of trying to look after you myself."

"Well, it's about time you gave that up." Now she did laugh, but not with amusement. "But I certainly don't need you to call my parents. I'm a big girl."

"Then act like one!" Jeanine gave an indignant *harrumph*. "I'm sorry, but I'm leaving for Paris tomorrow as planned. You can ruin your own vacation but not mine."

"Have a great time," Leah said, sincere if not enthusiastic. "And don't worry about me. I know what I'm doing."

"All *I* know is that you better be in London tonight. I'll see you later." The phone clicked and the line went dead.

She grimaced. For the benefit of her audience, she said, "Okay, Jeanine, enjoy yourself. I'll see you then. Good-bye."

She pushed the Off button on the receiver and looked at the others. "That was my friend Jeanine. She's going to Paris tomorrow."

"But you and Mr. Traymore will be staying with us?" Lady Isabella asked, lines etched in her face. She seemed genuinely concerned.

Leah looked at David. "That's what you want?"

"I do."

"Very good," her ladyship said, giving Leah no time to interject an opinion. "Why don't you go upstairs and settle in? You've had a trying day."

Leah almost whimpered with relief. She had to summon up all of her willpower to keep herself from grabbing David and running up to their room. Their tentative footing in the household required a little more politeness than that.

"Thanks very much," she said. "Can we help you put away your family records first?"

"No . . . I still have some investigating I want to do." Lady Isabella drew out a leatherbound book from the pile on the table. "Have you seen this volume before, Miss Cantrell?"

"No. The birth records we checked were all in large ledgers. That one's much smaller."

"Yes." She stared at the cover. "This volume is among a few family archives we keep locked in a safe in the library. I daresay tonight is the first time in decades that anyone has opened that safe. The lock had to be well oiled before the combination would work."

Leah glanced toward the stairs, then back at their hostess. "My lady, I know David appreciates all the effort you've made on his behalf, but please don't feel you have to comb through every document in the house. If your records held any clues to his birth, we probably would have found them already."

"I'm not so sure of that." She looked up, her sharp gaze darting between the faces of her guests. "There is one thing I'd like you to tell me again before you retire: How did you say you two got drenched this afternoon?"

They looked at each other, silence hanging over the room while Leah tried to come up with a reasonable excuse for falling in the spring.

Meanwhile, David said simply, "We fell in the spring."

Leah's stomach flip-flopped as she waited for a new on-slaught of inquiry. Instead, her ladyship nodded, showing neither surprise nor curiosity. "I thought so. Well, we shall talk more tomorrow. Good night."

"Good night," they chorused. Leah let her shoulders sag.

She pulled David toward the staircase, eager to escape further questioning.

He must have been overwhelmed by the evening's events, himself. As they mounted the stairs and walked through the hall, he didn't say a word about having to share a room with her.

Chapter 17

DAVID STRODE INTO the bedchamber, swatting a lock of hair away from his eyes. He waited for Leah to close the door behind them, then tugged at the riotously decorated cravat on his twentieth-century costume. The knot only seemed to tighten. "I don't know how I kept my countenance through that debacle."

"You were great." She turned the lock on the door handle, testing to see that it latched. "I almost fainted, and I'm not as involved as you are."

"His lordship's disclosures nearly landed me on the floor as well." Too unnerved to worry about the dictates of propriety, he stripped off his jacket and tossed it onto a chair. "Imagine Solebury actually altering his will to favor *me* with his unentailed properties! Can the tale be credited?"

"I don't see why not." She crossed the room and sat down

on the bed. "I'm sure the family curse is a lot of bunk, but the contents of your father's will must be documented."

"Yes. And, if you recall, just before we left him, he said he had an important matter to discuss with me." The memory pierced him with the first real regret he'd felt since departing from the past. That his sense of loss centered on his father startled him. He would not have accepted Solebury's attempt at amends anyway . . . but he would have liked to receive the offer.

"He must have been talking about his will." Leah leaned back on her elbows and kicked off her slippers. "Would the unentailed items have amounted to much?"

"Items?" He let out a short laugh. "Leah, the items consisted of *properties*—additional estates."

Her eyes rounded into sea-green pools. "Estates? You mean something along the lines of this one?"

"Much like Solebury, though none of the others are—or were, rather—quite so extensive. Still, the current marquess said my father intended to leave them *all* to me." He shook his head in awe. "Can his account be accurate? If so, I may well have received a larger inheritance than William."

"Wow." She dropped back on the mattress, covering her mouth with one hand. "And you lost all that when the spring brought you forward in time. Damn it, you lost your inheritance because of *me*! If I hadn't come into your life and caused you so much worry, you never would have followed me here. You would have been a rich man."

"No." He stepped toward her, but the sight of her body sprawled on the bed halted him. The scant modern dress she wore hugged her waist and hips, ending right below the knee to reveal both her shins and ankles. He looked away, steering his thoughts back to the matter at hand. "I would not have taken his money. But, I have to confess, I am over-whelmed by the enormity of the gesture."

"Then his action does mean something to you?"

He swallowed against a tightening in his throat. "It is as though, for once, he *chose* me. . . ."

"Over William? Yes, he did. Really, when you think about it, he never chose William. All he did was choose to marry William's mother."

"And that was more his family's choice than his." Surprised to hear such charitable reasoning emerge from his own mouth, he stopped speaking and turned to the window. Dusk had settled, but brilliant lamps, fueled—Leah had explained—by electricity, illuminated the park. The powerful lights set dew sparkling in the grass like glittering fairy dust. Even on a moonless night one would be able to see every stone on the lane.

"I'm not as surprised as you," she said from the bed. "I knew that your father loved and respected you. Despite the mistakes he made when he was young, he understood enough to recognize a worthy son . . . as well as an unworthy son. Quite frankly, I admire him for trying to keep his property away from William. What an ass."

"An ass!" He swung around to look at her. "I had the impression you found him . . . rather charming."

"Charming?" She smirked, rolling onto her side to face him. "Right. Don't tell me you thought I'd fall for that insincere chivalry he reeks."

"I don't know." He scarcely believed his ears, but the amusement on her face looked genuine. Could she indeed not have been attracted to his brother?

"Oh, please." She rolled her eyes toward the ceiling. "Give me a little more credit than that."

"But if William's attentions didn't affect you, why did you decide to discard your ring when he asked about it?"

"My ring?" Her eyebrows crunched together, then parted again. "I guess I did mention that plan to him, but I made the decision before meeting him. You mean you thought I wanted to let *him* know I was a free woman?"

He shrugged, prompting a tinkling laugh from her. Her amusement might have mortified him, if the good news hadn't left him too pleased to care. "The conclusion seemed reasonable at the time."

"Not at all, I'm afraid." She watched his face, her smile softening. "Did you really think I preferred him over you?"

The caressing tone she used implied the opposite, and he felt his blood quicken.

"He is, by far, the more eligible."

"Is he?" Her eyes gleamed, glints of green contrasting with the burnished flecks in her loose hair.

She entranced him. He wanted to know if he meant anything to her. "Is he not?"

"Well, he's not even here. But you must realize that even in the nineteenth century, you came out ahead of him." She paused, but when he waited for more, she obliged him. "Between the two of you, you have all the integrity, more good looks, and, after what we learned tonight, most of the wealth."

He had hoped for a more personal answer, but her logical approach brought a new point to light. Until that moment he had not thought of one important privilege his father's amends would have afforded him: the means to offer for Leah. She appeared to care for him, and, if she felt only half what he did for her, she might have consented to be his wife. If so, he could have had her immediately—without having to spend years trying to establish himself. Now he had to wait . . . and who knew for how long? He knew nothing of the world in which he'd have to build his fortune.

"Why the grim face?" she asked. "I thought my overt flattery would please you. I'd be insulted by your lack of response if I didn't know you're probably as exhausted as I am. Do you realize how long we've been up? The time transport extended our day."

He looked into her eyes and knew the important thing was that he had the *chance* to win her. He had never wanted anything handed to him. Whatever was worthwhile in life was worth working for.

"I am weary, now that I think about it," he said.

"Have a seat." She drew up toward the headboard, leaving space for him at the foot of the bed.

His gaze dropped to the mattress—on the *one bed* in the chamber. He glanced about, wondering where he could sleep. The two wooden chairs in the room looked hard and unsteady, useless for constructing any sort of pallet.

"Not on one of those uncomfortable chairs—over here." She patted the spot beside her.

He hesitated. She looked so enticing, languishing on her side, her slim waist and the lush rise of her hip enhanced by the posture. Her lips curved in an encouraging smile.

All at once, he recalled the discussion they'd had the night he brought her back to the gatehouse. She had hinted at a "future" society where unmarried adults might make love without socially ruinous consequences. Good Lord! Now he lived in that world with her! Lady Isabella's pairing them together for the night testified as much. The implications stirred his loins, set his heart racing. Dared he join her on the bed?

"It's all right, David." Her smile faded into sober lines. "We've sat next to each other before."

And ended up in each other's arms! He continued to balk, wondering how one conducted modern lovemaking. Should he tell her he loved her? He did love her, he realized, but in a world where unmarried couples cavorted freely, the sentiment might have become laughable. What exactly did she expect from him? Coming from this free society, she probably had experience in this arena—perhaps even more than he, considering all the years he'd spent in the military.

Whatever the answers, his uncertainty didn't unsettle him enough to decline her invitation. He stepped forward, gaze locked with hers. Gingerly he sat down on the bed, leaving a prudent space of six inches between them. He didn't have the audacity to lie back as she had.

"Let me help you with your tie." She sat up and unknotted his cravat, her fingers skimming the skin under his chin. His neck felt hot as she slid the long, narrow cloth out from his collar. "You smell good."

"I do?" His voice sounded husky to his own ears. She wasn't naive, and she would know where his thoughts had strayed. Might she actually expect him to make love to her? He fought to slow the tightening in his groin. "I shouldn't think so, after all of our traveling."

"That fresh springwater must have rinsed away the dirt of the road." She leaned closer, her breath warm on his throat. "You don't smell like that cologne you usually wear."

"I apologize—"

"No, I like your natural scent." She smiled and lowered her gaze, the first indication that she felt shy as well. When she reached to unbutton his collar, he detected a trembling in her touch. At least some of her boldness, he deduced, came only with an effort.

"What do I smell like?" he murmured.

She continued undoing his shirt, centering her gaze on his

chest rather than meeting his eyes. "Like David Traymore—warm and brimming with life."

He took her chin in his hand and tilted her face up to look into her eyes. "Leah, I am not certain how to go about this. . . ."

"Oh, yes, you are." Finished with his buttons, she focused her gaze on his mouth. She reached up and grazed a finger along his lower lip. "I know you're perfectly certain what to do."

Her confidence convinced him he did. He slipped his hand up from her chin to cradle the side of her face. Her hair felt silky on his fingers, her cheek soft and warm against his palm. He leaned forward and touched her lips with his, savoring the taste of her, relishing the faint scent of rosewater that still lingered about her.

He intended to bridle his passions, but he didn't count on her hungry response. She returned his kiss with all the ardor he had meant to delay, kindling embers that burned deep in his body. Her lips parted, inviting him to meet the moist warmth of her tongue. He dipped into her mouth and withdrew to taste her lips, repeating and varying the motion like an ever-changing dance. She matched him at every move, their minds and bodies rapt in instinctive unison.

"Let me help you undo your dress," he whispered against her mouth. Still kissing her, he reached around and slid his hand across her shoulder blades. He found the tab he sought and pulled the zipping device downward. The ease of the task made him smile against her lips. "With these modern fasteners, you no longer need my help."

"I like having it, anyway." She spoke softly, breathlessly. "Help me some more."

"My pleasure." He gave up her mouth in order to look at her. Her hair hung free, flowing like claret to create a brilliant frame for her creamy complexion. One side of her dress had fallen to expose a perfect shoulder.

He dropped his gaze to her *décolletage,* grazing her exposed collarbone with the backs of his fingers. As he slipped his hand under her loosened neckline, the draped fabric fell from her other shoulder.

Modern undergarments left little unexposed, and he let his fingertips glide down the sides of her barely swathed breasts. Marveling at her graceful form, he ran his hands over the contours of her ribs and the yielding warmth of her slender belly. As he pushed her dress downward, he skimmed her firm thighs, then retraced a path up over her hips and waist.

She reached back and undid her sparse bodice piece, the slackened garment revealing more of her luscious curves. He slid his hands up to savor the soft flesh, and the garment fell from her, unveiling her lovely breasts.

With one last hard stare into her eyes, he slid his arms around her body and lowered her onto the mattress. He took one pink nipple in his mouth, the tender tip instantly pebbling against his tongue.

She sucked in her breath and pulled him closer, digging her nails into his back. Intoxicated by her taste, her warmth, her scent, he lost himself in a swirl of sensation, devouring her like some sort of magical elixir laced with sugar, fortified brandy, and rose petals.

She wriggled beneath him, conforming to him snugly. He felt her fingers in his hair, tightening as her body flexed against his. She slid her hand down his jaw and lifted his face up so he looked at her.

"Come up here," she whispered.

He lingered in parting with her breast then moved up to take her mouth again. She kissed him back, squeezing her hand between their bodies to unfasten his breeches. The binding fabric gave way, and he felt the dizzying warmth of her hand on his aching shaft.

Spellbound, he deepened his kiss. She pressed her hips into his, the timeless movement blinding his mind with the demands of instinct. He had none of the patience he ought in order to make love to her properly. He couldn't wait any longer.

"Leah." He moaned and pulled back to look into her eyes. "Leah, it feels as if I have wanted you forever. . . ."

"Shhhh." Her gaze bored into his eyes, and her breath came in puffs. Before he knew what she intended, she shimmied out of her strange connected stockings, then reached up to slide his shirt off his shoulders.

Quick to join her, he kicked off his shoes and scrambled out of his breeches. With a hungry survey of her naked beauty, he swept her into his arms again and fell down on the mattress with her. She parted her legs, and he sank between her thighs, his entire body pounding with consciousness of the precipice they perched upon.

"Kiss me, David," she murmured.

He stretched to take her lips again, keenly aware of the soft heat engulfing his loins at the core of her body. She squirmed to fit more snugly around him, and he pressed back, feasting on her mouth. She wriggled again and, with no thought or self-guidance, he felt himself dip inside of her.

They both gasped. Staring hard into her wide eyes, he pushed into her, captivated by how slick and hot she felt. She closed her eyes and let her head drop back, pressing her hips upward to take him deep inside her. She *wanted* him, and the knowledge made him mad with hunger for her. He should have been careful, should have been considerate, but he could think only of getting into her deeper, harder, till they became one in body and soul.

He needn't have concerned himself for Leah's sake. Before he reached a critical state, she cried out and shuddered beneath him. Frenzied by her moans and the dizzying contractions of her body, he thrust deeper into her, quickly following her with his own shattering orgasm.

He spilled his seed deep within her, holding her tightly. For that instant, nothing else mattered—nothing on earth, nothing throughout time—only that he and Leah had become one.

When he could, he opened his eyes and saw that she watched him. Her face pinkened and dewy with perspiration, she looked radiant—like an angel or an enchantress. He wiped traces of tears from the corners of her eyes, longing to ask why she cried but preferring to make his own conclusion. He hoped her emotions had matched his own.

He kissed her gently and lifted his body to lie beside her. She snuggled into his chest, and they lay in silent communion for some time. He wanted to tell her he loved her but didn't know whether he would sound daft or antiquated. Instead, he kissed her hair, stroked her arms, wondering what the future held for them. Would she marry him? *Did* people still marry, given that sex out of wedlock was accepted? She had told him her parents had married, but only due to her own conception.

So, an illegitimate child was still considered undesirable. His stomach turned over, ending his brief period of absolute contentment. A bastard was still unacceptable in this society. *He* would be unacceptable.

"What is it, David?" Leah asked. "You're all tense."

He tried to swallow the sour feeling but had no success.

"Leah, how does your society view someone . . . someone born like me—out of wedlock?"

"At a time like this, you're worried about being illegitimate?" She hugged him. "No one's going to know anything about your birth, anyway. We can't very well tell people the truth."

"But you and I know the truth. And I don't want to lie to others. I shall conceal what I have to, but I won't pretend I am something other than what I am. I am a bastard now, as surely as I was in the nineteenth century."

"All right, if that's the way you feel, but you still have no reason to worry. I'd say there's pretty much no stigma attached to that label anymore."

"You'd '*say*'?" He frowned at her. "That sounds ambiguous. I suspect there is a stigma, Leah, or why would your parents have felt compelled to marry against their will?"

She shifted onto her side, propping herself up on one elbow to face him. "That was more than a quarter-century ago, and my parents are sort of old-fashioned anyway."

"So your father does not look kindly upon bastards?"

She grinned and shook her head. "I don't think he cares either way."

"I disagree. If he married your mother to ensure your legitimacy, then he must care."

"I doubt that avoiding social stigma was his only concern. There are other reasons to bring a child up with two parents—supportive reasons, both financially and emotionally. Besides, what do you care what my father thinks? You don't have to answer to him."

Ah, but he did, if he wanted to marry the man's daughter. But her statement made it clear she wasn't thinking of marrying him—even after their soul-wrenching lovemaking.

Her indifference dismayed him. He had her tonight, but he wanted her forever. How long would she want him?

"Come here, David," she said, wrapping her arms around him. "You look so worried. Forget about my father."

"It is not so simple—"

"Then let me make it simple." She dug her fingers into his hair and pulled him toward her, taking his mouth in a ravaging kiss. Her tongue captivated him, and the press of her body against his enthralled him.

In short, her tactics worked. With her sensuality engulfing his whole being, he cared not one whit about her father—nor anything else but her.

Chapter 18

SOMETHING WOKE LEAH up—a rapping sound of some sort. Blinking against the sunlight, she focused on David, still asleep beside her. She smiled and snuggled closer to him, forgetting the noise. He was *here*—in her bed. She knew it must be late, but she let her eyelids close. There was no reason to get up . . . ever.

Someone tapped at the door—again, she realized.

"Miss Cantrell?" a hoarse whisper penetrated the cracks. "I'm terribly sorry, miss. Are you awake?"

"Yes," she whispered back, lifting her head. Lady Isabella had probably sent a servant to get her lazy guests out of bed. But whoever it was had asked for her and not David. She wondered why. "Just a minute."

She tried to slip out of bed without disturbing David, but he felt her movement and stirred. He squinted in the sun, his hair stark black against the pillowcase. Sleeping had erased any remnant of his frequent frown. He looked around the room, probably trying to remember where he was.

"Go back to sleep," she murmured, smiling. She'd never seen him look so vulnerable and felt a tug of love so unrestrained it scared her. What would she do if the past took him back? Maybe if he simply avoided the spring . . . but she didn't know whether he'd *want* to avoid it. If he wanted to return to the past, could she convince him to stay? Or could *she* go back with him? She thought she would, if it was the only way to be with him.

A tap sounded again. "Miss Cantrell?"

"I'm coming." She leaned over and kissed the little black bristles that grazed his cheek. His skin felt hot on her lips, and he smelled familiar and comforting. He watched with a sleepy smile as she put on his shirt and cracked open the door.

"Yes?" she asked a uniformed maid who fidgeted in the hall.

The freckle-dusted young redhead wrung her hands. "Terribly sorry to wake you, miss, but your father's on the telephone."

"My father?" She jerked the door open wider.

"Yes, miss. The housekeeper told him you were still in bed, but he's quite insistent on speaking to you."

A sick lump rose in her throat. "Did he . . . did he say why he's calling?"

The maid shook her head. "I don't believe so, miss, but the matter seems urgent. Otherwise, we wouldn't have disturbed you."

Her stomach lurched at the thought of several possible disasters at home—then she remembered Jeanine's threat to call her parents. Of course. Jeanine had talked to her father.

How else would he have known to call her at Solebury House?

She looked back to see if David had been following the conversation. He'd propped himself up on his elbows, the familiar frown restored to his face. She guessed her own expression looked similar.

"Don't worry," she said to him. "I have a good idea what this is about. I'll be right back."

She pulled his shirt more tightly around her and ducked into the hall, closing the door behind her. The maid led her to a nearby alcove furnished with a chair, table, and phone. The girl scurried away as Leah picked up the receiver.

"Hello?"

"Leah!" her father's voice boomed across the Atlantic. "What the hell's going on over there?"

She rolled her eyes and cleared her sleep-clouded vocal chords. "Why, I'm having a wonderful time, Daddy. What a surprise to hear from you. I guess Jeanine must have told you where to reach me. Did she tell you I'm enjoying England so much I've decided to spend my whole vacation here?"

Maybe my whole life, she thought.

"Enjoying England! Is that how you describe this stunt of yours? From what Jeanine says, England's enjoying you—or at least one English punk is."

"Punk?" Despite her tension, she giggled. Her father apparently pictured her with one of the mohawked fashion plates that had haunted Piccadilly Circus in the eighties. "So you're convinced I'm dating Sid Vicious?"

"Very funny, Leah, but you're not *dating* anyone. You're acting like a lovesick teenager, clinging onto the first idiot who pays any attention to you." Her father's voice cracked. His anger must have run deeper than she'd expected. "Well, you better come to your senses fast, girl. What on earth are you thinking, staying behind in a foreign country all alone? Jeanine is worried sick about you!"

Her brief amusement faded, replaced by annoyance. "There's no reason for Jeanine—or you—to worry. I'm not alone, and, for a foreign country, England isn't very foreign. In fact, London reminded me a lot of Philly."

"I don't care what London reminded you of. You're not even in London. You're traipsing around the middle of . . . of wherever you are. I always knew you didn't have much sense, but at least up till now you were never one for rebound romances. What a time to start! I can't believe you trashed a whole vacation for some pasty-faced Englishman. Who is this jerk who has you making a fool of yourself?"

"I'm not making a fool of myself—and I'm not on the rebound, either." Her grip tightened on the receiver. Her father had a knack for filling her with self-doubt, but this time she knew her own mind. "As a matter of fact, I've been making some of the smartest decisions of my life."

"Wasting thousands of dollars worth of travel is smart? And shacking up with some fellow you just met?"

"I'm staying with his *family,* Dad."

"As though you know them any better! Good God, Leah, they could all be ax murderers."

She held back a humorless laugh. "I don't think so. They're an old family—a lot more respectable than any I know at home. They're even titled."

"So what does that mean—they're rich? Is it their money that has you out of your senses?"

"All of my senses are intact." She felt heat rising under the collar of David's shirt. "Anyway, the Traymores don't have money."

"So you're impressed by this title thing—or some other

sort of English pomp. Whatever this new buddy of yours has, you'll see it slip through your fingers quick enough. He doesn't know you and can't possibly care about you. He probably expected you to move on to Paris by now. Since you haven't, he'll get tired of you any day. Then you'll come running home and subject your mother and me to a month's worth of moping."

Only a few weeks ago his tirade would have leveled her. Now she puffed up her chest, furious that he put no trust in her judgment. "I'll tell you what, Dad: If I have a reason to mope, I'll make sure I don't bother you with it. And if I end up happier than ever before, maybe I'll still leave you alone. Is two thousand miles far enough away for you?"

"You're threatening to stay in England?" His voice shook. "Well, that plan'll last about five minutes! Hold on. Someone else here wants to talk to you. *He* should have better luck getting through to you."

"*He*? Not Mom?"

But her father had gone.

"Leah?" a familiar baritone asked.

Her stomach churned as soon as she recognized the voice. "I'm sorry, Kevin, but I'm not in the mood for this. Can we talk some other time?"

"Wait, babe, I need to know what's going on with you."

"I'm having a wonderful time, as the postcards always say—but, sorry, I *don't* wish you were here."

"Look, babe, I've really missed you since you left." He had taken on his *sensitive* tone, the one that never quite sounded sincere to her. "Having an ocean between us has put a new perspective on things."

"It sure has. But the fact remains that you broke off our relationship. Since I have no desire to rekindle those doused embers, we have nothing to talk about. Tell Dad not to bother wasting another one of his quarters."

"Wait, Leah! When will I hear from you?"

"I don't know. Maybe I'll be in Philly in a few weeks. Maybe I'll just send you a wedding invitation. Cheers!" She hung up the phone and took a deep breath, startled by the words that had tumbled out of her mouth. She'd implied she and David might be getting married. Might they?

The door to their room swung open, and he stood in the frame, nude from the waist up. Wisps of hair sprinkled his well-muscled chest, dwindling as they arrowed down his torso. The faint trail lured her gaze downward, ending at the low-slung waist of his borrowed pants. If they'd been a size larger, they wouldn't even have stayed up. . . .

She grinned. For her part, she was ready to apply for the license.

"Why in creation are you smiling?" he asked, his own features forming a frown. "From your raised tones, I gather you and your father had a row. Is there a problem at home?"

"What does it matter? There isn't one *here*." She got up and slipped her arms around him, running her hands over the smooth, hard muscles of his back. "Did you sleep well?"

"Better than I should have done." He glanced up and down the hall and steered her into the bedroom. "We had best come back inside. Between the two of us, we have scarcely enough clothing on for one."

"Yet still too much," she said, kicking the door shut behind them. She reached to unbutton his pants.

"Oh, Leah." He grabbed her hand and pressed her palm flat against his belly. "Tell me why your father called."

"Jeanine got him riled up." She spread her fingers across his warm skin, rubbing her thumb over his firm abdominal muscles. They rippled at her touch, and she smiled. "I guess she told him I'd lost my head over a perfect stranger—*perfect* being the operative word."

"Not for your father, I daresay. Naturally, he cannot approve of me."

"*I'm* the one he doesn't approve of. He doesn't even know you." She leaned forward to kiss his chest, but he caught her chin and forced her to meet his gaze.

"He knows your other suitor, though—the one who gave you the ring?"

She tilted her head to one side, surprised by the tightness in his tone. "Did you hear me talking to Kevin?"

"Is Kevin his name? And your father and he were together?"

She shrugged, letting her focus drop back to the scattered curls on his chest. "They probably called from work. They sell cars for the same dealer, both having a talent for . . . persuasion, to put it nicely."

"Your father clearly favors this Kevin fellow." He ran a hand through his hair. "How far has this gone, Leah? Have they spoken about a marriage settlement? Is that why you left the States?"

"Oh, David." She grinned, gently pushing him backward toward the bed. "We don't have marriage settlements nowadays—not where I come from."

He studied her eyes, evidently not convinced. "Leah, we must discuss this. Your father's wishes have to be considered—"

"Right now, *my wishes* have to be considered. I insist on it." She gave him a forceful hug that amounted to a tackle. They fell onto the mattress, and she kissed him hard until the furrows in his forehead softened.

His response turned hungry quickly, but she pulled back to look into his eyes. Brushing his hair away from his face, she said, "Unless you want to present a case for considering yours?"

He pulled her back to his mouth, apparently no longer interested in discussion.

"So you managed to rise and shine in time for dinner," Lady Isabella remarked as they entered the dining room hours later. She and the marquess had taken their places at one end of the table, but so far only the bread had been served. Her ladyship picked up a roll, poising it between thumb and forefinger. "Have you been tapping at the walls for hidden passages all day, or is the honeymoon too sweet to leave off?"

There was a new edge of hostility in the woman's voice, and Leah glanced at David to see how he reacted. He looked down at the hardwood floor, his cheeks singed with red. She guessed Isabella's implications embarrassed him too much to surprise him. He didn't know enough about contemporary moral standards to realize he should be offended. She supposed she'd have to be the one to respond.

She took him by the arm and lifted her chin to look down at their hostess. "Judging by your tone, I take it we've outstayed our welcome. Well, we won't impose on you any longer, my lady, your lordship. Thank you for your hospitality. Come on, David. Let's get our things and go."

"Nonsense!" the marquess exploded, very loudly for a man who looked so frail. "How could my boy outwear his welcome in his own house? And, my dear Miss Cantrell, your company is a pleasure. Isabella, what bee have you got in your bonnet? Why would you try to embarrass Davy and his young lady like this?"

Her ladyship pursed her lips, setting her roll back down

on a chipped Wedgwood plate. "Jonathan, I've tried to explain to you that this young man is not your son—"

"I'll hear no more of that talk!" His normally pale complexion streaked with pink. "Now, you put an end to these insulting insinuations."

"Jon, please. I don't want to upset you, but I—"

"Apologize now, Isabella!" The redness in his cheeks spread and deepened, and Leah began to worry he might have a stroke or a heart attack.

Lady Isabella must have had the same thought, because she swallowed and turned to her guests. "Pray pardon me. Won't you have a seat? *Please.*"

All Leah wanted was to get out of there, but at the moment calming the marquess seemed the most important thing. She and David looked at each other, and he stepped forward to pull out a vacant chair placed to Lord Solebury's left. When he motioned for her to sit, she did, blinking away her reluctance. He took the seat next to her.

An expressionless manservant entered the room and splashed a dollop of red wine into his lordship's glass. He waited for the old man to sample the vintage and nod his approval before pouring for the rest of the table. When finished, he lifted one eyebrow to his employer.

"Have you taken care of that little task I assigned you, Warner?" the marquess asked.

"Yes, m'lord."

"Very good." Lord Solebury watched him leave the room, then looked at David. "I've had Warner gather up your personal papers. You should find your birth certificate, passport, and such in your room when you retire."

David shot a wide-eyed look at Lady Isabella, who frowned, then gave him a slight nod.

"Thank you, sir," he said to the marquess. He lifted his glass and took a sip, eyes focused on the wine.

His lordship glanced at his sister, as if waiting for her to challenge him. She turned her attention to buttering her roll, and he looked back to David. "Mrs. Pickford is searching through the attic for the trunks containing your clothes. Of course, she'll need to launder them before you can wear them again. No doubt they smell of camphor."

Leah downed a gulp of wine. How far could this game go? The longer she and David stayed at Solebury House, the more complicated the situation got. She slid a peek at him, but he kept staring into his glass, giving no clue whether or not he also wanted to escape. He probably didn't. The modern-day Traymores served him as a sort of anchor in unexplored waters—but how stable an anchor?

The marquess took a sip from his glass and set the drink down to wobble on the table. "I also spoke with my solicitor today. He's drawing up a new will for me."

Lady Isabella gasped. "Whatever for?"

He glared at her. "Obviously, Davy has to be reinstated as my heir. And I warn you I won't tolerate any arguments about this, Isabella."

She bit her lip. "Arguing with you is the last thing I want to do, Jon, but I cannot simply stand by while you hand over your estate and title to an impostor."

"Davy is not an impostor!"

"He is, Jon." She leaned forward to put a hand on his arm, but he pulled away. "I realize these two young people seem nice enough, but I reviewed more of the family records last night, and I know they've assumed false names from our history. I can't imagine how they heard family stories that I myself can barely remember—perhaps Mr. Traymore is indeed a distant relation of ours. But he's definitely not your son, and this young woman is certainly not Leah Cantrell."

As Leah and David sat speechless, the marquess's respiration quickened and his pale eyes bulged. "Isabella, why are you doing this? Have you lost your wits?"

Her ladyship drew in a shaking breath. "Jon, dear, forgive me, but I must ask you to think back to the story of the sixth marquess. Do you remember the name of the girl who disappeared with his son? It was *Leah Cantrell.* I knew the name sounded familiar as soon as we met this young woman, but I couldn't place it until I reread the marchioness's journal. I'm certain these two mean to swindle you."

His lordship's small body now rocked with each breath. Leah debated whether she should run and get a servant to call an ambulance. As for Lady Isabella's accusations, she couldn't imagine how to answer them. David's silence showed he had no idea, either.

Lord Solebury held up a trembling finger. "You yourself have pointed out what a shocking amount of debt this estate has amassed, Isabella. I am, quite frankly, ashamed to leave the boy a legacy that may well never prove anything but a burden. Under such circumstances, what could anyone hope to gain by posing as my heir?"

His sister hesitated, again swallowing. "I have a few suspicions."

David got up. "Pardon me, but while I can assure your ladyship that Miss Cantrell and I mean no ill to you or your brother, I fear that only our departure will conclusively demonstrate our goodwill. Leah, love, come with me."

"No!" The marquess slammed his fist on the table, rattling the crystal stemware. "You will not leave me again, son. Isabella, see what you've—oh!"

Lord Solebury clutched at his chest. His sister sprang up, her chair skidding backward to crash on the floor. She rushed to her brother's side, shouting, "Warner! Mrs. Pickford! Anyone, come quickly!"

The servants appeared at the door immediately—probably having had their ears pressed to the other side.

"Call an ambulance," Leah said, rising and moving aside so David could stoop between her and the marquess.

"No, ring up Dr. Allen," her ladyship directed. "He'll be here sooner. And fetch his lordship's medication."

The housekeeper and the man who'd poured the wine ran off, leaving behind only the freckled girl who had woken Leah. Once again the maid was fidgeting and wringing her hands.

"Find his lordship's chair, Mavis," Lady Isabella commanded, and the girl rushed out the door.

"Forgive me, my lord." David took the marquess's hand between both of his. "Please believe I had no thought of upsetting you. You must try to calm yourself now, or your illness will only worsen."

Lord Solebury's head drooped, and he didn't respond.

The door burst open again, and the older female servant bustled in. "Here are his lordship's pills, ma'am." She had already opened the bottle and held out a handful of glistening capsules.

Lady Isabella snatched one and placed it under her brother's tongue. She took a goblet of water from the table and held it near his bluish lips.

"Try to drink some of this, dear."

After a few seconds his breathing calmed and he took a sip from the glass.

His sister picked up a napkin and dabbed at the perspiration on his forehead. "I'm sorry, Jon. I'm so sorry. I overstepped my bounds. Of course, David will stay here. I'll make no more objections. Your affairs are your own concern."

The marquess closed his eyes and sat back, breathing deeply but more easily. His medication had helped quickly. After a few more breaths, he opened his eyes and looked at David. "I apologize . . . I shall be myself again shortly. I hope your aunt hasn't upset you too much, my boy. She's an old woman and has strange ideas. You must try to forgive her."

"There is nothing to forgive," he said. He met Lady Isabella's gaze before looking back to Lord Solebury. "She has your best interests at heart, as well she should."

"Yes, yes, I know she does." He reached out and patted his sister's hand. "No harm done, Isabella. I'll be fine. And Davy will be staying—won't you, my boy?"

"Of course."

Leah's jaw dropped, but she clamped her mouth shut again. Naturally, they would have to stay. Lord Solebury's health wouldn't withstand any further stress right now. They would have to figure out a way to disillusion him as gently as possible. It wouldn't be an easy job.

"Mavis is bringing your chair around, Jonathan." Lady Isabella's lower lip still quivered. "Would you like to wait for Dr. Allen in your bedroom?"

"Might as well. I've not much of an appetite now. Have a tray sent to me later, Mrs. Pickford, won't you?"

The housekeeper nodded. The door opened, held by Mavis while the man called Warner rolled a wheelchair into the room. He and David helped his lordship into the seat.

Lady Isabella arranged a blanket on his lap and took her place behind the chair. She addressed David and Leah without expression. "I shall see my brother to his room and take my dinner with him. There's no need for you two to interrupt your meal. Jonathan will be fine now. He has these little attacks once in a while. He always recovers swiftly."

She steered the chair toward the door, again held open by the maid.

"You will let us know what the doctor says?" David called after them as they moved into the hall.

Isabella looked back, eyes narrowed, then nodded. Leaning down to her brother, she said, "Excuse me a moment, Jon. I want to fetch my wine."

She retraced her steps, letting the door swing closed behind her. Retrieving her glass, she gave David and Leah a hard stare. "You're not going to find anything, you know."

They exchanged puzzled glances.

Lady Isabella sniffed. "Don't you think each generation before you has already examined every inch of this place? Jon and I did so ourselves—when we were *children*. When we grew a little older, we came to see our gullibility. As adults, you two would see yours, as well, if only you would use your heads. Enjoy your meal."

She swept through the door, letting it bang shut.

David looked at Leah. "Do you suppose she suffers from a milder version of her brother's senility?"

"She must. What else could explain that last warning?" Unsteady on her feet, Leah sat down and sipped her wine. "She seemed sensible up till now, but our showing up must have added a lot of stress to her life. And reading about us in Phoebe's diary must have been strange for her. Maybe, subconsciously, she suspects who we really are. That would be enough to drive anyone to the brink of a breakdown."

He swirled his wine, watching the miniature whirlpool in his glass. "I hope we haven't done too much harm here. Perhaps I shouldn't have accepted their invitation to dinner yesterday. I let my curiosity overtake my common sense."

"No, David, don't question your decision." She scooted her chair closer to his and put her arm around his shoulders. "I think it was more than curiosity that kept you at Solebury House. The Traymores are your closest family—and, from what we've seen, you're theirs. Maybe they need you. Maybe they're part of the reason you've been brought to this century."

He looked up at her, and his frown began to melt. "Do you truly believe so?"

"I think it's very possible."

He smiled slightly, brushing her cheek with the backs of his fingers. "What a pity that Lady Isabella and the marquess must spend their golden years watching their home and their heritage crumble. If there is anything at all I can do to help them, I certainly will."

"Of course you will. If there's any way to help, I know you'll find it."

But what could he do? she thought. Saving an estate like this would take a fortune. A wave of sadness washed over her, and she tried to hold it off by leaning forward and kissing him. His lips were warm and tasted faintly of bordeaux.

The bang of the door opening made them jump apart as the manservant returned with two steaming covered trays. "Your dinner, madam, sir. Pray pardon the delay."

Reluctantly Leah sat up in her chair and picked up her napkin. Warner set down her food and uncovered the plate, but she stared ahead without seeing. David would have enough trouble learning how to support *himself* in these times, let alone rescuing his relatives.

She sighed. Life in the nineteenth century had seemed difficult. Who would have thought that returning to her own time could possibly complicate things more?

At least she and David were together. She only wished she knew for sure that time wouldn't steal him away from her again.

Chapter 19

DAVID STOOD AT the window, watching the orange streaks of dawn warm into gold. The sunlight formed halos around the highest oak leaves, and rays penetrated the treetops to glitter in dewdrops on the lawn. Beauty spanned before him, and beauty lay sleeping behind him—so why must ugliness teem inside of him?

His conscience had woken him early and pulled him out of bed, away from the impossible luxury of Leah's body. Her soft breathing beckoned him yet, but he didn't dare look back and permit the gentle rise and fall of her breasts to captivate him. He wouldn't allow her complexion to entrance him or her hair, magnificently strewn over the sheets, to beguile him.

He had no right.

No matter what the century, it couldn't be right for him to share her bed. He should have had to *earn* that privilege. Before even presuming to court her, he should have made his fortune, so he'd be able to support her in a proper manner. Then he should have gained her father's approval, rather than throwing himself in the way of the man's wishes for his daughter. And, of course, he and Leah should have taken marriage vows before all their friends and family. Nothing was as it should be, and under such circumstances, he couldn't believe she was his.

He *didn't* believe it.

Linen rustled behind him, and the antique bed creaked. Tiny hairs on the nape of his neck stood on end, but still he didn't look back.

"David? David, come back to bed."

He froze, but he could feel his body pulling toward her. Almost involuntarily, he turned, and she gave him a sleepy smile. He *had* to go to her, though he swore not to let himself slip back between the sheets. Instead, he perched on the edge of the mattress—even that felt wrong—and took up her hand. Simply touching her fingers made his own tingle.

He turned her hand over and kissed her palm, then let her fingers slide free. "Good morning."

"Good morning." She bolstered herself up on one elbow, her hair spilling over her bare shoulders. "Come here and give me a kiss."

He hesitated only a second, then leaned forward to kiss her lips. Her brow furrowed.

"What's wrong?" She sat up, pulling the covers around her shoulders like a cape. The makeshift neckline plunged deep between her breasts, revealing an expanse of flesh he shouldn't have been entitled to see.

He turned away, picking up a box of modern disposable handkerchiefs from the nightstand. Absently, he fingered the soft, sheer paper—so much softer than cloth. "I am . . . rather preoccupied."

"Couldn't you sleep? It's not even six-thirty." She put a hand on his shoulder, and he closed his eyes, nearly shuddering under her touch. "Have you been worrying about the marquess and Lady Isabella?"

"Yes." He latched on to the excuse rather than admitting his real fears—fears he knew she didn't share, having been born and bred in this strange world. Besides, the explanation she'd provided for him held some truth; he had thought about his relatives' dilemma as well as his own. Unfortunately, he knew how to address neither.

"*I* have an idea how to help them," she said, an eagerness in her tone prompting him to face her again. She grinned, taking her hand from his shoulder to sweep her hair back behind her ears. "It came to me in a dream. I'm not sure how practical it is, or if your family might consider it beneath their dignity. But they *are* desperate, and lately my dreams have proved unusually insightful. I think it might be worth a try."

His curiosity had been piqued. "What is your idea?"

"To make Solebury House into a bed-and-breakfast." His face must have shown his confusion, because she went on to explain, "A bed-and-breakfast is like an inn but offers a homier, more comfortable atmosphere. In a case like this, it would, of course, cater to an upscale clientele. I think it could bring in a decent amount of revenue."

"You are suggesting we convert Solebury House into an inn?" He blinked in disbelief. "Surely, you cannot be serious."

"Why not?" She blinked right back at him. "Older homes are converted into bed-and-breakfasts all the time. They're very popular."

He frowned. "I doubt that a nobleman such as the marquess would want to delve into trade—especially an area of trade that would exploit his family home."

"You may be right, but I know that other noblemen do it." Her eyes sparkled, making him want to believe in her scheme. "I saw a TV show on this exact subject. They toured several old English manors homes, now open to guests and operated by the aristocratic families who own them."

Lord, her mind worked quickly—seemingly more quickly than ever, now that she was in her own time period. She spoke more strangely than ever, too, perplexing him with the words she used and the concepts she presented. He wondered if contemporary nobility could possibly have opened themselves up to dirtying their hands in trade—or was Leah even further removed from the attitudes of the nobility than he? He tried to think like a twentieth-century man but found himself at a loss. Reevaluating her statement, he asked, "What is a 'TV show'?"

She laughed. "Oh, right. I forgot you haven't yet encountered that little miracle of modern technology. But, if you don't mind, I think I'll put off introducing you to a remote control for a while. The point is that these days it's not uncommon for Lord Snob and Lady Toplofty to lounge in their parlor, declaring in their Oxford University accents how much they love sitting down with intriguing houseguests from all over the world. Who knows? Maybe Lord Solebury and Lady Isabella would like that kind of life, too. They already allow tours here, so they can't be completely against opening their doors to the public."

He remained skeptical but did not wish to dampen her spirits. "Well, we shall have to present the idea to them and see what they say."

"Yes, let's do that." She stretched forward and gave him a

kiss. "I have a really good feeling about this. I know it seems too easy—and maybe a little distasteful to you. But it's better than losing the house, isn't it? I have all sorts of ideas for the different rooms. In my dream, the house was beautifully restored—a lot like Phoebe and your father had it, but with a few modifications. I can't wait to talk to the marquess and Lady Isabella about it."

"They may require some convincing." In fact, he suspected her enthusiasm would suffer quick deflation as soon as they broached the subject.

"Then we have our work cut out for us. Let's start by making a respectable appearance this morning—maybe even getting downstairs in time for breakfast." She grinned again.

He agreed, taking the notion rather more seriously than she. Their lack of decorum the day before had shamed him. Today he intended to conduct himself with more propriety.

She set about taking a shower—one of the most wonderful new amenities David had yet experienced—and he wasted no time in shaving with the amazing electric instrument Lord Solebury had lent him. As he finished examining the job he had done, a knock sounded at the chamber door.

"Your clothing, sir," the servant called Warner announced when David answered. He and the woman named Mrs. Pickford filed into the room, arms filled with freshly laundered and pressed apparel. The younger maid, Mavis, followed, carrying two large portmanteaux. She explained they had been forwarded from London by Leah's traveling companion.

He thanked the servants, directing them to stack the late heir's possessions on the bed. To refuse the clothes would only upset the marquess. In any case, the dead viscount no longer had use for them, while *he* certainly did. With only a minor pang of guilt, he closed the door behind the servants and returned to inspect his new wardrobe.

The contemporary clothes impressed him. He admired the tiny, perfect stitching and the variety of fabrics and prints. Their simplicity suited him as well—no elaborate cravats to entangle or skin-tight breeches to squeeze into. Best of all, the garments fit so comfortably. He imagined the styles might be a few seasons outdated, but Leah could tell him which costumes remained most suitable.

"My luggage!" she exclaimed when she emerged from the bathroom, enveloped only in a towel. Her legs looked longer than ever under the meager covering. "How did these get here?"

"Your friend had them sent," he said, trying to avert his gaze as she rushed to the cases. "The servants brought them up, along with Viscount Traymore's belongings."

She lifted the smaller bag onto the dresser and unzipped the top, rummaging through the contents. "Makeup, blow-dryer, a jacket . . . Jeanine isn't so bad, after all. After this, I can almost forgive her for calling my dad. Let's see what your namesake has passed on to you."

On glancing through the late viscount's wardrobe, she remarked that the man had shown good taste. "Not too stuffy for an aristocrat, though I don't see one pair of jeans here. You'll have plenty to wear for job hunting."

She helped him select an outfit for the day, and he took his turn in the shower while she chose her own clothes. They went down to breakfast in twentieth-century style. A short pale green frock complemented Leah perfectly, and David felt sophisticated—rather attuned to the contemporary era—in comfortable black trousers and a well fitted long-sleeved shirt.

Lady Isabella greeted them with civility, and the marquess hailed them warmly. His good coloring and lively manner attested to a full recovery, and everyone avoided mentioning the episode that had led to his attack. Instead, conversation centered on such benign topics as the mildness of the weather or the flakiness of the crescent rolls.

After they had consumed a good number of the rolls, Leah sat back, sipping coffee. She winked at David and gave the others a smile. "David and I have been trying to come up with ways to save the estate, and I think I have a possibility. It's only a rough idea, but I'd like to present it to you, if you don't mind a stranger putting her two cents in."

David shrank, bracing himself for an onslaught of angry words if their hosts took Leah's suggestion for an insult—an outcome he judged likely.

"You're hardly a stranger, my dear." Lord Solebury spread marmalade on a slice of toast with a notably steadier hand than he'd used the night before. "Practically family, I like to think. We'd be honored to entertain your ideas."

She smiled, and David had to admire her confidence, misplaced or not.

"Would you ever consider converting Solebury House into a bed-and-breakfast—that is, a sort of country inn for guests of quality?" she asked, unnerving David with her bluntness. "Naturally, you'd keep part of the manor closed off for private use, but the rooms opened to guests could earn you a substantial amount of money—a lot more than the tours you conduct now."

Lady Isabella's mouth curved downward, much as he had expected. "Kind of you to take an interest, Miss *Cantrell,* but I'm afraid the estate is too far gone for such a plan to work. Few of the bedrooms are even habitable."

The sarcasm tainting her voice didn't appear to daunt

Leah. "David and I would be willing to help with repairs and whatever cleaning needs to be done."

The marquess shook his head, though he looked more regretful than annoyed. "I'm afraid Isabella is right, dear. Your offer is generous, but your efforts could never be enough to succeed. The roof of the east wing collapsed last month, and many of the chambers there are now exposed to the elements. We don't have any capital for repairs, let alone for the additional help such an undertaking would require."

Surprised that neither of his relatives had brought up the issue of pride, David asked, "If the capital could be raised, would you have other objections?"

The marquess lifted his brows and shrugged.

"The question is irrelevant, Mr. Traymore," Lady Isabella said, "unless you have hidden riches you are willing to invest in the project. I don't suppose you happened to stumble across a diamond mine while lost in the African jungle after the yacht capsized? But you don't recall any of that, do you? Perhaps when your memory returns, you'll realize you have a treasure stashed away on a small Mediterranean island. Then we can discuss plans for a bed-and-breakfast."

He felt heat creep up his neck and looked down at his plate. Leah, he noted, had gone silent.

"We appreciate your concern," the marquess said in a gentler tone. "Perhaps if we think more on the matter, we'll come up with a way to implement Miss Cantrell's plan."

David lifted his gaze again. His lordship truly seemed to take no exception to operating a business out of his home! The well bred must be a different breed in this age, perhaps having disposed of their false pride entirely—no, likely not entirely, but considerably. Either way, he liked them much better than aristocrats he'd known in the past.

"Did you hear something?" Leah asked, glancing toward

the doors to the hall. "Raised voices, maybe, somewhere in the distance?"

No one else had, but a moment later, David, too, thought he heard faint shouting. He and Leah glanced at each other, then Warner entered, looking rather harried.

"Pray, pardon." He swept a lock of graying hair from his eyes. "Miss Cantrell has callers. Her father, from what I can gather, and a gentleman named, er, Kevin, I believe."

Her mouth fell open, and she leaped out of her seat. "My father is here—*in England*? What on earth is he thinking? Where is he, Mr. Warner?"

Her ashen complexion reflected the same range of sentiments that coursed through David. He could scarcely credit the news, though Leah had explained to him, in a simplified way, about the speed of air travel. Good Lord! The thought of her father's disapproval had disturbed him before, but now he must face, utterly unprepared, the man whom he had wronged—not to mention Mr. Cantrell's favorite, Kevin. Surely, one or the other would demand satisfaction from him. How ironic it would be if he had traveled two hundred years through time only to perish in a duel. Slowly he rose to his feet.

"I've shown the gentlemen to the main drawing room," Warner said. "They, uh, don't seem inclined to wait, though I informed them you were at breakfast."

"Oh, they won't have to wait." Lips pursed, Leah shoved her chair under the table. "Please excuse me. I'd like to deal with this as quickly as possible."

The marquess smiled, oblivious to the tension that suffused the room. "Please, Miss Cantrell, ask your guests if they have had breakfast and, if not, welcome them to join us. What a pleasure it will be to meet your father!"

"Yes, I'm anxious to meet him as well," Lady Isabella

said, her mouth twisted into a wry smile. "If they've already eaten, please urge them to stay until my brother and I can join you in the drawing room. We'll only be a few minutes. We wouldn't want to miss out on an introduction to Mr. Cantrell. Your father's name is also Cantrell, I presume?"

Leah was clearly too distracted to indulge her ladyship's gameplaying. She nodded to the party in general and pushed through the doors that led into the hall.

"Pray, pardon me," David said and hurried after her.

As they approached the entrance to the drawing room, he glimpsed a burly middle-aged man pacing the carpet. Telltale auburn hair identified him as Leah's father, though his locks were thinning and cropped short. A sandy-haired younger man—Kevin, of course—sat on the settee, one of his legs shaking nervously and his features a study in anxiety.

Milksop, David decided instantly, his lip curling. Let the fop challenge him to a duel!

Kevin looked their way, starting as he spotted them coming up the hall. His eyes widened, searching Leah's face briefly before focusing on David for the merest second. The coward didn't even hold his gaze, looking quickly back to Mr. Cantrell. What's more, the cur continued on his arse, proving himself as ill-mannered as he was cowardly. This was the man Leah's father had chosen for her?

Mr. Cantrell turned as they entered the room. He halted his pacing and glared at his daughter. "It's about time! Get your things, Leah. We've come to take you home."

She stared at him, slowly shaking her head. "I don't believe this. I *cannot* believe how far you will go to try to control me. The pair of you!" She made a sweeping gesture that encompassed both men. "Well, I'm sorry, but I'm not the same little mouse you almost talked out of coming to Europe at all. I'm here and I'm staying right where I am."

Red splotches surfaced on her father's face. "So, after all the worry you've caused us, this is the greeting we get? Leah, do you realize how much time, effort, and money we've spent coming here to get you?"

"Well, if you don't want all your time, effort, and money wasted, I suggest you head for London and tour the city. You'll find that more productive than trying to interfere in my life!"

David cringed, torn between admiration for her spirit and a dread of what such sauciness would earn her. No father would tolerate his daughter's addressing him in such a manner.

"I don't know what's come over you, girl, but it's going to end right here." Mr. Cantrell spoke through a tight jaw. "I suppose you think you're all high and mighty now that you're shacked up with the Duke of Earl here. This fellow is your new boyfriend, I take it?" He looked to David. "Well, your Worship, do you make a habit of seducing American tourists? Ever had to deal with any of your conquests' fathers before?"

David felt his cheeks grow hot. "I assure you my intentions are all that is honorable, sir. I mean to demonstrate my good—"

"Yeah, yeah, yeah. Spare me the bullshit. Just because I've never been on this side of the Atlantic before, don't think I haven't heard what type of morals you Europeans have. I know what you think of American girls. Well, my daughter is one girl you won't take advantage of any longer."

"*No one* is taking advantage of me." Leah's eyes smoldered into a dark shade. "Not David and not *you*. I make my own decisions."

"Not when your decisions are stupid." Mr. Cantrell stepped closer to her, scowling down his nose.

She made no move to retreat. "They're more sensible than any I've ever made before."

"Moving in with a guy you've known three days is sensible?"

David stood stunned, scarcely believing they continued to trade such barbs. Any father in the nineteenth century would have dragged his daughter away by now. And what could Leah be thinking, exacerbating her father's fury? At this rate, they would never gain Mr. Cantrell's blessing.

"Leah, please," he interrupted. "This is no way to try to alter your father's views. If I could have a word with you in private—"

"Over my dead body!" Mr. Cantrell bellowed. "You've had all the private time with my daughter you're going to get! This is a matter between her and me."

David frowned. He rather thought it a matter between Mr. Cantrell and himself—and possibly that oaf Kevin, had he shown any propensity to do more than gawk from the settee.

"Then leave him out of this, Daddy." Leah turned to David. "He's right. You shouldn't have to be subjected to this. Why don't you wait for me in our room? I'll come up after these two have gone."

Their room. His cheeks burned again, and he braced himself for Mr. Cantrell to slam his fist into one of them. Leah had admitted outright that they'd shared a bedchamber. She had confirmed, in front of her father and his favorite, that the two of them had slept together.

Yet the blow didn't come.

He looked to Kevin, whose lips puckered as though he'd eaten sour grapes—nothing worse. The fop turned his face away without getting up, let alone issuing a challenge.

"Well?" Mr. Cantrell tapped his foot on the floor.

David felt as though he had traveled not only through time but to another planet. He was perfectly capable of standing his ground—but only when he knew where his ground was.

He hesitated. "I shall, of course, honor your wishes, sir, though I do wish you would hear my piece."

Mr. Cantrell crossed his arms over his chest, unmoved by the request.

What more could David say? If the man refused to listen, he had no further recourse. He turned to Leah. "I will be in the garden." Under no circumstances could he await her in the bedchamber, as she had suggested. "Please send for me directly, if you or your father should want me."

He bowed and stalked from the room, continuing out the front door and into the park. He strode through the gardens without purpose, his mind brimming with emotion. Confusion, frustration, *shame* . . . how had he come to this point? He had always striven to compensate for his birth by conducting his life with the utmost honor. But blood always told, did it not? Now he'd debased himself entirely, taking a woman out of wedlock and against her father's wishes. How had he sunk to such depths?

Snapping out of his reverie, he found himself at the head of the path that led to the spring.

The spring. Of course.

Obviously, his life had gone awry because he was not meant to live in this century. He had to return to his own time. He had to relinquish Leah. As painful as the duty would be, it was the only way to end the injury he did her and her father, the only way to restore his own honor. He had to go back to the nineteenth century, where he knew how to tell the difference between right and wrong . . . in short, where he belonged.

He looked back at the house once more and felt a sharp stab of reluctance. Lord, how he wanted to be with her, more than he ever had before, more than he ever would want anyone else again.

But he would not allow her or himself to fall any further from grace. Swallowing the aching lump that had risen in his chest, he turned and walked into the woods.

Chapter 20

LEAH HAD TO defend herself through a marathon argument before her visitors finally agreed to leave. Even then, her father assured her they'd be back. They turned down Lord Solebury's invitation to spend the night in favor of getting a room in the village. This, her father explained, would give her "a chance to think" before they returned for round two.

"By then you should have come to your senses," he said, climbing into a rented car in front of the manor. "I expect you to be ready to leave with us tomorrow."

Kevin stared at her through a rolled-down window on the passenger side. The puppy-dog slant of his eyes gave him the look of a high-school drama student—and not one at the top of his class. "Please remember everything we've had together, Leah. Three years is a lot of history."

She nearly laughed. "You think we have a lot of history?

Well, we don't, because nothing happened in all those years. Our relationship didn't develop and neither did you or I. We had three years of stagnation."

"But you've only known *that* guy a few days." With a pout, he motioned toward the house. "What makes you think you'll 'develop' with him?"

"I've already done more growing with David than you'll do in a lifetime." She crossed her arms over her chest. "*Two hundred years'* worth!"

The sound of the ignition cranking kept him from answering—though she doubted he had much to say for himself anyway. In fact, before David had left, Kevin had been unusually quiet, probably intimidated by his rival's glares. She held back a smirk at the thought—not very nice of her, but, damn it, he'd put her through hell plenty of times. Let him suffer for once, assuming he had the capacity.

Her father leaned in front of him to look out at her. "We'll be back soon, Leah."

She didn't bother answering, and he ducked back and put the car into gear. As they pulled away, she walked to the front steps and waited until they'd rode up the drive. With a sigh, she leaned back against a wrought-iron railing.

Where was David? Guilt pricked at her as she remembered telling him she'd meet him hours ago. At the time she hadn't expected to get caught up in such a long argument. He'd said he'd be in the garden, but she couldn't see him from where she stood. She doubted he'd still be outside after all this time, but she skipped down the steps to take a look.

The rose garden, beautiful in spite of a thriving weed population, had only bees to enjoy it. She walked past the fragrant bushes and swept her gaze across two overgrown terraces. Several stone benches, crumbling among the thicket, all stood empty. She wandered along the side of the house and came across a weather-battered gazebo. Still, she didn't see David. He'd likely gone inside hours ago.

As she retraced her path, her sense of guilt multiplied. She should have made sure she got away from her father and Kevin sooner. Their sudden appearance had to be strange for David.

She hurried inside and did a quick search of the first floor but met no one. Rushing upstairs, she checked their room, but he wasn't there, either. As she turned to leave, she noticed the wardrobe was partly open.

His half of the closet looked empty.

She stepped forward and slid the doors apart. Her clothes still hung where she'd put them, but David's things were gone. With a sick twisting in her stomach, she went to the dresser and yanked each drawer open. One after the other proved empty—no sweaters, socks, underwear, ties. And Viscount Traymore's papers were nowhere in sight.

David had left.

But how could he? She sank down on the bed, her chest tightening. Maybe she should have seen this coming. When she told him she was going to throw Kevin's ring in the spring, he hadn't even cared. She should have known right then that he didn't return the feelings she had for him. And this morning, when they first woke up, he'd been distant, staring out the window, reluctant to kiss her.

She flopped onto her back. Obviously, he didn't love her. He must have felt some attraction, of course, but that didn't mean much. What nineteenth-century man, used to all the women he knew being either married or virgins, wouldn't respond to a woman who practically threw herself at him? His response simply hadn't been enough to withstand the stir her father kicked up. No, that would take more than simple attraction.

Where had he gone? She rolled off the bed and went to the window, staring out toward the patch of woods that hid the spring. A shiver ran down her spine. Had he gone and wished himself back in time? No, he wouldn't have taken Viscount Traymore's clothes unless he meant to stay in the current century. But maybe he'd packed them up and given them back to Lady Isabella. Or maybe Isabella herself had taken her nephew's things from the room.

She spun around and checked the dresser tops and night-stands for a note. She turned over both pillows to see if he'd pinned a letter there. Damn him! He didn't even care enough about her to scribble a brief explanation of why he'd left. Would he have told Lord Solebury or Lady Isabella his plans? Probably not, but she had to find them and ask.

As she burst through the bedroom door, she almost knocked down Mavis. The maid barely managed to keep her footing and hold on to the basket of laundry she carried.

"Mavis! I'm so sorry." Her voice came out breathless. "Do you know where the marquess and his sister are?"

"Her ladyship is havin' a lie down and asked not to be disturbed." The girl paused to shift her basket from one hip to the other. "Lord Solebury is in his room as well, but I daresay you can see him, if you like. Lord—er, Mr.—that is, your friend is already in there with him."

"David is?" Her shoulders slumped with relief. Then she considered that he might only be saying good-bye. She had to act quickly. "Where is Lord Solebury's room?"

"Straight that way." Mavis nodded her head in the direction she'd come from. "The third door on the left is his lord-ship's dressing room. Through that is the bedroom."

"Thanks." Leah hurried down the hall.

The door Mavis had indicated was open, and Lady Isabella stood inside, her face turned toward the door to the inner room. When she saw Leah, she held a finger up to her lips, then looked back toward the bedroom.

From where Leah stood, she couldn't see into the other room, but she could hear David's soft-spoken words. "So you believe a father and son should, above all, strive to express their love for each other?"

"Oh, yes." The marquess's voice was hushed, too—far more serene than usual. "Men have never been very good at expressing their feelings—Englishmen, especially. And we Traymores must be among the worst of our gender. Did my father ever tell me he loved me? Never! Of course, I knew he did. Or I *believed* he did. Perhaps I didn't, quite. I always seemed to be trying to prove myself to him, trying to *win* his love."

Leah told herself she should walk away and leave Isabella to eavesdrop alone, but she didn't want to miss talking to David. She had to try to convince him to stay with her, to at least give her a chance. She debated whether she should spoil Isabella's entertainment by letting the men know they weren't alone.

"How did you attempt to prove yourself?" David asked Lord Solebury.

"In all the wrong ways, I'm afraid. I tried to assert myself, show what grand ideas I had, how well I could conduct my life on my own. Years later, when *my* son reached maturity, I realized my father would have better appreciated my coming to him for advice. I know I felt that way about my son."

"Your son?"

Despite herself, Leah leaned closer to the door. The marquess had referred to his son in the third person. Had he realized David wasn't the viscount?

"Yes. I can't tell you how many times I wished he would have—I'm sorry. I mean you would have . . ." His lordship paused. "This is very odd. You and I never used to speak like this. Now, after so many years without contact between us, I feel almost as though I'm talking to another man. I hope I haven't offended you. I assure you that I cherish and respect you as much as ever."

Lady Isabella's eyes narrowed, and she looked to Leah.

"Pardon me, your lordship," David said, "but perhaps you should consider that I may be another man. I've told you that I don't recall a life as your son. I would be honored if I could, but I simply don't."

Leah froze, waiting for the marquess's rare serenity to shatter. A long minute passed while she watched Lady Isabella stretch her neck closer to the door, her thin eyebrows pinched together above her nose.

"Doubtlessly, this absurd sense of unfamiliarity is due to all the years that have passed since we've seen each other," Lord Solebury said. "Your memory may be faulty at the moment, but who could you be other than my son?"

"Perhaps we should leave that question open."

The lines in Lady Isabella's forehead smoothed. She blinked rapidly, avoiding Leah's gaze. Finally she murmured, "Perhaps we ought to make our presence known."

"Definitely." Preoccupied with her own problems, she couldn't feel much excitement over the progress David seemed to be making with his family. She swept a hand toward the bedroom door. "After you, my lady."

Isabella knocked on one of the wooden panels and pushed the door open. "Pardon me. I'm terribly sorry to interrupt. I wondered if you wanted to come downstairs for tea, Jon."

Leah stepped in behind her and looked straight to David. His gaze met hers, and he nodded a stoic greeting that made her ache with hopelessness. He got up from his chair, but his movements were lethargic. If he'd loved her, he would have sprung up the second she walked in the room. He would have broken into a big grin at the mere sight of her.

"Is it teatime already?" Lord Solebury asked, propped up in the bed. "David and I have had such a wonderful chat that I lost track of time."

"Your conversation must have been stimulating." His sister's voice wavered, drawing Leah's gaze away from David. The woman's eyes shone. "You're looking very . . . lively, Jon."

"I *feel* lively." He laughed, and Leah realized he did look more alert and composed than she'd ever seen him. No wonder his sister was emotional. "I can't remember the last time I've had such a rich discussion. David has got my intellectual juices flowing again. Funny, he never used to be so philosophical."

Isabella nodded, biting her lip. "It's been a long time since you have, either."

He smiled and turned to Leah. "My dear young lady, I hope you and your father have resolved your differences. I'm afraid that in trying to protect our children, we fathers often end up unduly interfering in their lives. I've had ten years to contemplate similar ways I wronged my son. Perhaps I should share some of my regrets with your father."

David shook his head. "I fear we can hardly fault Mr. Cantrell with undue interference."

Leah frowned, wondering how he could possibly make such a statement. Before she could ask, the marquess spoke.

"Cantrell . . . Leah Cantrell." He rubbed his chin. "You know, Isabella, you're right. That *was* the girl in our family legend. What a remarkable coincidence."

"Quite." His sister gave Leah an accusing stare but pressed her lips together, presumably using all her will to keep from speaking her thoughts out loud.

"It *is* my real name," Leah blurted. "I have a valid passport to prove it. And my father can confirm my story. He has a passport, too."

Lord Solebury reached out and patted her hand. "Of course it's your name, dear. Few of us have names that are entirely unique. I consider the fluke concerning yours an omen. I think it shows that your destiny is tied to this family's."

She swallowed and glanced at David, whose eyes didn't reveal a thing about his thoughts.

"Perhaps we should all get ready for tea," Lady Isabella said. "Mrs. Pickford doesn't like to hold the meals she works so hard to prepare."

"Of course." David pulled his gaze away from Leah's. "If you'll excuse me . . ."

She sighed. Now she'd get to speak to him. The knowledge left her half-relieved and half-afraid.

"Certainly." Lord Solebury gave him a wide smile. "Thank you so much for the chat."

Lady Isabella eyed her brother, holding her lower lip between thumb and forefinger. When she glanced at David and saw him watching her, she let her hand drop. "Yes . . . thank you. I believe you've done my brother good."

"The pleasure was all mine." He gave one of his old-fashioned bows. After a short, electrically charged lapse in conversation, he asked, "When should we be downstairs?"

"In about a quarter hour," Isabella said. "I hope that gives us all enough time to prepare."

"Certainly." With another general bow, he turned and left the room.

Leah murmured, "Excuse me," and darted after him. As soon as they stepped into the hall, she said, "I need to talk to you."

He glanced at her but didn't stop walking.

Knees wobbling, she willed herself to keep up with him. *He couldn't really be leaving, could he?* Maybe he didn't have anything to do with the clothes disappearing.

"Do you know that all your things—the viscount's things—are gone from our room?" she asked.

He continued up the hall, showing no surprise and, even worse, avoiding her gaze. "I asked Lady Isabella if I might move to my own chamber."

"You did?" Nausea stirred inside her, a feeling all-too familiar. She'd been through this with Kevin so many times. Whenever their relationship had begun to open up and grow, he'd always slammed the door on all possibilities. The confidence she'd gained over the past few weeks melted, and her voice came out small and weak. "Why?"

He still wouldn't look at her. The old cynical curl pulled at his lower lip. "Don't make this any harder than it is, Leah. Where is your father?"

She stopped outside the door to their room, startled by his quick change of subject. Suddenly the heat of anger flared up her neck, burning away her feelings of helplessness. *He wasn't going to crush her.* She was her own person, a whole person, capable of living happily on her own—and capable of calling him on his evasion tactics. She stood there until he stopped and turned to face her.

"This is about you and me," she said. "Don't try to change the subject."

"You should have gone with him." His stare was hard, his eyes untwinkling.

She shook her head. "Don't you dare tell me what I should or shouldn't do. I make my own choices."

He looked away, running a hand through his hair. "I only

meant that you should honor your father's wishes. It's the right thing to do."

"Oh, really? That's the best attempt you could make to dodge the real issue? Well, you couldn't have picked a more ridiculous argument. As if *you're* an expert on filial honor! When did *you* ever honor your father?"

He scowled at her. "This is entirely different. The man is only trying to protect your interests."

She let her arms go limp at her sides. "Why not simply say what you mean, David?"

He only stared.

She stood waiting for him to say something. But what exactly was she waiting to hear? That she meant so little to him he was willing to forget about her the minute her father gave them a little grief?

She opened the door behind her and stepped into *her* room. "You know, I'm glad you already took your things out of here. Now, I don't have to listen to any more of your ridiculous excuses and hypocritical advice while you move out."

The tilt of his eyes began to look sad right before she blanked out his face with a slam of the door.

She flopped belly first onto the bed, convinced the emotion she'd discerned must have been pity. Well, she didn't need his pity. She didn't need anything from him, not now that she'd learned to rely on herself.

A sniffle escaped her without warning, and she hid her face in the pillow. Damn it, her love was worth more than this. She was worth fighting for.

A tap sounded on the door, and she froze.

"Leah?" David called softly.

She gulped her tears down hard. If she answered, he'd be sure to know she was crying.

"Leah?"

Another minute passed, then she heard the sound of his footsteps fading in the hall. She hiccupped and pulled the pillow over her head.

Even a self-reliant person had to cry once in a while.

Chapter 21

DAVID STOOD STARING at the door Leah had slammed in his face. He clamped his jaw tight to keep from calling to her a third time. He really had no right to address her at all. Had he not unleashed enough chaos in her life? Only that morning he had vowed not to cause her further trouble.

He fought an urge to pound on the wood or even kick through the panels. His resolve to leave her alone would have been easier if he'd been able to return to the past. The spring, however, had not cooperated. When he'd gone to the clearing, he'd found nothing but a dried-up hole.

The relief he'd felt had made him wonder whether he could have gone through with the plan anyway.

Now he had another opportunity to show he had honorable intentions. But walking away from her door proved nearly as difficult as it would have been to step back into the past.

The time portal is closed, a voice in his head persisted. Fate had chosen to keep him in *this* century, and he felt certain he had a purpose here. Could that purpose not rest with Leah?

The wooden door hung before him, not physically impenetrable but morally so.

"Fool," he hissed to himself, closing his eyes to keep the barrier from taunting him. If he had a purpose, it surely centered around the marquess. Any effort he could make to comfort his lordship would be a noble pursuit. Chasing a woman intended for another man could only be deemed self-serving.

He opened his eyes and stalked off toward his own quarters. When he tried to close the door after him, the edge caught on the frame and wouldn't shut. He yanked harder, venting his frustration on the wood. This time the door slammed into place, bringing back the image of Leah's angry countenance as she had slammed her door. He grimaced and tried to blot out the impression by surveying his new room.

Dimly lit and poorly appointed, the chamber suffered in comparison to the one he had shared with Leah. The narrow bed looked lumpy, and a musty odor plagued his nostrils. As he wrinkled his nose, a draft blew through a crack in the window behind him, making the tiny hairs on the nape of his neck stand on end. He doubted the "uninhabitable" rooms in the west wing could have been much less inviting.

Then again, no chamber would have pleased him now— not without Leah to share the space.

A clock chimed in the hall, reminding him to dress for tea. He grappled with a sticking dresser drawer. Even inanimate objects seemed to be mocking him, but he knew the real struggle lay within him. His base yearnings kept him from thinking constructively. He should have been planning how to help his relations save their estate—or, at least be able to live their golden years in comfort.

He snatched a random tie from the drawer, peering into a cheval glass to wrap the cloth around his neck. As he looped a simple modern knot together, the mirror made his movements look backward and wrong—rather like this alternate time period distorted his judgment. He had to admit, though, that his decision to go the marquess and try to cheer him had proved a happy exception to his blundering. Something good, something truly meaningful, had come out of their talk, and somehow *he* had instigated that good.

"Is that not proof of where your purpose lies?" he asked his reflection. He, David Traymore, had actually helped Lord Solebury gain some peace of mind. His lordship's vagaries had lessened as they discussed the family history, and the marquess had grown downright sharp when the conversation turned to the meaning of family. Lord Solebury had *needed* to talk about his lost son, and David had been the one to elicit the catharsis.

His fingers stopped working as he thought back on how the marquess's calming had progressed. With his own eyes, he had seen the man healing as he confided his regrets. What's more, he had to confess that he, too, had experienced a sense of healing. As his lordship spoke, he had understood the inevitably of a father's making mistakes along the path he chose . . . as any man made mistakes.

As his own father had.

He stared hard into his reflected eyes, so much like those of the sixth marquess. His, however, began to look bright, and he refocused on his fingers, reaching blindly toward the drawer for a tie tack.

"Damn!" he muttered as a pin pierced his finger and rekindled his vexation. He fumbled with the emblem but couldn't connect the clasp. Catching his own flickering gaze again, he glowered and tossed the tack aside. What did he care for such trivia?

He went down to tea with his tie flopping on his shirt.

Leah never appeared for the meal, nor did she come down for dinner, sending word through Mavis that she felt unwell. Again, he fought against his longing to see her, though the need grew more painful with each passing hour. His only condolence lay in his advancement with his family. Lord Solebury remained alert throughout the evening, and Lady Isabella's attitude toward him continued to warm.

Nonetheless, he sighed with relief on finding Leah in the breakfast room early the next morning. She sat alone at the table, poking a fork at a dish full of omelet. When she looked up to where he stood at the entrance from the hall, he noticed that shadows ringed her eyes, rendering her fair complexion even paler.

"You really *are* ill." His gut sank and he stepped inside the room. He had to stop himself from rushing to her side. "Is there . . . is there anything I can get for you?"

Her gaze dropped to her plate. "I don't need anything from you."

"Look alive," Lady Isabella called out from behind him in the hall. As he moved aside, she wheeled the marquess in his chair into the breakfast room.

His lordship's cheeks glowed with health, and his gaze flit attentively over his surroundings. Isabella, too, looked animated and happy. The "good morning" she wished Leah even sounded sincere.

Mavis bustled in behind them, balancing a tray filled with rolls and another with marmalade, sugar, and a creamer. In a little flutter of activity, everyone took a seat and set about arranging food on their plates.

"We missed you last night, Miss Cantrell," Lord Solebury said. He paused to bite into a croissant. "I hope you're feeling better this morning."

"I am, a little, thank you." She gave him a wan smile. "I didn't sleep all that well. Frankly, I'm not looking forward to seeing my father this morning."

He frowned. "I'm so sorry you two aren't seeing eye to eye. Forgive me, dear, but I must claim the privilege of experience and advise you to give him the leeway he won't give you. What if someday you became separated from your father and didn't know if you'd ever see him again? God forbid, unforeseen things happen. In such a case, would you have regrets? Might you wish you had done things differently?"

She stared at him, balancing a forkful of eggs in the air. David realized she had indeed faced such a situation when she had been thrown into the past. For the first time, he perceived what an ordeal she must have endured. Unlike him, she'd had no one with whom to share her apprehensions. He wished more than ever he had listened to her story and offered her his support. Instead, as ever, he had failed her.

The marquess set down his roll. "I know such an event is hard to imagine when you've never met with the like, but—"

"No." She swallowed, though she still hadn't taken a bite of her food. "No, I *can* imagine it, and you're right, I would have regrets. I do already. I'll try to talk to my father. I'm sure he won't make it easy for me, but I'll do what I can to get through to him. I promise."

As if on cue, Warner appeared in the doorway. "Mr. Cantrell is here. He requests a visit with the whole family, whenever convenient for all of you."

Leah's fork dropped, clattering on her plate. "*Requests* a visit?"

"Yes, miss." Hints of a smile pulled at the corners of his mouth. "And the younger gentleman isn't with him this morning."

Lord Solebury clasped his hands together in front of him. "Wonderful news! Do ask Mr. Cantrell to join us for breakfast." As Warner ducked back out, he smiled at Leah. "It looks as though your father won't be quite as difficult as you expected."

The furrows in her brow endured.

Warner returned with Mr. Cantrell, who hesitated in the doorway. Face tilted slightly downward, he eyed his daughter from under bushy, red eyebrows. Two pairs of sea-green eyes exchanged a long look, then Leah leaped up and hugged him. He patted her back, looking rather awkward.

She left off her embrace and turned to the others, moistening her lips. "I think you all met my father briefly yesterday . . . Bob Cantrell. Dad, you remember Lady Isabella, her brother Lord Solebury and, uh, David Traymore."

Mr. Cantrell nodded to his hosts and then to David, who noted that his gaze lingered longest on him.

He nodded in return, wondering what to expect next. Unquestionably, the man had changed his approach, but any further conclusion would be folly.

Leah looked to her father and gestured toward the place next to hers at the table. They took their seats, and Warner poured coffee for the new arrival.

"Thank you." He took a sip and sat back in his chair, though his downcast gaze negated the ease of his posture.

"Right off the bat, I want to apologize to all of you for my behavior yesterday. I had no business storming in here the way I did."

David scanned the room, observing Lord Solebury's approving nod and Lady Isabella's scrutiny of the speaker. Leah eyed the empty sideboard, meeting no one's gaze.

"I had plenty of time to think last night," Mr. Cantrell continued. "I didn't sleep a wink with Kevin's snoring. In fact, maybe it was his snoring that got me thinking. Spending twenty-four hours straight with that nitwit has made me wonder how Leah managed to bear three years with him. Take him off a car lot and away from the sports page, and he doesn't have a damn thing to contribute to a conversation. And you'd think the world were coming to an end just because he couldn't get ranch dressing with his dinner last night."

Startled, David stole a glance at Leah. She looked at her father, but her expression remained impassive.

Mr. Cantrell cleared his throat. "Anyway, what I'm trying to say is that I'd like to start over, to listen and find out why my daughter cut her tour short to stay here. I guess maybe I overreacted by coming after her, but as long as I'm here, I'd like to get to know you all—to make sure she's all right, you know? Then I'll go home."

The marquess smiled. "Your concern is admirable, Mr. Cantrell. Certainly, too much is preferable to too little. Let me try to assuage your worries by assuring you your daughter is an honored guest here. Of course, you're likely wondering more about David's intentions toward her."

All eyes moved to converge on David. He glanced at Leah, but she looked away.

"They are honorable, sir." With a pang of guilt, he looked down, touching his napkin to his mouth. His *intentions* were honorable; his conduct, however, had not been. "Unfortunately, I cannot assure you of much more right now. At the moment, my financial circumstances are rather, er, straitened. I mean to turn that around quickly, however."

He looked up and saw Mr. Cantrell studying him. Suddenly the man emitted a snort of laughter.

"Hell, but you're a serious fellow, aren't you?" He shook his head. "All this talk about intentions and money! Do you think I expect you to marry Leah after knowing her four days?"

David had rather thought he did and, if not, couldn't imagine what Mr. Cantrell *did* expect. Did the man mean to allow his suit or not? He tried to catch Leah's eye, but she wouldn't meet his gaze.

"I feel as though I've know her for centuries," he murmured.

At last she looked up, a line forming between her brows. He wished she had appeared even the least bit pleased, but he could hardly expect it after he'd avoided speaking to her the day before. Furthermore, he could say nothing to make amends for his behavior. Indeed, he wasn't sure he could behave differently now. He still didn't know whether her father would let him court her—and even if so, his current state of destitution would delay the privilege for years.

"Romantic, too," Mr. Cantrell said, his mouth twisted in a smirk. "I'm beginning to understand why she's not in Paris with Jeanine. Women always suck up this kind of nonsense. Leah, I hope *your* head's not already full of dreams about marrying this fellow."

David, keenly aware he'd been insulted, waited for her response. She only pulled her gaze away, however, looking back to the sideboard.

Her father's brows shot up. "I'll be damned. I don't have a clue what's going on here."

"Welcome aboard," Lady Isabella said, tapping her chin with a finger. "Perhaps we *all* need to acquaint ourselves better. I'd like to have a little dinner party tonight. I hope you and your young friend will join us, Mr. Cantrell."

"I'd be happy to." He let out another short laugh. "But are you sure want me to bring Kevin? I'd think you'd want to give your boy an edge over the competition. Or don't you want him marrying a commoner?"

"Dad, please." Leah sent him a pained look, while her father chuckled at his own joke. David, meanwhile, sat mute, feeling a perfect fool.

Mr. Cantrell stood and patted his daughter on the shoulder. "Don't worry, honey. I'm going now, so you can eat the rest of your breakfast in peace. Lady Isabella, Lord Solebury, thanks for your hospitality. I look forward to tonight."

Isabella gave a wan smile. "As do we."

"I'll show you out," Leah said, rising as well. She took her father's arm and practically dragged him toward the doors to the hall.

Mr. Cantrell stopped again, however, standing in the entrance, and turned back to David. "It should be interesting to see you and Kevin *duke* it out. Are you a duke, Dave, or do I have the wrong title?"

"Viscount," Lord Solebury interjected while David stewed to himself. *Disastrous encounter!* "My *son* will be marquess upon my death, of course, but no higher rank than that, unless he earns one by some great feat of his own."

David stared at him. The marquess had called him son again, but he had put a curious emphasis on the word, as though trying to make a point.

"Come on, Dad," Leah begged, yanking her father into

the hall. Before the doors swung closed after them, David's gaze met Mr. Cantrell's a last time. The man's grin had faded.

He gathered up his scattered pride and turned back to Lord Solebury. "I thought we agreed to leave the question of my identity open."

"That was yesterday." Lord Solebury lifted his cup without its rattling in the saucer. He took a long swig of tea. "Today I'm prepared to close the matter."

"But I told you I cannot claim to be your son—"

"Oh, I know you're not my son."

Isabella gasped, while her brother gave David a cunning smile. "Of course, you know it as well, though I understand why you haven't revealed your true identity. You see, I had this very strange, very vivid dream last night—a nightmare, really, full of swirling colors and engulfing waves."

David held his breath. Could the marquess indeed have deduced the truth?

Lord Solebury watched him closely. "When Isabella and I first met you and Miss Cantrell, you were both drenched in water. You'd taken a dunk in the spring, hadn't you?"

He nodded.

"You were also wearing some rather odd, old-fashioned attire, weren't you? Early nineteenth-century, I believe."

David felt a chill, despite the warmth of the room.

"Jon, what is this all about?" Lady Isabella asked. "What do the spring and nineteenth-century costumes have to do with anything?"

Her brother smiled at her. "Quite a bit, my dear. You'll see when I explain why Miss Cantrell has the same name as the girl in our family legend—and, for that matter, why David shares his name with the sixth marquess's son. Quite simply, they *are* the two in the legend."

The look on Isabella's face could have soured milk—and David felt as though he had swallowed a quart. If she asked him to deny Lord Solebury's conclusion, he would not be able to oblige her.

But if he tried to convince *her* the marquess spoke the truth, he was certain he'd fare no better.

Chapter 22

LEAH STOOD ON the front steps, watching her father drive away in the rental car. His change of attitude had been a relief—almost a miracle—but he'd still managed to humiliate her as only a parent could. Not that she really blamed him for calling David's bluff on his supposed "good intentions." No, she was *glad* her father hadn't let him get away with that drivel. She only wished he hadn't asked *her* if she'd been thinking about marrying David. Lying had never come easily to her, and her silence had probably given away the truth.

The car disappeared among the trees, and she turned back to the door. What game had David been playing, anyway? Trying to put on a good face for her dad? Maybe, in his hopelessly antiquated mind, he'd expected her father to call him out for *sullying* her. He'd probably implied he would marry her in order to avoid meeting her father with pistols at dawn.

Too bad things didn't work like that anymore.

With a grimace, she stepped inside and closed the door. If she wanted her honor preserved, she'd have to do the preserving herself—and in a far less dramatic way.

She paused in the hall, reluctant to go back and face David's playacting. After three years with Kevin, she'd had her fill of insincerity. But living well was the best revenge, and that meant showing those who hurt you that they couldn't keep you down. *David* was the one who had treated *her* badly, not the other way around. She wouldn't allow herself to hide from him.

Resolved, she took a deep breath and lifted her chin high. She strode back to the breakfast room and pushed through the double doors.

To her surprise, no one paid attention to her entrance. Lady Isabella sat glaring at Lord Solebury, who, in turn, gave her a self-satisfied grin. David was also watching the marquess, his eyes narrowed and his gaze intent. She caught herself staring at him and looked away.

Obviously, something had happened while she was gone. She hoped everyone's lack of noticing her meant that she wasn't involved. Unsure whether to join the others or leave them in privacy, she stopped in the doorway.

Lord Solebury turned and nodded to her. "I'm glad you've returned, Miss Cantrell. Please take your seat. I have an announcement that should interest all of you."

So she did have some stake in this. She sensed Lady Isabella's gaze boring into her and knew David was watching her, too. Without looking at either, she obeyed his lordship's request and went to her chair.

The marquess pushed his plate to the side and folded his

hands on the table. "I spoke to my solicitor yesterday, informing him of David's appearance and confirming that my will secures him as heir. David, since you'll be assuming my son's identity, you must remember to call yourself Viscount Traymore from here on. Upon my death, you will, of course, receive my title—only two hundred years later than you rightfully should have."

Leah's jaw fell open. "Does this mean you . . . ? But how . . . ?" She trailed off. He couldn't possibly know the truth, and any question she voiced would only raise suspicions.

"Yes, I know who you are." Lord Solebury smiled. "While you were out of the room, I explained that the truth came to me in a dream last night. Admittedly, I don't quite understand all of it. For example, your father is clearly a contemporary American. Does that mean you are from the current time period?"

She glanced at David, who shrugged in response. But why did she care what he thought, anyway? Looking back to the marquess, she nodded.

"Of course she is, Jon!" Lady Isabella slapped her palm down on the table, rattling the juice glasses. "Just as we all are, including *Mister* Traymore. Now, please leave off this absurdity. You were doing so well up till now."

"I still am doing well." He turned back to Leah. "The legend records that a gamekeeper saw you and David disappear into the spring in 1815. I must assume that you somehow visited the nineteenth century before returning to the present again with David. But how? In my dream I saw you nearly drown. Does the spring have something to do with the time travel?"

His line of questioning intimidated her. Lady Isabella would never believe the truth and would therefore label her a liar. Still, she didn't like having to hide the real story, and at least in this century she didn't have to worry about being thrown into Bedlam. She nodded again.

"Good God, Jon, you're falling right into their trap!" Lady Isabella jumped up and leaned over the table on her hands. "Don't you see? This must be what they intended all along—to swindle their way into an inheritance!"

"Please, Isabella, reseat yourself. You'll drive your blood pressure through the roof." The marquess watched her until she complied. "Now, what would these two have to gain by this scheme you've laid out? You've informed them yourself that the estate is mortgaged to the hilt. We'll likely have to sell before this young man even inherits. I'm only ashamed I haven't been able to sustain some vestige of hope for Solebury's future."

Isabella gave David a hard stare, which he met squarely. Looking back to her brother, she said, "It could be your title they're after."

"In this day and age?" He waved off the suggestion. "Today's young people have little interest for titles. They're more likely to scorn such relics of social inequality."

"Not all young people, I'm sure, and your title isn't the only possible motive. Perhaps these two have heard the tales about hidden treasure." She wrinkled her nose at David and Leah. "Stuff and nonsense! If that's what you're after, you're bigger fools than I thought. For two centuries generations of Traymores have searched for that imaginary fortune. We all outgrew that folly along with childhood. Shouldn't you two be past the age of gullibility?"

Her gaze stopped at Leah's eyes, piercing them until she felt she had to answer.

"I don't know what you're talking about, my lady."

Lady Isabella snorted and looked away, her lips pressed together.

"She's referring to the other legend about the sixth marquess," Lord Solebury said. "Do you two know the story?"

David shook his head. "Nothing of it."

The marquess steepled his fingers in front of him. "Well, I've already told you how your father tried to divert assets away from your brother and *to* you."

"To *him*?" Isabella sniffed and crossed her arms over her chest. "For heaven's sake, Jon, this is ridiculous!"

Lord Solebury kept his gaze on David, who nodded his acknowledgment.

"After you disappeared, your father was forced to take alternate steps. He stockpiled a good deal of his wealth and hid the goods from his heir."

"All myth!" Lady Isabella declared. "Don't bother getting your hopes up."

Her brother rubbed his chin. "No, wait a minute. I don't have it quite right. The story goes that the marquess originally hid the goods in fear of an attack from Napoléon. But after Bonaparte died and all danger had passed, your father kept the treasures hidden, waiting for your half brother to reform his ways. The boy never changed, and the marquess carried the secret of the hiding place to his grave."

Leah shivered. The foreboding feeling she'd had when David's father stripped the house had been valid. She wasn't surprised that William had never reformed—or even that his father had hidden all that wealth from him. But when she looked to David, she saw he had his hand over his mouth, which hung open with shock.

"You say my father initially concealed this hoard from Napoléon?" he asked.

"Yes." Lord Solebury lifted an eyebrow. "Do you know something of the treasure, after all?"

"Oh, yes, I know *something*." For a moment David simply blinked at him. Then he let his body drop back in his chair. "I know the hiding place."

They all drove to the gatehouse, which was in such a deplorable state Leah felt like crying. She didn't doubt they would find the missing goods within its crumbling walls. The discovery would bring this whole adventure full circle and confirm the real purpose behind the time travel. She tried to be happy for the Traymores, at least the elder ones, but she still couldn't help resenting David for dumping her.

As he pried a sheet of plywood from the back entrance, she stole a glance at his profile. All the trauma she'd gone through had ended up benefiting him, yet he'd abandoned her. Someday he would be a wealthy marquess, prospering in England, while she would be back in Philadelphia . . . doing what?

Everything she could to keep her mind off him.

The plywood broke free with a loud crack. With a little jimmying, David opened the door behind it. He held it while Lady Isabella wheeled the marquess inside, then motioned for Leah to follow them.

Excitement sparkled in his eyes, but it had nothing to do with her, and she looked away from him.

"After you," she mumbled, a bitter note creeping into her voice. "It's *your* big moment."

"*Our* big moment," he corrected, nudging her forward with a hand on her back. Despite herself, she shuddered under his touch. "You unlocked this entire adventure, Leah. Now go on and discover what your quest has yielded."

Nothing. My so-called quest has dangled everything in front of me and left me with nothing.

She reproached herself for self-pity and trudged into the kitchen. Limited in space to start, the room was now cluttered with broken furniture and rusty appliances. A walk-in fireplace on the far wall had been clogged with two old refrigerators, both with the doors removed. Evidently, the Traymores didn't like to throw things away.

A step leading down into the main hall required David's taking charge of the wheelchair. Leah took the opportunity to drop behind him, as well as the rest of the group. While they filed through the house, she stopped at the door to the parlor and looked into the room where she and David had first kissed.

Unfurnished and lacking decoration, the sight made tears sting her eyes. Here, so long ago, she and David had shared a magical moment, brimming with excitement and expectations. The present moment, in contrast, was as empty as the room. Like the once comfortable furnishings, her hopes had been usurped by dust and cobwebs.

She crossed the threshold, walking up to stand in front of the fireplace. Even decades of neglect hadn't damaged the stone construction, and she smiled a little when she thought how much a good fire could still brighten the room. She ran a finger along the mantel. The wood beneath the dust and grime looked in good shape. Maybe the gatehouse could be restored—though it seemed more likely that whatever wealth the Traymores found would go into the main house.

What did it matter anyway? she asked herself, turning her back on the hearth. Whatever renovations they made, she wouldn't be here to see them.

Faint squeals echoed from somewhere off in the house, and she decided to go see what they'd found. She followed the sounds of laughter and exhilarated voices down the hall and stepped into a room she'd never seen before. The others had crowded around an opening in the wood-paneled wall, nestled between two built-in bookcases.

"Leah!" David crunched her against his chest, pressing a kiss on her forehead. "Solebury is saved! You'll scarcely credit the quantity of treasures my father amassed here."

Taken off-guard, she let her arms slide around his body. For one brief moment his strong hold felt like security, like *love*. Then she remembered he had left her. She loosened her arms and backed out of his grasp.

He didn't seem to notice, glancing back toward the opening with one arm still around her waist. She fought to keep from melting into him and forced her attention to the other side of the room. The older Traymores, each holding a kerosene lantern, peered into the passage, blocking her view.

"See for yourself." David pushed gently against her back, urging her forward.

Knees wobbling, she stepped up behind Lord Solebury's wheelchair. In the flickering light she saw a hall-like passageway, both sides lined with sealed trunks and bundles wrapped in linen. Near the front, a large ancient Greek statue had been uncovered and, beside that, several exquisitely executed paintings. Across the floor a small open trunk held a glittering pile of gold coins.

"Good God."

"I feel like Howard Carter on first looking into King Tut's tomb," Lord Solebury said, grinning up at her. " 'What do you see?' Caernarvon asked him. He replied simply, 'I see wonderful things.' "

"I hope we shan't be cursed like Carter and Caernarvon," Lady Isabella whispered.

"Dear Isabella," the marquess said, laughing, "I thought you didn't believe in such nonsense!"

Leah noticed the woman's lantern was shaking dangerously. She pried the handle from Isabella's fingers and set the lamp to the side. "Maybe you should sit for a minute, my lady. Here—I'll use one of these old sheets to wipe the window seat clean for you."

While she hurried to dust off a spot, David helped Isabella cross the room.

Lord Solebury wheeled himself behind them. "As one who *does* believe in the supernatural, I can assure you we wouldn't be affected by such a curse, Bella. Only those not entitled to the goods they find are punished by curses. David's father *meant* for him to inherit the bulk of his estate. Now, with the help of some magnificent force we'll never understand, his wish has been fulfilled."

A chill of awe trembled down Leah's spine, wiping out some of her bitterness. The marquess was right. A miracle had happened here, and she'd been lucky enough to play a part in it. David hadn't fallen for her, but he didn't *owe* her his love. Maybe he wasn't even capable of that kind of attachment, since he'd led most of his life feeling unloved. After living through that, he deserved whatever satisfaction his newfound family and status would bring him. Though she couldn't be happy for herself, she found she could be happy for him.

"I'm glad your father and his young friend are coming to dinner tonight," Lord Solebury said to her as David fussed over Lady Isabella. "We have so much to celebrate. Bella, we shall have to send Mrs. Pickford and Mavis out for the makings of a very special meal—and for some good champagne. An occasion of this magnitude calls for nothing but the best."

"I'll do what I can to help with the groceries and cooking," Leah said, thinking out loud. "We'll make this a very special evening."

Since this dinner would probably be her last at Solebury House, the idea seemed doubly appropriate. The next day she would go when her father did, either joining him for the trip home or moving on to meet Jeanine in Paris. Meanwhile, keeping herself busy would help her avoid dwelling on what—or whom—she'd be leaving behind.

In her peripheral vision she saw David bending over Lady Isabella, his face lit with a smile that made him look more gorgeous than ever.

Cooking wouldn't do a lot to help her forget that face . . . but what other choice did she have?

Chapter 23

HELPING PREPARE FOR the celebration turned out to be more of a boost than Leah expected. With the household overflowing with exhilaration, even she had to soak up some of the good feelings. In the old-fashioned kitchen her companions' spirits were as warm as the oven-heated room. Mrs. Pickford had relaxed her normally reserved manner, sharing personal anecdotes as well as tips for achieving flaky pastry and level cakes. Mavis, for once looking at ease, helped Leah set a fantastic table in the dining room—complete with vibrant centerpieces made up of untamed blooms from the gardens.

Before going upstairs to dress, Leah stopped to take in the festive scene. Savory smells of roasting meats and baking goodies wafted in from the kitchen—along with the muffled footsteps of someone approaching in the hall.

Mavis appeared in the arched entrance, carrying an armful of dinner tapers for the mass of candleholders she and Leah had hoarded into the room. As the maid filled the unmatched but charming holders, she grinned at Leah. "Better than Christmas, isn't it, miss? I never imagined this old house could be so cheerful."

She nodded, her own smile only a little bittersweet. "This is an important occasion."

"And to think this is only the beginning." Mavis plugged in her last taper and adjusted the placement of the holder on the table. "When we open the bread-and-breakfast, *every* meal will be a special occasion."

Leah's smile faded. "The bed-and-breakfast?"

"Yes, miss." Eyes twinkling, she repositioned a bloom in the center floral arrangement. "Lords Solebury and Traymore were discussing the idea in the drawing room while I dusted, so I overheard some of the plans. What a marvelous way to maintain the house once it's been restored—and just think of all the pleasure our future guests will reap from Solebury Manor. You came up with a wonderful suggestion, miss."

"Thank you." Leah bit her lower lip. Envy stung her again, as much she tried to suppress her selfishness. The Traymores were going to implement *her* plan—without her there to share the work or the rewards!

"Won't it be a pleasure to do this every day for guests from around the world?" Mavis walked toward the hall again, stopping in the archway. "Of course, *you* wouldn't want to spend all your days cooking and arranging like you did today."

"I think I would," Leah said, though she wondered whether she could answer objectively or if the grass just looked greener wherever David stood. But running a bed-and-breakfast definitely would have been more satisfying than her current job as an assistant manager in a department store. Even her goal of teaching didn't appeal to her the way operating the bed-and-breakfast did. Instead of bored students, she would have been dealing with delighted guests all the time.

"Let's hope it doesn't begin to feel like work when we have to do it every day." Mavis shot her another grin and took off up the hall.

"I wish I'd get a chance to find out," Leah said to herself.

The grandfather clock in the drawing room struck five, reminding her she didn't have much time before dinner. She went upstairs to get ready for the evening, glad she had something else to keep her busy.

She'd known ahead of time what she would wear: the only dressy attire she'd packed for her trip. With a brief scan of her wardrobe, she pulled out a classic "little black dress" with a cutout back. Maybe dressing to kill would help counter the gloominess of her mood—*and maybe it would make David think twice about leaving her.* She didn't really expect to change his mind, but any gain she made would be better than nothing. It would increase the chances of his thinking of her in the future—when, just maybe, he'd be more ready for a relationship.

Hanging on to that thread of hope, she treated herself to a long shower. Afterward, she took her time with her makeup, crafting a flawless "natural" look. With unpracticed hands, she somehow managed to harness her hair into a French braid. As she was twisting two wisps around her fingers to make them curl on her cheeks, a knock came at the door.

"Miss Cantrell?" Lady Isabella's voice intoned, deflating any hopes that David had come to see her.

"Come in, my lady." Leah glanced in the full-length mirror, smoothing her form-fitting skirt. "The door's open."

Isabella entered, wearing a long floral-print gown, complemented with fat sparkling sapphires clasped at her throat and ears—found, no doubt, among the treasures in the gatehouse. She smiled at Leah. "You look lovely, dear. I'm pleased to see you're wearing black. Your dress will go splendidly with these."

She held out a velvet box and opened the hinged lid. Inside was a dazzling matched set of diamond—yes, unquestionably *diamond*—earrings and necklace.

Leah couldn't begin to estimate the combined carats set in the pieces, let alone their value. Just thinking about the prospect of wearing them, she held up a hand to her throat. "Oh, my lady, thank you so much, but I couldn't possibly—"

"Of course you can, dear." Isabella removed the necklace, placing the box on Leah's dressing table. "Turn around, so I can put this on you."

"Really, I . . ." She swallowed, actually *afraid* to wear the precious jewels. What if something happened to them?

On the other hand, she recognized a once-in-a-lifetime chance when she got one. Her gaze seemed caught on the twinkling gems. "Are you sure you don't mind lending them to me?"

Isabella laughed. "Quite sure—not that I claim them for my own. Everything we found today belongs to David, since without him—and you, of course—Jonathan and I never would have located them. This is the least reward you deserve for your part in saving the estate. Now, do turn around."

She gave in, lifting her thick braid with trembling fingers.

Her ladyship strung the jewels around her neck, heavy and cool against her skin. Isabella clasped the back, then reached for the earrings, handing them to Leah. "I'll let you put these on yourself. You look beautiful, dear. I hope this makes up—partially, anyway—for my poor treatment of you. I'm sorry I distrusted you."

Leah tore her gaze away from the multicolored sparks at her throat and smiled at her. "You had every reason not to trust me. I'm only glad the whole truth is out now."

Isabella chuckled. "And I'm glad David's been so busy cataloging and securing his finds that he didn't have time to present you with these diamonds himself. If not, you might not have accepted my apology so quickly."

"Of course I would have." She looked away, eyeing the still-boxed earrings. "Is that what he told you—that he was too busy to see me?"

"Oh, no. He said nothing. I gathered as much myself. You know how men are. When they get involved with a task, they have no mind for anything else." Gaze fixed on her, Isabella tilted her head to one side. "Don't worry, dear. When he sees you in that little getup, cataloging items will be the last thing on his mind."

Leah tried to smile but felt her lips quiver. Her throat constricted and kept her from answering.

Isabella reached up and grazed her cheek with the back of her hand. "I nearly forgot how difficult being young is. Trust in my wise old opinion, dear. And don't forget to put on those earrings. I'll see you downstairs."

Leah watched her leave, blinking to hold back tears. Her ladyship had a gentle side she would have liked to get to know. Maybe they would keep in touch. She hoped so.

She picked up the earrings and leaned toward the mirror, a little startled by the elegance of her own reflection. With fumbling fingers, she put on the diamond drops and stood back, taking a deep breath. She never would have imagined she could look so sophisticated.

The precious gems called for a more made-up face. She added a coat of mascara to her lashes and dabbed on a richer shade of lipstick. Pouting cabernet-colored lips at her mirror image, she shook her head in wonder. "Perfect. If this doesn't give him second thoughts, nothing will."

When she stepped into the hall, she could hear voices drifting up from the drawing room. Hesitating at the top of the stairs, she made out enough to tell the rest of the party had already converged. She contorted her mouth into a stiff smile and sauntered down to the drawing room.

Her gaze flew straight to David, sinfully gorgeous in a black tux. He stood talking with her father and didn't see her enter the room. Lady Isabella sat on a sofa with her brother, and Kevin slouched across from them, strategically positioned before a tray of hors d'oeuvres. He glanced her way and looked back down, showing more interest in the food. Apparently, her declaration in the driveway had ended his attempt to win her back. She'd be happy if she never had to speak to him again.

David looked over as she crossed the floor, his gaze barely sweeping down her body before he reined in his focus to her face. He bowed and came up with a smile that almost looked formal—not exactly the gaping awe she'd hoped to inspire.

"Ho, aren't you dressed to the nines!" Her father joined them and gave her bare back a slap. "Dave here's been telling me about the hidden treasure you found. So, it turns out I was wrong about your blowing off your trip, wasn't I? You've had a hell of an adventure, while Jeanine's stuck trying to swallow snails and flag down snooty waiters."

She tried to smile but had a feeling she'd only come up with a grimace.

"Dinner is served," Mr. Warner announced from the doorway.

They all moved into the dining room, where her father made a fuss over the "pretty" table setting. She got seated next to David and tried not to stare at him. Each time she weakened and looked, he caught her in the act and gave her a rigid-looking smile. Where was the passion she'd seen in his eyes for those few short days they were together?

She didn't have it in her to confer much in the way of conversation. Her father and David dominated most of the talk throughout dinner, trading opinions about the future bed-and-breakfast and the car dealership Daddy managed. Lord Solebury and Lady Isabella added their viewpoints, but she and Kevin spoke only when someone questioned them. She supposed Kevin couldn't be enjoying himself, but he made no effort to talk to her, so she didn't give him much thought.

After dinner they went back to the drawing room, where David again paired up with her father. Leah kept to herself, staring into a glass of wine. Her last night at Solebury House and David wasn't paying her one iota of attention. She hadn't yet told him she intended to leave the next day, but she doubted the information would make much difference. Still, she did want to take him aside and inform him in private, so she could see his reaction. Even if she ended up giving away how much she loved him and making a total fool of herself, she had to try to talk to him one last time.

She got up and walked across the room to where he and her father stood. At the first break in conversation, she asked, "David, can I speak to you in private for a minute?"

He raised his eyebrows and looked a question to her father.

Daddy shrugged. "Go ahead. Don't mind me."

"Let's go out on the terrace," Leah said before she lost her nerve.

David looked at her father again, then back to her. "I have one more matter I want to discuss with your father. I shall be with you in a moment."

Her fingers tightened around the stem of her wineglass. So much for her irresistible outfit, let alone the possibility of his having real feelings for her.

"Fine." She took her drink and went out onto the terrace alone. If he didn't follow, she knew she'd have to accept she meant nothing to him.

The spring air chilled her exposed back and arms, but the heat of her anger kept her from shivering. A good five or more minutes passed, and David didn't come. Her last hopes dwindled with the wine in her glass. When she'd downed the remaining gulp, she glanced back into the drawing room.

Through the weathered French doors, she saw David and her father bent close together, engrossed in talking. Daddy made a motion with his head, and the two of them walked out of the room, disappearing from her view.

Her jaw dropped. Well, there it was—the final insult! He'd forgotten all about her.

She turned and stared out into the rose garden, the heavy scent of the blooms teasing her nostrils. Damn, she would miss Solebury almost as much as she'd miss him.

Suddenly she got an urge to see the spring one final time. She needed to say good-bye to the water sprites or whoever had engineered her adventure. True, they could have given her a better return for the gold coin she'd sacrificed to them—but all she had wished for was to know who'd originally owned the coin and if they got their wish. Now she knew David had thrown the coin into the pool in 1815 . . . and he had all he could possibly wish for.

She set down her glass and stepped into the garden. The chirping of crickets accompanied her on her walk, again reminding her what a wonderful place Solebury was. She had gained a belief in magic here . . . and a new respect for wish-making.

Next time she made one, she'd be sure to word the thing carefully.

Chapter 24

"I HAVE NEVER known a woman quite like your daughter." David took a deep breath and lifted a decanter of burgundy from the desk in Lord Solebury's study. As he refilled Mr. Cantrell's goblet, a droplet or two splashed onto the floor, but at least his grip *appeared* steady. He had never asked a man for his daughter's hand—never imagined he would have occasion to do so. Now he wished he had a better idea of how one handled the trick.

He held out the goblet, hoping his companion didn't notice the liquid's quivering. "Beside Leah's extraordinary outward beauty, she has an unmatched inward grace. She doesn't prejudge others—and, above all, I admire her self-reliance."

Leah's father accepted the drink and looked down into his glass. "I have to admit she's a lot more independent than I realized. I never thought she'd go through with this trip to

Europe, let alone decide to stay in England by herself. For a girl who's never really been out on her own, that took guts. Of course, I didn't see it that way at first. She and Kevin only broke up a few weeks ago. I assumed she was on the rebound."

David didn't quite understand the term but forged on with his speech. "I know that you have favored Kevin over me—"

"I wouldn't say that." Without making visual contact the man tossed back a gulp of wine. "I mean, I've always thought Kevin's all right. He's never really given me any reason not to. He works hard at the dealership—that sort of thing. But he's not necessarily a favorite of mine."

The statement encouraged David. He had seen Mr. Cantrell's annoyance with Kevin but hadn't known quite how little leverage his rival had. Still, the question remained of how much headway he himself had made with Leah's father. Could a single evening of conversation win him the kind of respect he required?

He sipped his drink to ease his dry mouth. "Indeed?"

"I only brought him along with me as sort of the lesser of two evils. I didn't like the idea of some playboy taking advantage of Leah." Mr. Cantrell looked up at him and grinned. "That's how I pictured you, if you can imagine. Here, you turn out to be about the most serious, business-minded young fellow I've ever met—not exactly the playboy type."

David allowed himself a cautious smile. The term *playboy* was unfamiliar, but he felt certain the word didn't describe him.

Leah's father stepped around the desk and seated himself in the chair behind it. "I apologize for making that kind of assumption about you. I'll have to apologize to Leah, too. She told me she made the decision to stay here with a clear head, but I didn't believe her till I got to know you and your family. I mean, I know there's an attraction or whatever between you two, but not the kind of thing I was afraid of. You have a very nice family. No wonder Leah chose to stay here rather than travel on with Jeanine. Jeanine can be a little overbearing at times."

David heard only half of his words, staring into his goblet. "You mentioned my being business-minded, sir. Do you believe the plans for the bed-and-breakfast are sound?"

His companion nodded. "I'm sure you'll earn plenty enough to maintain this place, even as massive as it is. I still can't get over the hidden treasure. It's like something out of a movie. It must feel good to suddenly find yourself out of the hole, eh?"

"Inexpressibly so." He cleared his throat. "You, uh, understand, then, that my financial situation has drastically changed from when we spoke this morning?"

"Well, of course. That goes without saying." Mr. Cantrell lifted his glass but stopped before drinking, eyeing David sharply. "Wait a minute—you're not about to start talking about your 'good intentions' again, are you?"

He couldn't help but look away. "The marquess and I spent the entire afternoon cataloging assets and calculating what capital we shall need for mortgage payments and restoration. The results are quite clear. I can unquestionably provide for your daughter now. Lord Solebury will attest to it, and we're prepared to show you figures, if you wish."

Leah's father rose again, rubbing his brow. "Let me make sure I understand this, though I keep telling myself I must have it wrong. You're saying you want to marry my daughter?"

He nodded, wishing the man would end his mounting tension with a simple answer: *Would he give his blessing or not?*

"After such a short time?" His would-be father-in-law scratched the red fuzz on his head. "I mean, you've known each other what—four or five days?"

David's stomach rolled, but he tried to smile. "However many days, each one has been extraordinary. Moreover, I shouldn't want to give this Kevin fellow any further opportunity to court her. He has already had an advantage over me, sir—several years' worth."

Mr. Cantrell let out a short laugh. Shaking his head, he said quietly, "Wait till her mother hears this."

David frowned. Perhaps Leah's mother held Kevin in more esteem than her father did. "Do you believe your wife will have objections, sir?"

This time the man's laugh rang out. "To Leah marrying a rich and handsome English lord? I don't think so!"

So the mother would not prove an obstacle. He waited to receive permission to pay his addresses, but still Mr. Cantrell dallied over his wine, chuckling to himself. Finally David cleared his throat again. "I . . . I should like to offer for your daughter tonight, sir."

"You don't say?" The smirk on the man's face looked more like amusement than gladness. "Well, this is one for the books! Wait till I tell the guys at the dealership."

At last David could wait no longer. "Sir, please, do I or do I not have your permission to address her?"

"My permission?" The grin on his lips finally faded, replaced by a vague O shape. Silence seemed to hang endlessly between them, then he laughed again. "Hell, yeah."

Leah stared down into the arid hole where the spring had gushed. The mud at the bottom was now dried and cracked.

Around the edges, moss had browned and hardened. She should have known the pool would be gone. The lost treasures had been returned to the Traymores. The need for magic had passed . . . for *them*, anyway. *She* could still use a miracle.

A breeze skimmed the nylon covering her legs, and she pulled her arms tightly around her torso. The night had become cold—though maybe it wasn't the air, but the . . . finality. Like the spring, her hopes had dried, gone lifeless.

"I knew you'd be here," a soft male voice said amidst the crickets' chorus.

Though she hadn't heard David come up behind her, somehow his presence didn't startle her. He always seemed to show up when she went to the spring.

She turned around and immediately wished he hadn't come. Shadows hid his features, but even his silhouetted form sent a shot of longing through her. In this very spot she'd felt his arms around her for the first time. She ached to feel that warmth again.

"I came to say good-bye," she said, looking down at her feet. "I was too late. The spring's dry."

"Good-bye? To the spring? Then you presumed it would dry up—and yet you appear disappointed." He stepped forward and lifted her chin so she had to look into his smile, a smile that showed he shared none of her grief. "Don't tell me you will miss being thrust into unknown eras, nearly drowning in the process. I know I shan't."

She swallowed, split between wanting to break free of his torturous touch and wanting to savor every last trace of contact. "No, that's not what I'll miss. . . ."

"You are thinking of Phoebe and my father?" His smile vanished, and his fingers slid from her face. He turned and stooped beside the spring hole, grazing the dried moss with the back of his hand. "I have regrets there, as well."

She touched her chin, where she imagined she could still feel the pressure of his fingertips. In her preoccupation with losing him, she'd forgotten about *his* losses. How could she have thought he had everything, when the father he might have had—for the first time—was gone forever, dead almost two centuries. "I . . . I'm sorry. It's a shame you and your father had to separate just when you'd really begun to value each other."

"If only I had been a bit quicker to see . . ." He trailed off, staring into the night. "No, I couldn't possibly have seen that wretched business in any other light. Even now I cannot forgive his spurning my mother. *She* accepted the choice he made, yet I cannot. Mama deserved better treatment."

"Of course she did."

"What pains me most is knowing how different matters might have been—indeed, almost were." He stood and faced her, his jaw set hard. "Today I learned how very close my father came to marrying Mama before his family interfered. Among the items at the gatehouse I found a betrothal ring engraved with her name. The inscription is dated 1784, the year before I was born. Leah, I was very nearly a *real* son, not a bastard but a nobleman, the legitimate heir to Solebury."

As she watched emotion flicker across his face, she winced in sympathy. "But you *are* all that, David—even legitimate, now that Fate has positioned you to take your place as viscount. A greater power has restored everything originally denied to you. It's all rightfully yours. I really believe so."

"I am not certain *I* do." He clenched his fists. "One thing I do know, however, is that I've been conveyed here to put this estate to rights. Thank heavens for your clever thinking, Leah. I shall never believe I deserve this fortune, but at least the bed-and-breakfast will allow me to share Solebury's pleasures with the world."

She smiled. He did have a good heart, even if he hadn't found a place in it for her.

He combed his fingers through his hair. "Forgive me, love. When I followed you here, I had no intention of carrying on about myself. I wanted, firstly, to apologize for the way I treated you yesterday—for upsetting you so."

She froze, taken off-guard by the endearment and unsure whether or not to admit how *much* he'd upset her. If she spelled out her feelings, she would let down the thin veil of dignity she had left—and her confession wouldn't change his lack of love for her. Tears burned her eyes, and she turned her back to him.

"I suspect my reasons for moving to another chamber may not have been as clear to you as I supposed." From behind her, he placed his hands on her bare shoulders, prompting goose bumps to rise until his touch warmed them. "The differences between your upbringing and mine are proving great indeed. I've had particular difficulty comprehending your father's expectations, but tonight he and I seem to have reached an understanding."

Her father again? Obviously, David came from a hopelessly male-oriented culture. While she stood here pining for his love, all he cared about was her father's views and opinions! She spun around and frowned up at him. "What does my father have to do with anything?"

"That's what I've been trying to determine." He smiled and reached up to one of her earrings. His fingers brushed her ear lobe, sending shivers down the nape of her neck. "Diamonds become you, Leah. I believe Phoebe wore these the day she and my father were wed. She would have liked you to have them now."

"To *have* them?" The outrageous statement threw her off track—probably his intention. He couldn't have meant *have* the earrings. He must have meant *wear* them. She put her hand to her throat, ensuring the necklace hadn't slipped off. "Lady Isabella lent these to me, and I'll return them the minute I take them off. God, I shouldn't even have worn them out here. What if I lost one of the pieces in the woods?"

"I know you will take better care than that." He let go of her shoulders and reached into his jacket. "Isabella can tell you whether she meant them as a loan or a gift, but I have something I certainly mean for you to keep. I only hope, above all things, that you will agree."

She watched him take a small velvet box out of his pocket. The idea of keeping Lady Isabella's diamonds was out of the question, but she would love to have a little souvenir from David—and of Solebury. Knowing the item must have come from the estate, she held her breath.

He opened the box, but his hand still hid the piece from view. As he took it out, the moonlight caught on a precious jewel, sparkling like fairy dust. When he held up his hand, she saw the ring, a large diamond with smaller gems sprinkled along a beautifully worked band.

"Oh—" Her voice caught in her throat. The ring was magnificent, not a souvenir but a treasure. She couldn't speak and could barely think a coherent thought. Of course, she couldn't possibly accept it. It couldn't be right. She really wanted a memento of him, but she couldn't take *this*.

"I hope you don't mind that it carries someone else's name." His gaze, when she looked up to it, seemed to pierce right through to her soul. "Perhaps that can be altered. Allow me to try it on your finger."

Before she could protest—maybe she didn't want to, not yet—he'd lifted her left hand and slipped the ring onto her finger. The band fit perfectly. For a long moment they both stared at her hand in his, adorned with the glittering diamond, like one of those perfect, retouched photos in someone's wedding album.

"The name it bears is my mother's." His voice came out low and soft. "You will see the inscription when we have better light. I don't imagine she ever got to see it."

Her gaze shot to his. "This is the betrothal ring? You would give *me* your mother's betrothal ring?"

He nodded. "I would hope to make it yours—to signify *our* betrothal."

Her lips parted but nothing came out. *Could this really be happening?* She felt her hand began to tremble in his.

He closed his fingers around hers. "I don't know how people decide to wed in these times. Your father seemed to think I had lost my wits when I asked his permission to address you—but in the end he did not object."

"You asked Daddy's permission? Wait—was that why you've been spending so much time with him?" Suddenly a wonderful warmth simmered up inside her, and the beginning of a smile tugged at her mouth.

His gaze felt heavy on her, intense. "He assured me your mother would offer no objections, either."

A giddy little giggle bubbled up her throat. "No one will offer objections!"

"Not you?" The moonlight glinted in his eyes, lifting some of their intensity.

"Least of all, me." She pulled free of his hand to crush him in a hug. His body was warm and solid, and she could feel his breath come out in a ragged sigh—relief. He'd been unsure *she* would have *him*! Her eyes filled with fresh tears. "Oh, David, I thought you'd decided to leave me. If you didn't mean to leave me, why did you move out of our room?"

He kissed the top of her head, holding her tight against his chest. "Your father's arrival reminded me how dishonorably I'd been conducting myself. I had no right to share your bed without making you my wife—but I hadn't the means to offer for you. I had no way to keep you."

"David, David . . . your perspective is *so* archaic." She tilted her face up to grin at him. "*I* was going to keep *you*!"

He looked shocked. "You were?"

"Yes, as long as the spring didn't suck you away from me again." She glanced over her shoulder at the hole and felt a new twinge of nerves. "It won't, will it? I mean, do you think it might gush up again, or will it really let you stay here? You don't think it will force you back to your own time?"

"History is written, Leah. The sixth marquess's bastard son disappeared in 1815 and never returned."

"So now you're the current marquess's legitimate son—but what if *that* David Traymore returns?" She still couldn't quite let herself believe Fate could be shining so brightly on her. All day she'd cursed herself for wasting her original wish in the spring. Had she wasted it or not? "Lord Solebury seems to think his son may only be lost."

He shook his head. "Isabella told me that they were all on the yacht when it capsized in the storm. Though the viscount's body was never recovered, she saw him go down for the third time. She is quite certain he is gone. His lordship has denied the truth for many years, but I believe even his thinking is changing."

She took in a deep breath. Yes, this was meant to be; she hadn't wasted her wish. She smiled. "Give me a kiss, my lord."

"Don't call me that." He leaned down and caught her mouth hungrily, officially sealing their fate.

When they paused, she whispered, "What should I call you?"

"You've called me David from the moment we met. I've always liked your informality." He grinned. "Your father goes a step further and calls me Dave. I like that as well. It has such a contemporary ring."

"Should we go back to the house and announce our engagement, Dave? Or shall we stay right where we are, alone?"

"I thought perhaps we'd stop by the gatehouse and plan the renovations." He put an arm around her waist, and they turned toward the path. "Would you consider our residing there once the building is restored?"

"I'd love to live there!" Another wish come true—any more and she would burst with happiness. "I already have some wonderful memories of the gatehouse. I'm glad the treasure is big enough to repair it."

"More than big enough." He pulled her so close they could hardly walk. "We can even restore the springhouse, if we want."

She glanced back one last time. The moon gave the building an eerie glow that made her shiver.

"I don't think so," she said. She was grateful for everything the spring had brought about, but she'd had enough mystical adventure to last her some time. "What do you say to getting a swimming pool instead?"

"Anything you wish," he said and leaned down to kiss her again.

TIME PASSAGES